SYDNEY SCOTT

EVERNIGHT PUBLISHING ®

www.evernightpublishing.com

DATING THE DAMSEL

Copyright© 2025

Sydney Scott

ISBN: 978-0-3695-1150-8

Cover Artist: Jay Aheer

Editor: CA Clauson

SYDNEY SCOTT

DEDICATION

For Ellie. Thank you for being my very own loving, sassy grandma.

SYDNEY SCOTT

Willow Creek, 1

Sydney Scott

Copyright © 2025

Chapter One

Gigi

The golden rays of the newly rising sun pouring in through the windows pulled a happy sigh from Gigi as she transitioned from mountain pose to downward dog, the muscles that had pinched and pulled during her hours of sleep stretching pleasantly. Virginia Davenport, or Gigi as she was known to just about everyone but her parents in the small city of Willow Creek, Georgia, loved to begin her day with some light yoga and a little meditation before heading off to work at The Happy Kettle.

The Kettle, a tearoom she inherited from her Grandma Mae four years ago, had been owned and operated by her paternal grandmother since Gigi's own father was in diapers. Mae Davenport hadn't been content with simply being the wife of a Southern lawyer and nothing else. Gigi's grandmother wanted much more for herself than to sit around and do nothing but look pretty and plan dinner parties. Mae had wanted something of her own, something she could contribute to the town she loved so much.

With fierce determination and a love of everything having to do with high tea, Mae bought a small cottage adjacent to the downtown area and transformed it into a tearoom where locals could enjoy something a little classier than the meals on offer at the greasy spoon diners that had lined the streets of the town back in the day. With the support of her husband and the local community that loved her dearly, Mae turned her dream into a reality and was a success for over fifty years.

Gigi worked side-by-side with her grandmother after she graduated with her bachelor's degree in hospitality from the state college and loved every minute of it. Gigi enjoyed being part of the town center and getting to know just about everyone in the community as they came and went from the small shop. She had also enjoyed being around such a strong, female role model, a woman who expected more from her granddaughter than just to marry well. When Mae finally passed at the age of eighty-one, Gigi took over as business owner and had been running it ever since.

Gigi's arms shook as she slid into a plank position, trying to breathe as regularly as possible for someone whose core strength was built on a bedrock of scones smothered in clotted cream for breakfast and leftover chicken salad sandwiches for dinner. As she held the pose to the best of her ability, Gigi thought about the tearoom and smiled. Owning her own business meant her days were long and filled with hard work, but she had always been up for a challenge. A lifetime of dealing with overbearing parents had more than prepared her for it.

When she first took over, the tearoom was in need of a few updates, so Gigi used some trust money she had gotten from her grandfather and poured it into the business, knowing doing so would make her grandmother proud. She had given the cottage a much needed facelift—a fresh coat of paint for the exterior, new landscaping, and some new paver stones for the patio garden in the front of the shop worked wonders for increasing foot traffic. All the updates she had made to the inside consisted mainly of adding some wainscoting to the walls and refinishing the wood furniture to give it a fresher look while keeping the charm that her grandmother had instilled in the business over the years. In truth, Gigi hadn't wanted to change much anyway because the shop was where she had spent a good amount of time bonding with her Granny Mae, and making any drastic alterations felt like taking a giant eraser to some of the best memories from her past.

When her arms and core had enough for the day, Gigi's knees hit the mat with a soft thud. After a deep breath, she rolled over into corpse pose to relax her body for a few minutes before she had to get herself ready for work. She had just started to feel the muscles in her body unwind and release some tension when the sound of her phone ringing pierced the air. Gigi turned and glared at the device, grumbling to no one in particular as she rolled onto her side and sat up. When she grabbed her phone, her brow furrowed at the name on the screen, any relaxation she had managed to accomplish in the last forty minutes gone in two seconds. The phone continued to ring while Gigi started to seriously contemplate how bad life would be for her if she ignored this call from her mother. Theodora Davenport wasn't someone who liked to be disregarded, especially by her own children, and would call repeatedly until she was finally heard.

Gigi inhaled deeply, trying to hold onto the last remaining traces of serenity from her yoga, and slid open the phone. "Good morning, Mama," she trilled. Mustering up enthusiasm for her mother was nearly impossible when the woman did nothing but come down on her all the time.

"Don't good morning me, young lady. Would you care to explain to me why I had to hear from Gladys Heller of all people that you and Tanner Lawson broke up?" Gigi rolled her eyes as her mother's voice went up another octave, the grating sound putting her instantly on edge. "Do you know how humiliating it is to hear gossip about my own daughter from that woman? You know she's been gunning for my seat as chair of the social committee of our charity organization. How could you do this to me?" Gigi could practically see her mom positioning herself on the fainting couch in her living room as she spoke. The woman could win awards for how dramatic she always was.

"Mama," she started patiently. Patience was always key when dealing with her mother, but unfortunately the woman always ensured those interacting with her were in short supply. "Tanner and I went on all of about two dates. You could hardly call it a break up when we weren't really together in the first place." The second date was a courtesy on Gigi's part. She chalked the first date up to bad timing or an off-day for the two of them, but the second was just as dull as the first. Gigi politely declined his offer of a third date thinking that would be the end of things. Clearly, she had forgotten about her mother's flare for turning anything having to do with Gigi's social life into a major crisis.

"And why is that?" her mother griped. "Tanner is

a partner at your father's law office and he's from a good family. You aren't going to be able to do much better than him in this town, Virginia, and I don't want to be an old woman by the time my grandbabies come around."

Grandbaby guilt? Wow, her mom was really busting out the big guns today. Usually she saved that for special occasions like Thanksgiving or whenever one of her cousins announces their pregnancy. "You're only fifty-five, Mama." Gigi pinched the bridge of her nose, the last vestiges of relaxation from her meditation and yoga session seeping from her body like the flavors from her custom loose leaf tea mixes into hot water with each minute this conversation continued. "Why don't you call and harass Ford about babies? He's a whole four years older than I am." Gigi winced, feeling a twinge of guilt for throwing her brother under the proverbial bus, but at the moment, she just needed to survive this conversation.

"Don't try to distract me by bringing up your brother. I give him an earful every time I talk to him, too," her mother huffed out.

Well, at least she wasn't the only Davenport to get harassed on the daily about marriage and grandchildren. Gigi sighed and looked at the clock in her small kitchen. She still had plenty of time to have breakfast and get ready for work, but she needed to get off the phone before her mom tried to set her up with another lawyer, doctor, politician, or any of the other boring professions worked by the sons of one of her friends.

"Look, Mama. I really am sorry I didn't tell you that things fizzled out with Tanner." She blew a breath out slowly, hoping to expel the irritation from her phone call with it. "We just weren't compatible."

Gigi was telling the truth. She and the young lawyer hadn't had much in common other than the fact that they both knew her dad. There was nothing particularly wrong with Tanner, he just didn't excite her the way she had always hoped her one and only would. There was no spark, between then, no fireworks when they touched, or really even the tiniest hint that they could be anything other than acquaintances. They also wanted different things out of life, so what was the point of going out on more dates? Tanner wanted to continue working in corporate law and have a pretty girl on his arm for every social event from now until the end of eternity. Gigi wanted more out of life than to be a trophy wife. She wanted fun, excitement, and maybe even a little bit of danger every now and then, but that wasn't how she was raised and it certainly wasn't something her mother or father would approve of.

Her mother hummed regretfully. "Well, I still think you two could work something out. Maybe we should all have dinner together sometime."

Gigi almost gagged at the suggestion, but instead of saying something to earn even more scolding or prolong the conversation, she just ignored her mother and tried to end the call. "Mama, I need to get going so I can open the shop. I'll see you at Sunday dinner. Love you," she said quickly, clicking off the call before tossing her phone onto the bed. There was no doubt in her mind that she would be hearing about that abrupt ending at said Sunday dinner, but sometimes you do what you have to in the moment in order to survive a call with your mother. With a groan of discontent, Gigi stood, tried to shake away the bad mojo from the call with a wiggle of her arms, and walked into her kitchen to make herself a smoothie.

As she moved, she glanced around her studio cottage, letting the warm glow of the sunlight hitting the ecru walls, bright blue curtains, and gray furniture, soothe her frayed nerves. Nothing got Gigi's hackles up quite like her mother getting on her case about her love life. Just because she was turning twenty-eight in a few days and had no viable prospects on the horizon didn't mean she was doomed to eternal spinsterhood or anything.

Apparently, her mom thought otherwise and was ready to get her back out there with Tanner as soon as possible. *Ugh,* Gigi thought to herself. She was just so tired of going out on dates with the same type of guy, one with the same kind of job, the same All-American look, and the same affluent family lineage that she too boasted, but never really cared about. Gigi didn't want that kind of guy, but she knew anything else would disappoint her parents, and she didn't want that either.

For all of their high expectations and guilt trips about her love life, Gigi's parents weren't all bad deep, deep down. They were pretentious and mostly concerned with money and appearances, but they had always supported her desire to go into hospitality and take over her grandmother's business, and without their help financially, she would never have gotten her degree or had the money to update her little shop. She would be eternally grateful for both of those things, so dating her parent's idea of her "perfect man" felt like a small concession to pay in return. At least it had. Now, things seemed a bit less black and white.

Gigi paused her ruminations and took another few cleansing breaths before she started to rummage around her refrigerator, pulling out yogurt, berries, and peanut butter before dumping them into her blender and hitting the pulverize button. If only her own conflicting emotions were as easy to disintegrate. She hadn't minded the dates her parents had set her up on through the years, but the older she got, the more she wanted to break free of their vision for her future and create her own. Her parents wanted her to have the perfect life, *their* perfect life, but she wanted something real. As she poured her drink into a tall glass, watching the imperfect lumps tumble out of the blender, Gigi wondered if her brother ever felt the same way.

Ford worked as a partner in their father's law office and had pretty much the same dating history that she did. He had been set-up with numerous society debutantes and law partners' daughters through the years, but he actually hadn't dated anyone seriously for a long while. Like her, Ford had a hard time trying to live life for himself and not their parents. Maybe they should look into getting a sibling discount with the local therapist to try and fix that. It wasn't the first time she'd had that thought and likely wouldn't be the last, but that was a solution to consider at another time when she wasn't already drained from the call.

Gigi drank her smoothie, letting the cool liquid numb all thoughts of dating and parental expectations as she made her way over to the bathroom to get ready for work. After a quick shower, she proceeded to perform her morning beauty routine of cleansing and treating her face, applying moisturizer, then doing her make-up before slathering her arms and legs with her peach scented body butter. It was a bit extravagant, and even though Gigi didn't necessarily want that kind of life anymore, she enjoyed her self-care a little too much to not splurge on her body products.

Once she was satisfied that she looked her best, Gigi stepped into her walk-in closet and put on her clothes for the day. It was mid-January, and there was definitely still a chill in the air, so she decided to pair her floral skirt with a white sweater. It would keep her warm enough in the fifty degree weather, and she was really only outside on the way to and from her car today, so she wouldn't feel the chill long. After styling her shoulder length, auburn hair in some loose curls, she gave herself an approving nod in the mirror before grabbing her phone, keys, and designer handbag and walking out to her car.

Dua Lipa's sultry voice poured through the car stereo as Gigi drove her powder blue Volkswagen Beetle from her beautiful yet modest home toward the downtown area. She sang along with the lyrics as she steered down Willow and Oak tree-lined streets before crossing the small bridge that went over the creek the town was named after. Willow Creek was more like a river most days of the year, but the city's founders probably didn't think that was as marketable, so a creek was what it was called.

Gigi smiled brightly and waved to Mr. Grady who sat out in a rocking chair in the front of his hardware store just as she was pulling into the small lot that sat between his place of business and her tearoom. "Good morning, Mr. Grady," she called happily to the older gentleman as he moved back and forth in his chair.

"Beautiful day, innit?" the older gentleman called back, his southern twang slightly more pronounced than her own. The sun reflected brightly off his white overalls, a stark contrast to the dark red brick wall behind him.

Gigi nodded and waved excitedly in response. "It sure is, Mr. Grady. You have a wonderful day now." Her business neighbor was all smiles as he tipped his straw hat at her. It was almost cliché how polite and Southern the whole interaction was, but that was what was nice about living in her small town. It may be a bit corny, but it was mostly in the best ways. Willow Creek was a good town with good people, and she was glad to call it home.

Gigi hummed while she walked, approaching the front walk of her tearoom and heading up the stone path before turning to glance over her shoulder at the auto shop across the street. Bob's Auto Shop was owned and operated by her friend Jo's father, Robert, but he wasn't who Gigi was looking for. There were a few other mechanics who worked at the shop besides Bob, and while all of them could probably have graced the cover of one of her friend Millie's romance novels, there was one mechanic in particular she was hoping to spy this morning.

Gigi took a small step backwards and glanced into the open bay door, tilting her head slightly to get a better angle and sighing dreamily as she took in the sight before her. A man with a very fine backside was currently bent over to inspect whatever lie underneath the hood of an older looking car. Gigi knew nothing about automobiles but she knew plenty about what got her engine revving and this man was definitely doing that. Gigi bit her lower lip and whimpered as he shifted his weight from one foot to another, popping his booty out on display. It was like he knew she was watching and wanted to give her a private show, or maybe that was wishful thinking, something to make herself feel better about ogling a total stranger.

The man straightened up and slammed the hood of the car shut. He took a rag out of the back pocket of his coveralls and started to wipe his hands as he turned around, their eyes locking the moment he was facing her. Gigi couldn't see much from this distance, but what she did see looked just as good as every other time she'd taken a look over at the man. His dirty blond hair was cropped short on the sides, but it was longer on top, just the right amount for her to tug on as they... She shook her head violently, blinking her eyes as rapidly as possible at the same time to try and clear the dirty images from her head. She shouldn't be imagining that sort of thing with a guy like him, no matter how gorgeous he was with his strong jaw, clean beard, and muscular build. *Inappropriate,* her mother's voice scolded in her mind. Gigi deflated, glancing over at him once more only to see that he was still staring at her, this time with the hint of a smirk on his face.

Busted. Gigi quickly turned to head back inside, but one of her heels caught on a flagstone and she tripped forward slightly, catching herself on the rail of the small patio fence. Her cheeks flushed with embarrassment, and she winced at how big of a klutz she must have seemed. Of all the times to almost face plant, it had to be when the hottest guy ever was looking her way. Nothing like humiliating yourself in front of your crush to make you feel like you're back in high school.

"You okay there, honey? It looks like you almost took quite the tumble," a gruff, but friendly voice called over from across street.
Gigi bit back a groan at knowing there was an additional witness to her indignity, turning to see Bob out front of his auto shop next to the man she'd been eyeing. She held up a hand in a shy wave. "I'm good, Bob. Thanks for checking." Her glance moved from Bob to the man next to him, and his head was bowed, but not enough to hide the smile on his face. *Wonderful.* "Have a nice day," she called out one last time before hurrying into her shop and locking the door behind her.

Gigi still had an hour until opening and a lot of paperwork and prep to do. With any luck, it would be enough to take her mind off of how silly she still felt. She wasn't really sure why it mattered what that man thought of her anyway. It wasn't like she would ever date the mechanic, even though she had felt more of a spark from him in her seconds long looking over at him than she had for any of her "suitable dates." She could just imagine the lecture she would get from her mother if she showed up to Sunday dinner with one of Bob's employees, but as she moved throughout the tea shop and got ready for the day, Gigi couldn't help but think that a little lecture from her mom just might be worth it for a guy like that.

Chapter Two

Cooper

The sides of Cooper Ellis's mouth twitched as he fought another smile. It had happened at least a dozen times over the course of the day as he once again thought back on what he'd witnessed earlier that morning. When he had finished inspecting the old Buick and turned around, the last thing he thought he would see was the beautiful woman from across the street checking him out. Cooper had seen the woman on a number of occasions and done a little looking himself, but he never thought that she would be interested in him.

The woman looked strait-laced and completely put together, and if word around town was to be believed, she was the daughter of one of the most affluent and influential families in the area. No way would a Davenport ever stoop low enough to date a guy like him, a guy who came from almost nothing and had hardly made more of himself at the age of thirty-three. Cooper sighed and the smile that almost was disappeared completely. No, the woman might like to look, but there was no way she would ever let herself get close enough to touch. He wanted her to though. *Badly.*

Cooper sighed again and dropped the carburetor he had been cleaning onto his work bench. He wasn't sure why the thought of never getting a pretty woman like the tearoom owner to say yes to a date was eating away at him, but it was like a bug in his brain that just wouldn't let up. Until a couple of years ago, he had been content with his personal life, one that consisted mainly of relationships that lasted a few months or hook-ups that didn't last more than a night. For a long while though, Cooper hadn't bothered with the dating scene at all.

Maybe it was his age or perhaps he'd just gotten tired of superficial relationships, but it seemed the moment he had turned thirty, the idea of anything less than permanent with someone else just didn't seem like it was worth the time. So he had made himself content with what he had—a good job, a nice place to live, a loyal canine companion, and a grandma who loved him more than anything.

Thinking of his grandma brightened Cooper's mood slightly. Grandma Maggie, or Mags as she liked him to call her, was as close to a mother figure as he ever got. His mom took off shortly after he was born, leaving him to be raised solely by his grandparents. He hadn't ever heard from his mom in the years since and as far as he knew, neither had his grandmother. Funnily enough, it never really bothered him much. Sure, there had been the occasional thought as to why his mother left, but he always felt it was more of an indictment on her character than his. His grandparents told him as much growing up, which helped, and they provided him with all the love and support a kid could ask for, only asking for honesty and hard work in return.

The pair didn't have a ton of money growing up, but the three of them had each other and that was enough. When his grandma wasn't working as a schoolteacher, she was encouraging him to read and teaching him how to cook. When his granddad, Gilbert, wasn't working around town as a handyman, he was showing Cooper everything he knew about cars and fixing things up around the house. Maggie and Gilbert Ellis hadn't been able to afford to give him much in the way of material possessions, but they gave him love, attention, and enough skills to turn him into a bit of a renaissance man.

Cooper could have gone into any number of professions with the skills and education his grandparents had provided, but he had always loved working on cars with his granddad, so after graduating from high school, Cooper attended the technical school one town over in Drysdale, earning his certificate in auto mechanics. He started working at a shop in the same town as his school, but when his granddad passed away seven years ago, Cooper moved back home to help care for his grandma. She was getting up there in years, and last year she decided it was time for her to move to a senior living facility.

Ole Mags was as sharp and spry as she ever had been, but she thought it might be good for her to be around more people her own age and not have to worry about taking care of her house anymore. Cooper would have taken care of it for her, but she insisted on selling. "Go out and get your own life and stop trying to live mine," she had told him before handing him a check for half the profits of the house sale. He tried to give the money back, but Mags wouldn't hear of it. Cooper didn't plan on spending a dime on the off chance she might need it back, so the money still sat untouched in his savings account. Mags had given so much to him already, the least he could do was keep it as a safety net for her.

"What's got you in a daze, Coop?" The booming voice of his boss, Bob, rang through the work bay and it brought Cooper back to the present. He stretched his neck from side to side, frowning at the pop in his joints but enjoying the tension release as he turned to face his employer.

"Nothing in particular," he told the older man. Bob had owned the garage for many years and while he looked every bit the strong, capable boss, Cooper knew that the work had been getting to him and he wan inching closer to retirement. He wondered who would take over ownership of the shop when that happened. *You could do it*, a small voice whispered in his head, but Cooper shook the thought away almost instantly. He wasn't cut out for that sort of thing anyway. Running an entire shop was a lot of responsibility, and Cooper was a working man, not a boss man.

"You sure about that?" Bob asked, his gray eyebrow waggling comically as a smirk played across his face. "I thought you might have been thinking about a certain tearoom owner I may have noticed you checking out earlier."

Cooper scoffed and turned back toward his work bench, feeling a blush color the cheeks underneath his beard. He tried desperately to not give anything away with his expressions, but that damn smile from earlier threatened to reappear, and the last thing he needed was his boss teasing him about a woman. "I don't know what you're talking about," he lied. The falsehood felt clunky as it fell off his tongue. He always had been a shit liar. "Might be time to get your eyes checked, old man."

Bob barked a laugh. "I'm not that old." Cooper peered over his shoulder and caught his boss running a hand through his mostly gray hair.

He shook his head at the older man and chuckled. "Bob, if you were a car, you'd be up on blocks with most of your good parts sold off for scrap." Cooper loved to give his boss a hard time, but the older man could dish it out just as well most days. It definitely kept work interesting and fun, two things he enjoyed most about his employment at the shop.

Bob laughed, tossing a rag at the back of Cooper's head. "I don't know why you think you can talk to your boss like that," he said with a smile. For as much crap as all his employees liked to give him, Bob remained one of the most jovial people Cooper had ever met. "The only person I let bust my balls that badly is my daughter."

The thought of the man's wily daughter had him smirking. "Who do you think I get all my best material from?" Cooper turned to face the man who was as close to a father figure as he had nowadays. His grandad would always hold that place in his heart, but it was nice to have the additional support. "Jo taught us all how to rile you up good."

"Figures," he muttered good-naturedly while scratching at his jaw. "I still wish she would settle down and marry one of you gearheads."

Now it was Cooper's turned to bark a laugh. "Are you kidding? You know she would eat each and every one of us alive and spit out our bones before using them to pick her teeth clean when she was done." He shook his head from side to side, his hair tickling his brow. "Not one man working in this garage could handle her temper."

"I know, I know," the man grumbled. Jolene Farrow was a force to be reckoned with, and while she was attractive, nothing on this green Earth could get Cooper or any of his co-workers to ask out their boss' daughter. Besides, he meant what he said. Jo was one tough cookie, and she needed someone who was an equal match. Cooper was self-aware enough to know that that wasn't him. He needed someone softer around the edges, someone like the woman across the street. Cooper never bothered to get her first name. Bob knew it, of course, and Cooper also knew that she was friends with Jo, but he never asked either of them about her or listened to town gossip too closely because he didn't want to give anything away. At the same time, some part of him thought knowing her name would make his feelings more real when they couldn't be that. No, it was a meaningless crush and nothing more. Better to leave that tiny mystery unsolved.

The bell dinged through the shop to let them know that someone had driven up to the outer bay doors. "Duty calls." Cooper gave his boss a mock salute and headed out to check on the new customer, raising a hand to shield his eyes from the blazing sun. You'd never know it was the middle of winter with the way the sun's rays refused to stop shining, but the chill that lingered in the air outside was a nice reminder. Cooper barely felt it through his coveralls, but he did feel it prickle against the skin of his face the further he walked.

The car that had pulled up was a sleek, black Jaguar F-type. Cooper gave out a low whistle as he strode over to the vehicle, marveling at the luxury he could never afford himself. The car was definitely high quality, and he wondered if the owner had gotten lost and was just stopping to ask for directions because they didn't often get cars worth this much rolling up to their doors. As he approached the bumper, a man stepped out of the driver's door, looking around with an upturned expression, like he would rather be just about anywhere else.

Cooper wiped his hands on a rag before stuffing it in his back pocket as he approached the older gentleman. If the car hadn't alerted him to the status of the owner already, the man's attire certainly would have. He was wearing a suit that probably cost more than two months' rent on Cooper's small home behind the shop. The sharp lines and cut of the light gray suit screamed money, as did the man's hundred dollar haircut. The older man's light brown eyes met Cooper's, a frown pulling down the corners of his mouth.

Ignoring the look of disparagement that was a familiar sight coming from anyone higher than his lower-middle class status, Cooper pasted on his customer service smile. "Good afternoon. How can I help you today?" Cooper asked, keeping his tone friendly.

"I'm not sure you can," the man muttered as he looked around. He then straightened up to his full height which just about matched Cooper's own six feet, looking intimidating in a way Cooper hadn't experienced in a long time, maybe ever. "My check engine light came on about a mile back and I thought it best to get it looked at right away." He held out a set of keys for Cooper to take, and reluctantly let go of them once Cooper's fingers had touched the metal. "I'll be at the business across the street when you're done."

The man turned to leave and Cooper tried not to laugh at the haughty attitude or assumptions Mister High and Mighty was making. It was something he'd been expecting and of course the man with obvious cash to burn did not disappoint. "Um, sir." The man turned around slowly, his brow wrinkled in annoyance. The expression had Cooper feeling defensive, not used to such behavior from their regular customers. It had been a long time since he had felt the need to shrink into himself, but the affluence and privilege that rolled off the man in waves made Cooper want to back up a step. "There's some paperwork you need to complete before we can look at your car, Mr...."

The man sighed, his attitude already well beyond the border or rudeness. "Davenport. Will it take long?"

Ah, that tracked. Between the car, the demeanor, and the mention of the tearoom, it made sense that he would be a Davenport. As much as he admired the daughter from afar, Cooper had never actually met a single member of the most talked about family in town because they ran in different circles, the reason for which becoming more evident the more the man spoke. "Well, Mr. Davenport. It will take about fifteen minutes to get you entered into our system, after that you'll be good to go."

Davenport glanced at his watch and shook his head. "That won't do." He reached for his keys and Cooper handed them back. "I need to be back at the office and your timetable doesn't work for me." He gave one last glance around the shop before pulling out his phone and starting a call. "Brenda. I need a car service to pick me up at Virginia's tearoom in thirty and someone needs to come pick up my car at Farrow's Auto and take it to the dealer in Atlanta." The rest of the call trailed off as the man walked across the street.

That whole interaction was a bust, but Cooper now had a name to go with the stunning face of the woman who he had taken a lot of notice of lately. Virginia. Cooper's face scrunched up as he turned the name over silently on his tongue. That name didn't seem to fit with the auburn haired beauty from across the way. It was too formal, too buttoned up even for her. He shook the thought away and went back into the shop. No need to think any more about the woman he would never have. He nodded to his coworker Carl who was currently wrist deep in motor oil as he worked on a sedan. "Hey, Carl. I'm taking my lunch break."

The man looked around the near empty shop and nodded. "Sounds good, Coop."

Cooper walked through the back door of the shop and the next fifty feet of grass and dirt until he came to the front door of his small house. Bob had said it used to be another small garage for the previous owner of the shop, but he didn't make use of it. When Cooper had first started working for the man and saw that there was plumbing routed to and from the space, he asked Bob if he could fix it up and rent it for himself. He hadn't wanted to live with his Grandma forever and a place of his own was just what he needed. Bob agreed, and after about a year of working on it as a side project, Cooper had a home all to himself. He didn't replace the garage door with a wall, choosing to instead update it with large, sliding glass doors. It let in so much light and air when the weather was nice, and he was pretty pleased with himself on a job well done.

He opened the front door and stepped inside, dropping his keys on the small entry table. The sound of nails clacking on the wood floors reached his ears just before his ten-year-old German Shepard came running toward him, sliding to a stop at Cooper's feet. He reached down and scratched behind the dog's ears, smiling at how the older dog still acting very much like a puppy most days. "Hey, Shep. You miss me?" The dog's tongue lolled out and Cooper took that as a yes. "How about some lunch, huh, boy?"

Shep marched into the kitchen and sat dutifully near the counter as Cooper washed his hands and gathered the ingredients to make himself a sandwich. He tossed a few slices of turkey at his dog and smiled when the animal lapped it up eagerly. "You act like I don't feed you enough," he chastised as he finished assembling his lunch and taking it over to the small table in the kitchen.

Cooper took a large bite, enjoying the tangy mustard as it hit his tongue. He glanced around his home as he chewed, appreciating the fruits of all his labor. It was a big, open concept space with only a small wall and some iron framing separating the kitchen from his bedroom and living area. Black cabinets and light brown walls accented the kitchen while dark wood and brown leather furniture took up most of the empty space in the other room. It was definitely a more masculine aesthetic, and Cooper wondered if a woman would be comfortable spending time here. It wasn't a large home, but it was enough for him and Shep, but that didn't seem to be enough for him anymore. If he ever did get serious with a woman, he would probably need to move to a larger home.

"I wonder where Virginia lives," he mused to himself and his dog, still finding the name she was given wholly unsuitable for her. Shep looked over at him, his head tilted in question. Cooper put down the remains of his sandwich. "That's the name of the woman I've been eyeing for the last little while. I didn't notice her before and when I did I was sure she would pass right out of my mind. That didn't happen and now I'm apparently so mixed up over her I'm talking to my dog." He lowered his plate toward Shep and let him eat the remnants of the sandwich. The dog ate it quickly and licked his chops when he was done. "What do you think I should do about it?"

The dog trotted over to the back door and scratched at it. Cooper chuckled and strode over to let his dog outside, watching as the large canine sniffed around for the perfect spot to go to the bathroom. "Serves me right for asking a dog for advice," he mumbled to himself.

Shep trotted back inside, looking very pleased with himself and Cooper shut the back door. He gave his very good boy a few more scratches behind the ears and took a final look around the home before he had to head back to work. He wasn't sure he could picture the prim and proper looking Virginia sharing this space with him, but boy, did he really want to try. "Not for you, Coop," he scolded himself as he walked toward the front door of his home, a heaviness in his heart that didn't exist there before. "Not for you."

Chapter Three

Gigi

After a wonderfully busy week, Friday night had finally come around, and Gigi was ready to celebrate her birthday with her two best friends, Jo and Millie. The three of them were all turning twenty-eight tomorrow and they had been celebrating their birthdays together for as long as Gigi could remember. It was tradition, one that started with slumber parties featuring milk and cookies evolved into alcohol infused nights out once they'd turned twenty-one.

The friends took turns picking the venues each year, but they all had veto rights, something that had come in extremely handy the year Millie picked a book signing as their destination and the year Jo had picked an all-male revue. Gigi hadn't been against that last one, but she stood in solidarity with Millie when their modest friend started turning beet red at the thought of watching a group of men dance around as they flung their clothes from their well-oiled, muscled bodies. Millicent Legare was probably the most bashful girl she had ever met, but Gigi loved her and even remembered the exact day they became friends.

It was the first day of kindergarten, and the teacher had asked each student to stand up, say their name, and their favorite color. Gigi knew that she and Millie were meant to be best friends when they both answered "rainbow" as their color. When they discovered that they also shared a birthday, both little girls knew it was meant to be. For as much as they had in common, there were also a lot of differences that made their friendship harder to maintain at times. Millie lived in the trailer park near the school, and anytime Gigi asked her mom if she could go play at Millie's house, her mom always insisted that while Millie could come to their house from time to time, she could never play at Millie's.

Gigi hadn't been sure why until a few years later when she started to notice things such as Millie's lunches consisting of little more than a slice of bread, or her clothes being threadbare and full of holes, and her light brown hair constantly tangled in knots. It had been pressed upon Gigi from a very early age that how the outside world viewed you was important, and it only took one glance at her best friend to see why her mom didn't want Gigi playing at her house. As a child, Gigi couldn't do much for her friend in the way of money, but she did start bringing extra food in her lunch bag, a sewing kit to help stitch up Millie's shirts and dresses, and a brush and hair ties to help her friend feel a little more put together. Millie was the sweetest woman Gigi had ever known, and she wanted her best friend to feel as special as she truly was.

Their other friend Jo arrived in Willow Creek a couple of years later. It was the middle of second grade when Jolene Farrow waltzed through the door in a pair of ripped jeans and a t-shirt advertising some baseball team. She wore her curly blonde hair short and hidden under a ball cap, something the teacher immediately noticed and made her remove. Gigi recalled Jo looking very put out by that only for the girl's expression to sour further when she had to introduce herself in front of the class. Her tiny chest puffed up and her chin jutted out as she stated firmly and simply, "I'm Jo, and I like sports and cars." She then nodded to the teacher and took the empty seat next to Gigi.

It took until lunchtime for Gigi to get up the nerve to approach the tenacious girl, but when she introduced herself and Millie, who had hidden partially behind her, they discovered that while she acted tough, Jo was actually pretty friendly and much more worldly than the two of them. She knew all sorts of things the other two weren't privy to and liked to share that knowledge freely. Gigi would later learn that girls did not in fact get pregnant through kissing as Jo had said, but at the time it had seemed like a revelation. Once Jo mentioned her birthday was also January 14th, Gigi and Millie knew they had found an addition to their little duo, and the three of them had been inseparable ever since.

Jo plunking down in the chair next to her pulled Gigi's thoughts from the past and back to the bar they were sitting in, waiting for the drag show to start. It was Gigi's pick this year, and the three of them had traveled to Atlanta to see the famous Heidi Haux perform. Gigi loved the artistry and pageantry that went into drag shows, and the fashion was always amazing.

"I think I'm going to go home with that guy at the bar." Jo's announcement came as she passed strawberry daiquiris to both Gigi and Millie before taking a sip of her beer. Gigi looked over her shoulder at the guy Jo was indicating and sighed. He looked like every other guy Jo always hooked up with—young, dumb, and ready to you know what. "You guys cool with that?"

"Why do you bother hooking up with these guys? You know it's never going to go anywhere." Millie's nose twitched in disapproval as she took a dainty sip of her drink.

"Yea, they're all the same himbos that offer one thing," Gigi added. Not that the one thing was bad, but Gigi wanted more than that for her friend. Jo spent all her time taking care of her dad, but she needed someone other than her friends to care for her every now and then too, and not just with a tumble between the sheets.

Jo snorted and leveled a glare at Gigi. "You're

one to talk. You always go out with the same stiffs that your mommy and daddy set you up with." She spoke the truth and as much as Gigi wanted to deny it, the accuracy of the statement stung. Jo took another pull from her beer bottle and shook her head, her golden curls bouncing as she did. "When was the last time you actually dated a guy that you were interested in, huh?"

Gigi shrugged a shoulder because she couldn't actually remember. Most of her dates were just to please her parents or for show, which was pretty pathetic when she really sat with the reality of that. She was turning twenty-eight tomorrow and could probably count the number of times she ended up doing something her parents hadn't instigated on one hand. Why shouldn't she do something for herself? Her mind wandered to the mechanic that she couldn't stop obsessing over. Thinking about his handsome face and kind eyes had a smile pulling at the corners of her mouth.

"Oh, that's it. Whoever put that spellbound look on your face is who you should ask out," Millie insisted excitedly. She pointed at Gigi before sighing happily and resting her chin on her hand, her own expression turning wistful. "You looked like you were in love."

Gigi tried not to roll her eyes at her friend's assessment. She definitely wasn't in love. Lust? Without a doubt, but love was a long way off. She didn't even know the man's name. Sure she could ask, but knowing his name would make him seem like a real possibility, and he couldn't be that. Could he? Hearing Millie sigh dreamily again made Gigi smile. She didn't blame her friend for thinking Gigi might be in love. Millie was the most sentimental of their trio, especially when it came to romance, and she wanted everyone to fall in love and live happily ever after with a house full of babies. Millie never tried too hard to find that happy ending for herself, though. Thinking of that made her also think about how she and her friends all seemed to be at a standstill in life, which gave her an idea.

"Let's set that aside for a second." Gigi grabbed a pen from her handbag and a napkin from the table, intent on transcribing what she hoped would be the brightest idea she'd ever had while slightly inebriated. "I have a proposition."

Jo leaned closer to Gigi. "Oh, yeah, baby. Talk dirty to me," Jo purred at her, the barley smell of her beer wafting over Gigi while Millie snorted a laugh.

Gigi shoved her friend's shoulder. "Save it for your himbos." Gigi's small jab earned a mock pout from Jo, but she knew her feelings remained intact. Jo was too tough to let a little light teasing get to her. She got herself back on track and started again, needing the support of her friends to help spur her into action. "So, we're turning twenty-eight this year, which is basically twenty-nine which might as well be thirty," she explained emphatically.

Millie started counting silently with her fingers while Jo gave her an assessing look. "I know I've had a couple of beers, but I think your math might be a bit wonky," Jo mentioned, placing her hand to stop Millie's. "Keep going."

"The point is that we aren't getting any younger, and we all seem to be in a rut of sorts." Gigi knew she definitely was. Her tearoom was doing well, but she wanted to shake up her business a little, do something different than just the traditional high tea. As for her personal life, it didn't need a shake up so much as a major overhaul.

Jo turned to the bar and waggled her fingers at the young guy from earlier, her eyes traveling up and down his body obviously without a hint of shame. "Speak for yourself, friend," she said out of the side of her mouth. "I'm in no rut."

Millie rolled her eyes and continued to sip her drink as Gigi plowed on. "You only bang fuckboys and leave before the sheets are cold. Just because you are getting some on the regular doesn't mean you aren't in a rut." She stared at Jo unblinkingly until her friend acknowledged the truth.

"Brutal, but fair," Jo sighed and turned away from her eye-candy, bringing her attention back to the table. "So what are you suggesting we do about it?"

"I'm saying that the three of us need to demand more of ourselves, you know? Do something a little out of character and see what happens. We'll challenge ourselves professionally and personally. I'll go first." She clicked open her pen and took a look around the bar. The lighting was dim, but the enthusiasm and anticipation was palpable, and she knew the energy would only get more electric once the show started. Decision made, Gigi started writing on the napkin, the excitement flowing through her making her fingers tremble slightly. "I'm going to host a drag queen brunch at my tearoom," she announced. "People shouldn't have to drive all the way to Atlanta to see one, and they're such great entertainment. I think it would be loads of fun and I bet my customers would too."

Millie's eyes widened to the size of dinner plates. "Are your parents going to be cool with that?" Gigi's eyes moved from Millie over to Jo, seeing an equally unconvinced look on her face.

Gigi bit her lower lip nervously. No, they absolutely wouldn't be cool with it. In fact, they would probably be pretty upset with her about it. Not because they were so conservative that they thought drag shows were bad per se, but the shows were considered controversial by some. The one thing Davenports didn't do was controversy, at least, not that could be witnessed by the general public or gossiped about.

After a moment of contemplation, Gigi felt her resolve strengthen. It was time she took steps to break away from what had become more of a burden than familial responsibility. "I'm doing it anyway," she declared boldly, feeling much more confident with the idea now that she'd said it aloud.

"Good luck with that." Jo pat her shoulder and raised her glass to Gigi. "I will speak fondly of you at your funeral."

Gigi laughed, causing her normally pristine writing to squiggle a little. "Shut up. They won't kill me." She thought about it a little longer. Her parents did take the family's standing in the community very seriously, and her actions would definitely be seen as besmirching the Davenport name. "They won't, right?"

"Kill? No. Disown? Maybe," Jo said bleakly. The thought of her parents disowning her was unpleasant. Despite all their faults, her family was important to her. Surely they wouldn't go that far over something so minor.

"Ford wouldn't let them do that," Millie announced with certainty to the table. Her head nodded curtly, as if her belief in the man was as unwavering as her love of romance novels. Gigi knew that Millie had developed a crush on her older brother the moment she laid eyes on him back when she was six and he was ten, but she thought she had gotten over it years ago. The lovesick look in Millie's eyes had her second guessing that.

Gigi hated to break the idealistic bubble Millie was currently floating in, but it wouldn't do any good to let her believe in a false reality. "I think you overestimate my brother's ability to stand up to our parents. He's just as much a coward as I am." She watched Millie's confidence in Ford diminish slightly at that statement and felt a twinge of remorse, but it was true. Ford did everything their parents wanted, even though Gigi was pretty sure it made him miserable. It was messed up. Both she and her brother should get to live their lives like they wanted, not the ones their parents outlined for them. A surge of renewed passion for her plan coursed through her body as the validity of that notion sunk in. "It doesn't matter. I'm still doing it."

"Yeah, balls to the wall." Jo smirked, clinking her bottle to Gigi's daiquiri. "I think for your personal challenge, you should definitely date someone who isn't a stuffed suit. You should go out with a blue collar guy. Like a construction worker, or a plumber, or…" Jo's eyes started to sparkle with mischief, but even without that visual cue, Gigi knew what her friend was going to say next. "A mechanic."

Gigi's cheeks warmed and she would forever regret mentioning the hottie from the garage to her best friend earlier that evening. She should have known better, but it was difficult to keep her feelings to herself when they seemed to want to burst out of her anytime she thought about the man. Jo's dad owned the auto shop after all, so Jo probably knew all those guys anyway. "I don't know what you're talking about," she mumbled before taking a sip of her drink.

"If that's how you want to play things, okay. I am writing down blue collar guy for you, though." Jo snatched the napkin and scribbled down Gigi's personal challenge before she could protest.

"Fine." Gigi resigned herself to her fate, not at all unhappy about it when she pictured the handsome man. Giving her friend a once over, she decided to counter with a little mischief of her own. "Then you need to date a guy that can actually handle you and not let you walk all over him like these younger guys do." She wrote that down under Jo's name on the napkin and glanced back up at her friend, narrowing her eyes. "And you have to lay off the hook-ups until you find him. Actual dates only."

Jo's mouth dropped wide open, the prospect of going without sex clearly terrifying her. "How am I supposed to relieve stress without my hook-ups?"

Gigi barked a laugh at the concept being so completely foreign to Jo. "I don't know. Exercise, yoga, a vibrator. You know, things the rest of us do." Gigi knew firsthand how to relieve stress without sex. It had been far too long since she'd shared a bed with anyone, but the thought of jumping into the sack with a guy after one or two bad dates left her feeling cold. She didn't need candlelight and romance like Millie, but she could do with at least liking the person.

"Fine. No more fuckboys." Jo continued to grumble as she crossed her arms over her chest, the act reminiscent of the toddlers Gigi sometimes saw in her tearoom when they didn't get an extra slice of cake. "You two should buy stock in silicone because I'm going to need to do some serious shopping to make up for all the sex I won't be having."

"Ew," Millie replied, shaking her head. Millie wasn't a prude by any means, but she was definitely more about the wooing than the screwing. Ever the romantic that one.

"I'm going to circle back to that in a moment, miss thing" Jo speared Millie with a sharp look causing Millie to sink a little lower in her chair as she sipped her daiquiri. Jo turned to face Gigi. "For my professional challenge, I'm going to try and get a promotion at work. I've been there for five years and I should be a team lead by now." Jo was in sports marketing and as far as Gigi could tell from having little knowledge of what that profession entailed, she was really good at her job. Jo was probably the only woman in her office, something the three of them were sure was the cause of her having been held back from getting a promotion. Gigi knew how hard Jo worked, so she hoped whatever plan she had in mind to get the respect she deserved worked.

"That sounds awesome, Jojo." Gigi wrote it down for her friend and turned her eyes to Millie, whose expression couldn't have been more terrified. Her friend looked like she wanted to crawl under the table and hide, but probably thought better of it when she realized that the sticky substance on the floor may be more than just spilled alcohol. "What about you, Mills?"

Millie avoided their gazes for a moment, shrugging a shoulder. "I don't know. I can't really get a promotion at the library, and I like my job as it is anyway."

Millie had been a librarian in Willow Creek since graduating from college. The woman was definitely in her element at the small public library, spending her days surrounded by books and sharing fantastic tales with children at story time. While it was true Millie couldn't get a promotion without the person above her retiring, Gigi remembered something her friend mentioned a while back and smiled. "What about the outreach program you had wanted to start? You had talked about delivering books to homebound members of the community or something." Gigi couldn't remember the exact details, only that her friend has seemed very passionate about the whole thing.

Millie twisted her fingers together, a nervous habit she'd had as long as Gigi had known her. It was a wonder she hand anything left attached to her palm with how often she did it. "I really want to do something like that, but I don't think we have the funds and I'd have to give a whole presentation to the board." Her eyes widened with fear the longer she talked about everything that would entail. "They probably won't go for it anyway."

Millie may doubt herself, but Gigi fully believed in her friend. "Sounds like a perfect challenge to me. I think you can do it." Gigi started writing it down under her friend's name. Millie was a strong and capable woman, but she had no confidence in herself as a result of her upbringing, something Gigi desperately hoped would change after their little endeavor. "You're totally going to make that program happen, Mills."

The fingers that had been tortured for the last minute now laid flat on the table. "Okay." Millie spoke quietly, a shy smile spreading across her face as she blinked up at her friends.

"Now, about your personal challenge." Jo's head tipped back as she broke out into maniacal laughter. Gigi knew Jo was playing things up for laughs, but wished she would stop when she saw the look of genuine terror on Millie's face. Jo did love to play pranks and get people riled up, but she would never do anything genuinely terrible to Millie.

"Oh, god. Please don't do anything too crazy," Millie pleaded, burying her face in her hands.

Jo stopped cackling and looked at their friend seriously as she drew her hands away. "I'm both flattered and offended that you think I would do something horrible to you."

"Sorry?" Millie said unsurely. The odds of Jo being serious in any given moment were fifty/fifty, so Gigi didn't blame the lack of surety in Millie's statement.

Jo chuckled and shook her head. "I was merely

going to suggest you go out on a date." Jo's brow furrowed as continued to scrutinize Millie. "When's the last time you went out on a date anyway?" Millie avoided their gazes once more and mumbled something under her breath, seemingly determined to avoid the topic for the rest of the evening. "What was that?"

Millie sighed heavily, her face a deep red. "I said four years," she stated with a wince.

Gigi and Jo looked at one another, mouths agape. Millie had never really talked very openly about her love life, so Gigi assumed that she liked to keep the details to herself, not that there were no details to share at all. She sat back in her chair, still a little shell shocked at the revelation and a little ashamed at herself for not knowing about it. "Why didn't you say anything?"

Millie shook her head, her coloring nearing an alarming shade of crimson. "I didn't want to sound pathetic, so whenever you guys talked about that stuff, I just deflected or busied myself with something else." Millie put her glass on the table, her body slumping as she readied herself for their commentary. "Go ahead and make fun of me."

Gigi reached over and squeezed her friend's hand, wanting to reassure her after what had obviously been a difficult confession. "We would never do that, Mills."

Millie glanced over to Jo who looked affronted for a moment and sighed. "Okay, while that is something I would do about a lot of things, I would never tease you about something that you are clearly self-conscious about," she conceded. "Why the no dating, though? I mean, you've got the whole cute, hipster librarian vibe going for you. I'm sure you could clean up on Tinder or Bumble."

Millie groaned lightly. "I don't want to meet someone on an app. I want to fall in love the old fashioned way like accidentally spilling my coffee on someone, or getting pulled over by a hot police officer and hitting it off, or I don't know..." she trailed off, biting her lip and looking at Gigi with reluctance. "Falling in love with my best friend's brother."

Gigi's little gut feeling from earlier was confirmed, but knowing she was right didn't make her feel any sense of victory. Millie still harbored a crush on her brother, and while Gigi didn't want to break her friend's heart, she didn't want her to waste her time either. She squeezed Millie's hand one more time, hoping the physical contact would help soften the blow of what she had to say. "Oh, sweetie. Ford is a great guy, but you're wasting your time on him."

Millie nodded slowly, her eyes looking the slightest bit watery. Gigi didn't bother attributing that the alcohol as Millie had been nursing the same drink all night. "I know I'm not good enough..." Millie started to say, but Gigi shook her head adamantly to cut off that line of thinking.

"Are you kidding? If anything, you are far too good for my brother." Millie was great and Ford was, too, but right now her friend needed to hear the hard truth. "But Mills, Ford basically lives under my dad's thumb and there's no way he'd date someone..." Gigi wasn't sure how to finish the sentence without sounding like a total bitch, so she didn't.

"Someone who grew up in a trailer park and has no family to speak of?" Millie finished sadly. The circumstances of her birth had always been a point of contention between Gigi and her parents, and that only concerned friendship.

"Yeah, that." Gigi scooted over and hugged her friend. Jo hopped up and wrapped her arms around the both of them, creating a cocoon of comfort that was as familiar as anything else in Gigi's life. "Sorry my parents suck so much," she admitted sadly.

"Not your fault." Millie blinked a few times and leaned out of the hug. Once they were all resituated in their seats, Millie grabbed the napkin and pen from Gigi. Her friend took a deep breath and started writing. She slid the napkin back over to Gigi having written the words *Join dating apps.* "I guess it's time I get my head out of my books and join the twenty-first century."

Gigi looked up at her friend and smiled. "Proud of you, sweetie." She knew it would be hard for Millie to try and date the modern way, but she was glad she was going to try. Her friends deserved happiness.

"Same." Millie smiled and looked over to Jo. "Proud of you, too, Jojo."

Jo smiled as well, but her happiness was clearly tempered by the trepidation she felt. "Thanks, but save it for if I actually make it through the rest of this week without hooking up with someone." She finished off her beer and sighed, gazing wistfully at the young man at the bar who now had his arm around someone else. "God, this is going to suck."

"No. It's going to be awesome." Gigi's promise came as the lights dimmed and the emcee came out onto the stage. The three of them were going to bust out of their ruts and make their lives better. "Speaking of awesome," she said as they all turned to focus on the announcer. The rest of the night was filled with laughter, applause, and admiration for the amazing Heidi Haux, and Gigi was happy that they got to celebrate with one another once again. While she knew the next year would bring challenges in both the ones they had set for themselves and some they may not expect, she was excited to face them head on.

Chapter Four

Cooper

A cool breeze blew through the carport next to Cooper's home, cooling the sweat on his brow and causing him to shiver. He was currently working on his silver 1979 Triumph Bonneville motorcycle, and despite the fact that the temperature was only in the high fifties, Cooper was getting warm from all the work he'd put into his vehicle that day. The bike had been his granddad's and he passed it down to Coop when he turned twenty-one.

The vintage cycle was a beauty, but like all classic vehicles, it required a great deal of maintenance to keep it in tip-top shape. He was just tightening the chain when his phone pinged with a message. The auto shop was closed, so he knew it couldn't be work. He dropped the torque wrench on the drop cloth that lay on the ground next to him and wiped his hands on a clean rag, the once white fabric now stained black. He slid his phone out of his jeans pocket and smiled at the message notification.

Gran: **Remember our lunch today. Don't leave me to the sharks, young man.**

Cooper chuckled at his grandma's phrasing. The "sharks" is how she referred to all the silver haired gentlemen in her senior living community. She had told Cooper on more than one occasion that they would circle the cafeteria and community center like the predator fish, waiting to smell blood in the water, or in their case, a single woman in need of some company. Mags insisted that the love she shared with his grandad was more than enough for one lifetime and vowed to remain single until the end of her days.

Cooper had tried to explain to her that one lunch

date didn't equal marriage, but she wouldn't hear of it. "You don't know these old men, Coop," she told him one day. "They're lonely and will take even the slightest glance in their direction as a declaration of love. Or at the very least, a sign that you're interested in sex." He shut the conversation down at that point and the two of them didn't talk about it much after that. The last thing he needed to picture was a bunch of grandparents trying to hook up. After shuddering at the memory of that conversation, he moved his thumbs across the screen to send a reply.

Coop: **I'll be there, Mags. Consider me your own personal shark deterrent.**

His phone pinged not a minute later. For being an older woman, his grandma had fully embraced technology and was surprisingly adept with all things computer related.

Mags: **Good. Be here right at 11:00, otherwise we'll get the ends of the meatloaf and I want a center slice.**

Cooper chuckled and shook his head as he typed. His grandmother knew exactly what she wanted and she would swat at anyone who dared get in her way, even him. Her tenacity was always something he admired, even if he was often caught on the wrong side of it when he was younger.

Coop: **Yes, ma'am.**

Cooper glanced at the clock that hung on the wall of the small carport. If he was going to make it over to Mags's place in time for meatloaf, he would need to start cleaning up. With a few final twists of his wrench, he finished tightening the chain and gathered up his tools. After putting everything in its designated spot, Cooper opened the door to his house only to be pounced on by his large dog. "What's up, boy? You need to head out?" The dog dropped back to all fours and trotted outside to do his business. Shep was acting a little squirrely and Cooper made a mental note to take him out on a run later to get all that energy out. The last thing he needed was for Shep to be bouncing around all night long while he tried to sleep. He had a long work week ahead of him, and he wanted to start it off with at least a solid eight hours.

After a quick shower and a good amount of time scrubbing away the grease from underneath his blunt fingernails, Cooper grabbed the keys to his truck and headed outside. It was a gorgeous day, something that would normally mean a ride on the bike, but he wanted to take the truck in case Mags needed him to run her somewhere. She had her own car and could still legally drive, but she didn't like to and while her computer skills were sharp, the same couldn't be said for her reaction times. Besides, dutiful grandson that he was, Cooper was happy to shuttle her anywhere she needed. Mags had done so much for him over the course of his life that he would gladly drive her all over the state if that's what she wanted.

Twenty minutes and one stop at the flower shop later, Cooper had driven across town and pulled into the parking lot of The Willows Senior Living Center, a mix of independent and assisted living apartments for the silver-haired crowd. Cooper had been here many times before, but as he looked out the window at the bright yellow buildings grouped in front of him, he still wished he had been driving over to the house he grew up in instead.

Cooper had thought of buying the small cottage style home from his grandma when she had decided to sell, but he hadn't had enough for a down payment. He was certain that his grandma would have made a deal with him, but he didn't want her losing out on any money that she needed to care for herself in her golden years. With a sigh for what might have been and a look in the rearview mirror to give himself a final once over, Cooper grabbed the bouquet of white tulips he had purchased for Mags and hopped out of the truck.

He had barely started to rap his knuckles on the door of her apartment when it swung wide open, his grandma waiting impatiently on the other side of the threshold, a hand propped on her outturned hip. Mags was a petite woman, standing no taller than five feet, but she still seemed larger than life to him. It was always an interesting juxtaposition. The formidable Maggie Ellis, a woman who wouldn't hesitate putting anyone and everyone in their place wrapped up in such a tiny little package.

She smoothed a hand over her short gray curls and pushed up her glasses, tipping her head back to look at him for all of two seconds before she snorted and shook her head. "Couldn't be bothered to wear more than jeans and a t-shirt, huh?" She then turned and walked back into her apartment.

Cooper sighed and crossed the threshold, making sure to secure the door behind him. "Nice to see you too, Mags." He presented her with the tulips and leaned down to kiss her wrinkled cheek, her skin feeling a little like the fine sandpaper he used at the shop. "I figured you'd be okay with the lack of Sunday best if I was here on time to get you that center cut of meatloaf you wanted."

His grandma smiled at the flowers and went into her small kitchen to put them in some water. "I can deal with your clothes, but it wouldn't kill you to wear a shirt with buttons every now and then," she called over to him as she arranged the flowers to her liking, placing them in the center of the coffee table of her living room when she was finished. "Girls like a fella who can look nice every once in a while."

He placed a hand over his heart in mock offense. "Mags, you wound me." He looked down at his faded denim and black t-shirt, her assessment seeming wildly off base as far as he was concerned. At least his clothes were clean and not covered in grease or motor oil, something that happened more often than he would care to admit. "I don't think I look half bad, actually."

Mags snorted once more. "Half bad is still not all good." She grabbed her purse off the coatrack by the door and signaled for him to follow. Like the Southern gentleman she's raised him to be, he offered her his arm as they left her apartment and started toward the communal dining hall. As they walked, Mags peered up at him and winked. "You know I'm giving you a hard time, right? You're a handsome boy despite your desire to keep that big, bushy thing on your face."

Cooper barely managed to refrain from rolling his eyes. "It's called a beard, Mags, and I keep it neatly trimmed thank you very much." His grandma loved to give him a hard time when it came to just about everything in his life, and he didn't mind it in the least because he knew she was mostly teasing, but her distaste of his facial hair had always been a point of contention. Cooper liked looking a little more rugged, but Mags always thought a man with facial hair had something to hide.

"It's a shame is what it is. Covering such a handsome face with all that scruff." He slowed his pace to not get her too winded. "Back in my day, boys wore their hair short and their faces clean."

Cooper held back his scoffing. "Well, back in your day hitchhiking was a thing and people wouldn't think twice about taking candy from strangers, so let's be happy we live in modern times." Cooper loved his grandma, but every now and then it seemed like their time together turned into another lecture about "kids these days."

"I never did that," she chastised as she swatted his arm. She stopped walking and tapped her chin, her cloudy eyes looking back to another time and place. "Come to think of it, I did hitchhike once when I ran out of gas on the 87." She shrugged her shoulders as though the revelation were no big deal. "Oh, well."

Cooper chuckled and opened the door to the dining hall for her. "Well, I'm glad you survived it, Mags." Not that it would have been difficult for her to do so. Anyone who tried to pull one over on her likely would have ended up with a black-eye or a split lip.

"Of course I did," she insisted, a wide smile pulling across her weathered face. "Even if someone had tried something, I would have been all right. I always carried a brick in my purse in case I ever ran into trouble."

Cooper snorted a laugh as she confirmed his suspicions. "Sounds about right." He steered the two of them through the large, cream walled dining hall and over to the line for food, grabbing a couple of trays for them. They passed through the line, grabbing rolls, mashed potatoes, veggies, and a nice center cut piece of meatloaf for themselves as well as a slice of the chocolate cake that was being offered for dessert. The spread at The Willows was pretty sweet considering it was essentially glorified cafeteria food, and after living off a steady diet of deli meat and stale bread during the week, Cooper looked forward to his meals there.

Mags started to reach into her purse, but Cooper batted her hand away and took out his wallet to pay for the meal. "I was going to treat." She huffed, a stubborn expression on her face. Even though she was at the age where she should do nothing more than sit back and relax, his grandmother was still always trying to take care of him. He may not have much in his life, but at least he still had someone who loved him, a gift he was determined to repay in any way he could.

"You can treat next time." Smiling, he handed over the payment to the cashier. Cooper probably wouldn't let her pay then either or any time after that, but he didn't want to start their meal off by bickering about money.

"You always say that and then you always pay." Mags grumbled her annoyance as they walked over to an empty table near the window. She really did know him well.

"What can I say? I like spoiling my grandma." He pulled out a chair for her and pushed her seat, taking the one across. Cooper plunked down in his seat and grabbed a forkful of mashed potatoes, enjoying the flavor of the buttery vegetable for a second when he looked over at his grandma. She was staring at him, her elbows on the table and her fingers steepled together. "What?" he asked around his mouthful of food.

"When are you going to get married?" Her face was completely serious as she asked the question as though it weren't totally out of the blue.

Cooper tried not to choke on his food and grabbed a sip from his water glass, shaking his head as he put down his fork. "Where did that come from?" Mags had never taken much of an interest in his personal life before, so he was a bit baffled as to why she was now.

His grandma sighed and picked at her veggies. "I'm getting old and I want to see you settled before I die."

Panic shot through his chest at the implication. "Is something wrong? I thought your last check-up went well." Cooper had been keeping on top of her health news the last few years and as far as he knew, everything had been great. The thought of losing the only person who cared about him had a pain shooting straight through his heart and he suddenly felt short of breath, his appetite vanishing almost instantly.

She waved off his concern with a flick of her wrist. "It went just fine. I'm as fit as a fiddle, but at my age just one wrong step off the curb could mean a broken hip and a one way ticket to the afterlife." She looked over at him, her dim gray eyes meeting his with concern, but none for herself. "I want to see you with a good woman before I go. I need to know that you're being taken care of."

While he was relieved his grandmother was all right, Cooper wasn't sure what to say to address her concerns. He wanted that too, a nice woman to call his own, but he just hadn't been interested in anyone lately. Suddenly his mind flashed to the tearoom owner, Virginia. No matter how much he told himself she wasn't an option, he couldn't get her auburn waves, sweet smile, and curvy body out of his head. Day or night, she seemed to be all he could think about.

"I can take care of myself, Mags," he told her with as much sincerity as he could muster. Cooper could look after himself, but that didn't mean it wouldn't be nice to have someone around to share the burden every now and then. Still, no need for his grandmother to preoccupy herself with his social life. Cooper reached across the table and squeezed her hand gently. "You don't need to worry about me."

Mags sounded less than convinced as she hummed with a twist of her lips. She took a bite of her meatloaf and looked around as she chewed. Cooper was happy that conversation seemed to be over, and just when he was about to ask her about her ladies' lunch group, she spoke again. "Why aren't you seeing anyone? There are plenty of single gals in this town. Or single guys if that's your thing."

Cooper dropped his fork again and dropped his head into his hands for a moment. Apparently, she wasn't going to let this go and he was going to have to explain himself like he was a child and not an adult closer to middle age than high school. "I like women, Mags." His head lifted and he ran a hand through his hair to buy some time. He wasn't sure how to put his feelings into words, something that had always been difficult for him, but he tried his best. "It's just that the type of woman I'm interested in wouldn't go for a guy like me."

His grandma frowned, looking affronted on his behalf. "And what type of guy is that?"

Cooper groaned, not wanting to talk about himself or this even a little bit, but he and his grandparents had always had an open and honest relationship, he had trusted them explicitly and that wasn't going to stop now. "Don't get me wrong, I'm very proud of what I do. Sending people off on their way to work or school or wherever safely and with peace of mind is an important thing." Cooper meant every word, but pride in his work didn't change the way the world worked, and there were still a good number of people who looked down on his profession. He shook his head sadly as he looked at his gran. "But I'm not saving the world, Mags. I'm just doing a job and at the end of the day, I make a decent salary, but not enough to impress anyone. Not enough to treat a woman to the finer things in life."

His grandma's frown deepened and she looked a little guilty. "I know Gilbert and I couldn't give you much growing up and we couldn't afford to send you to college, but we tried our best and we are both so proud of

the man that you have become and you should be, too."
She sighed heavily, the obvious disappointment she felt
causing his chest to squeeze. "I wish we could have given
you more."

Cooper held his grandma's hand as tight as he
could without hurting her, needing her to understand how
much his shortcomings had nothing to do with her and
everything to do with how the outside world viewing him
as less than still got to him. "Hey, Mags, look at me." Her
eyes met his and he felt like a heel for making her feel
bad about his upbringing. "You and Pops gave me all the
love and attention a kid could ask for. That was more
than enough." He blinked away tears that threatened to
fall as he thought about just how much care and kindness
his grandparents had shown him when his own mother
couldn't. "It was everything," he rasped, clearing his
throat that was thick with too much unspoken gratitude. If
Cooper lived a thousand years, he could never express
how much his caregivers meant to him.

Mags smiled at him and squeezed his hand back.
"Good." She picked up her fork and took another bite of
her food. "So, if love is more than enough, then you
should have no problem going after that girl you like."

Cooper reared back and looked at his grandma.
He had forgotten how shrewd the old gal could be and
she'd just backed him into a corner. Now that he had
admitted that love was enough, he didn't have his excuses
for not pursuing anything with Miss Virginia. "Well, I'll
be damned," he muttered to himself. "I suppose you're
right."

"Of course I'm right," she stated confidently.
"Now, look alive because I see old man Jennings looking
this way, and he's the last man I would want to spend an
evening with."

Cooper chuckled lightly, thankful for the subject

change. "Sure thing, Mags." He got up and took the seat next to his grandma and shot a glare at the old man that had been making his way toward their table. The man looked startled and backed off as soon as he caught sight of Cooper's expression.

"Atta boy," she praised happily. The two of them spent the rest of lunch catching up on what was new in each other's lives and the latest gossip from around the community, but any time there was a lull in the conversation, Cooper would think back to what he had said about love being enough. While that might be true for him, it might not be true for the object of his affection. There was only really one way to find out, but was he brave enough to try?

Chapter Five

Gigi

The Davenport house sat on the side of a hill overlooking the river that ran through most of Willow Creek, and while Gigi grew up in this house and had always loved the large cabin like structure, she wasn't looking forward to spending the evening there tonight. The house had always been imposing, but something about the large homestead was making her more nervous than usual. Perhaps it was the fact that she knew her mother would try to set her up again, and because she had made a pact with her best friends two days ago, she would actually have to stand up for herself and say "no." It had been easy enough to do with a cocktail flowing through her veins and the excitement of seeing the drag show with her besties to bolster her confidence, but now that she was sober and on her own, Gigi wasn't sure she could live up to her own hype. She had convinced her friends that they had been stagnant and needed a change, yet at the first possible obstacle, she was already floundering.

A knock on her driver's side window spooked her and she whipped her head around to face the person who had interrupted her spiraling. She exhaled in relief, her hand falling from where it had been clutching her chest when her eyes met the furrowed brow of her brother, Ford. He gazed at her quizzically for a moment. "What are you doing out here?"

Gigi sighed and opened her door, stepping outside into the crisp evening air. She pulled her coat tighter in a move both to protect herself from the cold and from what was sure to be an onslaught of questions and comments from her parents. "I was just avoiding the inevitable," she confessed to her brother as she locked her car and started up the stone driveway toward the front porch.

Ford sighed along with her as he ran a hand through his light brown hair. He was only thirty-two, yet the weariness he carried like a weight on his shoulders made him seem far older than that. "Well, better to get it over with, I guess." He shot her a smile of commiseration as they approached the porch. "It won't be that bad."

Gigi shook her head sadly at what would surely be true for him, but not for her. Ford was the golden child, her parents never really taking issue with anything he said or did. Of course, that may be because Ford pretty much said and did everything they told him to, but the way they were treated still seemed significantly lopsided in her opinion. Gigi went along with their plans for her for the most part, though she did have a tendency to deviate slightly wherever she thought she could manage it. The small tastes of rebellion had helped her make it through the last twenty-eight years, but now was the time for more than a taste.

"For you maybe, but I just know Mom is going to try and set me up with one of her charity friend's sons again." She laughed humorlessly at the prospect of another long dinner where the conversation was stilted and dull. "I've probably already dated them all."

Ford huffed a breath, looking less sympathetic to her plight than she would like. "At least she's not trying to convince you to get back with your ex." His voice was filled with dismay as he revealed a piece of gossip Gigi hadn't been privy to. Normally the tearoom acted as enough of a gossip center that she was one of the first to know about anything, and it coming as a surprise was unpleasant for multiple reasons.

Gigi stopped him with a hand on his arm. "Seriously? She wants you to get back with Presley?"

Presley was Ford's ex-girlfriend, and Gigi had been happy that he ended their ill-conceived relationship years ago. Presley was a status seeking, social climbing, terror of a woman, but because she came from "the right family," her many personality flaws were conveniently overlooked by their parents. Gigi was certain Ford had only dated her because he felt like he had to in order to live up to their parents' expectations, and she shuddered to think that her brother might actually consider getting back with that horrible woman.

Ford sighed heavily, his shoulders sagging further as the distance between them and the house grew shorter. "She won't stop harping on it. It probably doesn't help that I'm not really dating anyone else."

Gigi watched him look over toward the sunset, his gaze wistful. When he turned back to her, she narrowed her gaze. "Why aren't you dating anyone? It's been a long time since you had anything serious going on. Have you even gone on a single date since you broke things off with the she-devil?"

Ford's eyes darted away quickly, only meeting hers again after he'd schooled his features. "A few. I'm focusing on work now, so I don't have much time is all."

"Ford…" she started, but he held up a hand to stop her.

"Drop it, Ginny. Please." A pained expression flashed across his face as he pleaded with her using the special name only he called her. After another moment, Ford schooled his features, and while she really wanted him to confide in her, she wasn't going to push him any farther when their evening ahead was probably already going to be more than a little unpleasant.

"Fine." They walked up the steps to the expansive wraparound porch, both of their feet slow to make the climb. Before Ford opened the front door, she pulled on his arm once more. "You can talk to me about stuff, you know. It's a little annoying that you won't."

They had been closer when they were younger, but his work as a lawyer did keep him occupied quite often. It was something Gigi hoped would lessen with time, but the longer he worked for their father, the busier he seemed to be. Ford smiled sadly at her as he reached for the doorknocker. Despite both growing up in the house, they were always expected to knock and announce their presence. Just another ridiculous expectation from their parents. "Sorry, Gin, but my path has been laid out before me for a long time. I'm tired of walking it, to be sure, but I'm not sure what else to do."

Gigi hated seeing her brother looking miserable, but before she could talk to him anymore about it, the door swung open and their mother was in front of them, hands on her hips. "I didn't think you two were going to make it." Her eyes flicked from her two children to her jewel encrusted wristwatch. "You're late."

Ford removed his coat and helped Gigi out of her own before he leaned down and kissed their mom on the cheek. "Sorry, Mama. Traffic was surprisingly heavy for a Sunday." The lie rolled off his tongue easily as he winked at Gigi behind their mother's back. Apparently some good had come from all of his time in the courtroom defending large corporations, he was an expert bullshitter.

Gigi jumped on the excuse, nodding her head vigorously. "Yes, there must be some sort of rush on Sunday services this evening." She stifled the laugh that was bubbling up in her lungs and leaned in to give her mom a light hug.

The woman clicked her tongue skeptically. "That seems a bit odd, but at least the two of you made it at all." Fortunately she seemed to be done with their scolding as she whisked them off to the parlor for drinks.

Gigi sat in her usual spot near the large stone fireplace, wiggling down in the large chair that had been broken in over the years. She had spent a lot of time in this chair growing up—reading, doing homework, or chatting on the phone with her friends. Gigi ran her fingers over fabric, the soft, buttery leather comforting in a house that had provided so little of that over the last few years. A tray of drinks was placed on the coffee table in front of her and Gigi looked up to see her dad, his eyebrow raised in question.

Gigi stood back up immediately and gave him the hug he had been expecting. "Hi, Daddy." Genuinely happy to give him the affection she always hoped he would return, she wrapped her arms around his large frame. As intimidating as he could be, Gigi still found him more approachable than her mother, though that wasn't saying much. Clifford Davenport was tall and broad, with graying brown hair and brown eyes. He looked like an older version of her brother, which was made even more apparent as the two of them stood next to each other. "How are you?"

Her dad kissed the top of her head and moved over to the sofa to join her mother. "I'm well. Thank you, Virginia." He raised his glass in the air and the rest of them followed along. They always saluted to something at their monthly dinners, and as Gigi raised her cosmopolitan, she wondered what it would be tonight. "To the continuation of a prosperous year."

Gigi silently tipped her head at her dad and they all drank. Just once, Gigi wished they could raise their glasses to something more meaningful, but she should probably just stop expecting that to happen because it seemed that money and status were the two things her parents cared about most. She peered at her brother out of the corner of her eye and saw that he had already downed his glass of whiskey. Perhaps he didn't have an easier time facing her parents like she had previously thought.

Gigi decided to take one for the team and get the ball rolling by bringing the attention to herself. "Speaking of prosperous years, the tearoom is doing incredibly well. I thought that there would be a bit of a lull after the holidays, but business seems to be holding steady."

"That's wonderful, Sweetheart." Her dad smiled at her, pride evident from the twinkle in his eye to the upturn of his lips. "I think you got your grandmother's knack for business."

Gigi beamed at the praise. It didn't come around all that often, so she tried to soak it up like a sponge whenever she could to remember during the dry seasons. "Thanks, Daddy." Gigi hoped she inherited more than that, like Mae's determined spirit and ability to socialize with just about anyone, but she would take what she could get.

She hazarded a glance in her mother's direction and saw a thoughtful expression on her face. Her mom thinking while Gigi was talking was never a good thing as it always turned to scheming, and it almost always had to do with her personal life. "That is wonderful, dear." Her mom took a small drink from her gin fizz, her eyes far too calculating for what should have been a relaxing, family dinner. Gigi should know by now that Sunday evenings were never going to be that, but she couldn't stop herself from hoping. "It's too bad you can't turn that knack for business into a way to be more successful socially."

Gigi took a deep breath and tried to swallow down the frustration that threatened to surface along with the remnants of her drink. Couldn't her mom lay off for one evening? "Well, I went out with my friends on Friday night. That was a big success actually."

Her mother did not look entertained at Gigi's snarky reply. The woman really could do with getting whatever stick had been lodged in her rear end removed permanently. "You know that isn't what I meant. You just turned twenty-eight, Virginia. It's time you get serious and settle down with someone." Her mom pulled her rose colored pocketbook from the side table and Gigi cringed. It was her mom's version of a little black book, but it contained a list of all the society matrons and their eligible bachelor sons. The woman was like the most boring version of the Hollywood Madame, and Gigi was helpless to do anything other than watch in horror as her bony fingers flipped through the pages.

Gigi quickly shot a pleading glance at Ford, but he just shook his head at her. She had brought this on herself in a way, but she had hoped he would repay her for having jumped on a live grenade at the beginning of the night by distracting their mother. *Traitor*, she mouthed to him. He simply shrugged and tried to take another drink, not realizing his glass was empty. "Anyone else need a refill?" Ford asked, grabbing their father's now empty glass and heading over to the drinks cart. Complete coward.

"Ah, here we are." The announcement sent a chill down Gigi's spine as she watched in horror as her mom ran her finger down the page and came to a stop. "Giles Duncan. Thirty-five year old podiatrist and son of Hank and Beverly Duncan." Her mother's eyes sparkled as she looked over at Gigi, clearly satisfied at the result of her perusal. "The Duncans are a great family and their son would be an advantageous match."

"Advantageous match?" She looked around the room for help, but there was none to be found. Her father sat in complete solidarity with his wife and her brother was too busy drowning his sorrows to pay any attention to what was going on. "What century is this?"

"Come now, Virginia. Don't start sassing your mother," her dad scolded lightly, though she could swear she saw the hint of a smile on his face. Her father may ride Ford pretty hard, but he was slightly more lenient on Gigi, though in this case not nearly enough.

Gigi smiled politely at her parents. "I'm not trying to sass anyone, but I'm just a little tired of dating the same type of men all the time." She filled her lungs with air, trying to gather some courage along with it. Standing up to them was something that was long overdue and had to be done if she wanted to maintain even a shred of sanity. "I think I'd like to date outside of the normal pool. Maybe someone like a teacher, or an engineer. I'm a little sick of doctors and lawyers," she admitted without thought to the men in the room. She looked over at her dad and brother, smiling apologetically. "No offense, guys."

Ford chuckled and raised his glass to her. "None taken. I'm a little sick of lawyers myself," he replied boldly, probably due to the alcohol buzz he was already enjoying.

Their father's head darted to where Ford stood, his expression much sharper than it had been moments ago. "You don't seem to be sick of all the money and the nice house your profession affords you." Working in corporate law had afforded her brother a lot of things, but none of those material possessions seemed to bring him any kind of happiness.

Her brother looked sufficiently chagrined and tipped his head down. "Apologies, Dad. Just trying to lighten the mood." Ford looked at her and rolled his eyes so hard she had to stifle a giggle.

"Well, enough of that. This is serious business."

Her mother scolding them once again drew everyone's attention back to her. "I know you haven't been too keen on any of the young men that you've gone out with lately, but I think this Duncan boy could be the one."

Gigi highly doubted that, but she wasn't bold enough or drunk enough to say so. "While I can appreciate that, and your help, I still would like to try things on my own for a while. See how it goes." The shakiness in her voice gave away how nervous she was, but she hoped her parents would ignore that and drop the subject entirely.

Her mother narrowed her gaze on her and Gigi felt the need to sit up straighter and smooth out any wrinkles in her green cocktail dress, unable to shake the lifetime habit of needing to be look and act perfectly in her parent's presence. "Hmm. I will make you a deal." Gigi swallowed nervously and tried to clear away the image of her signing her soul away to the devil that popped into her mind. "I will put a stop to my meddling, but first you have to attend a dating event put on by my friend's charity organization."

The proposal was innocuous enough, but she knew better than to underestimate her mother. "What kind of dating event?" If her mom was going to try and get her to auction herself off or something equally as debasing, Gigi was out of there. Her tolerance for her parents' shenanigans did not extend to that level.

"It's one of those fast date things where you spend a little time with each person before moving to another table," her mom explained.

Ford laughed into his drink. "Speed dating?"

"That's it. Speed dating." Her mom looked back at Gigi and smiled. "Go to this speed dating event, and I will try not to bug you about your personal life for a little while."

Gigi exhaled slowly at the offer that seemed a little too good to be true. She didn't want to go to a speed dating event, but if it would get her mom off her back for even a little while, it would be worth it. Besides, maybe there would be some more down to earth guys in attendance and she could fulfill the pact she made with her friends at the same time. She smiled at her mom, happy at the prospect of mashing two potatoes with one fork. "Okay. I'll do it."

"Wonderful." Her mom clapped her hands together briefly and withdrew an invitation from her pocketbook and handing it to Gigi, her smile shifting from polite to almost sinister. "Here are all the details."

Gigi's eyes wandered over the slip of paper and widened. "It's on Valentine's Day?" Her eyes moved to the bottom of the page and widened further than she thought possible. Gigi had readied herself for an attack that evening, but she was clearly without skill when it came to battling an opponent as crafty as her mom. "And it's sponsored by the Feeding Families Fund and Beverly and Hank Duncan?" Gigi never seemed to remember just how manipulative her mom could be when it came to getting what she wanted.

Ford barked a laugh, his eyes bouncing as they pinged between Gigi and their mom. "Well played, Mama."

Gigi shot him a mutinous look as her mom spoke. "Don't be so quick to gloat, Clifford. I still need to talk to you about your own lack of dating prospects." Gigi's glare turned smug as she watched her brother's face fall and his head hang low at being called by his given name and having exposed himself to her ire. Served him right for reveling in her misery.

"Can we at least have some dinner before you pick apart my social life?" Ford asked as he dropped his empty glass on the tray.

"Very well." Their mom stood and the four of them walked through the hall into the dining room with Gigi and Ford trailing behind as though they were being marched toward the gallows. Since she had agreed to her mother's terms and would attend the dating event, her parents spent most of dinner ragging on her brother, and any time she felt the slightest bit of sympathy at him getting lectured about his love life or his work, she just remembered how he left her to fend for herself and smiled across the table at him.

As the two of them walked out to their cars later that night, Ford looked over at her glumly. "You could have stepped in a time or two back there," he grumbled.

Gigi tried not to laugh as she peered at him, a sardonic expression on her face. "I could say the same thing to you, big brother." They walked to their cars and Gigi stopped just shy of her Beetle. She looked across the roof to Ford as he gazed back over the hillside and down on the town. "Do you think we'll ever be able to stick up for ourselves? Do what we really want with our lives?"

Ford's head turned toward her slowly, a look of hopelessness painted across his face. "If either of us can do it, Ginny, it will be you." He nodded at her and slid into his Audi, driving off into the night.

Gigi slid into her own car and started back toward her home, thinking over her brother's final words to her. Could she really be brave enough to go after what she wanted? The image of a certain mechanic popped into her head, but Gigi shook it away as quickly as she could. She wanted to be brave, and not just for herself, but for her brother as well. She just wasn't certain she could do it. Her confidence in her plan to turn her life around had been up in the clouds, but one dinner with her parents had it down in the dirt once more. No matter what, though, there would need to be a pretty good reason for her to stand up to her parents. As she drove, Gigi couldn't help but wish that just doing it for herself would have been reason enough.

Chapter Six

Cooper

Wednesdays at the auto shop were always a little slow and boring, a bit tedious, but it did allow Cooper to show some of the younger mechanics a thing or two about taking care of cars that they didn't already know, something that he derived a good amount of satisfaction from. Cooper never envisioned himself as a mentor to others, and frankly, he still didn't, but feeling like he was able to impart some kind of wisdom, even if it was only about something as simple as how changing a car's oil when it's hot helps it drain faster or how maintaining a clean and organized work bench makes the day go by much easier, felt fantastic. Currently, Cooper was showing a few of his coworkers something a little more fun and a lot less work related.

"Okay. I think they're probably done now," Cooper shouted over the noise of the engine and signaled for Justin to turn off the truck he and his three coworkers were standing in front of.

Justin cut the engine and hopped out of his large truck. He sauntered over to the hood and watched closely as Cooper popped it open, the smell of cooked meat wafting out to greet them. "Grab me those tongs, will you, Roe?" he called over to Monroe Jenkins, the youngest mechanic of all of them at the tender age of twenty-two. Roe handed him the silver cooking tongs and Cooper grabbed the foil packets that had been sitting on the engine for the last little while. He dropped the packets on the tray being held up by Tommy and then proceeded to shut the hood.

Cooper grabbed the tray and walked the three of them over to the small picnic bench that sat under some old ash trees near the front of the garage's bay doors. It was the perfect spot for them to eat lunch and watch for customers at the same time. He placed the tray down on the table and pulled ketchup and mustard bottles from his coveralls, slamming them down on the table in triumph with a cocky grin on his face as he glanced around the group. "Gentlemen. Lunch is served."

Cooper watched with amusement as the guys tore open the foil packets and began to assemble hot dogs on the warm, buttered buns that had also been heating on the engine block. It wasn't the fanciest meal any of them would ever eat, but there was something great about eating a meal, no matter how modest, that you had cooked in your car, or on your car to be more specific. Cooper grabbed a dog for himself, and after adding a little ketchup and a generous portion of mustard, he took a bite and groaned when the meat popped between his teeth, the juices and savory flavor spilling onto his tongue. The tangy mustard and sweet ketchup added a nice touch, and as he enjoyed his small meal, he wondered what else they could cook on the engine during their lunch break in the future. Buttered sweet corn on the cob could be fun to try once summer rolled around he mused, consuming half of the hot dog in another bite.

Tommy looked over at Cooper, a mustard blob tracking its way down his chin. "Where'd you learn to do this, Coop?"

Cooper swallowed the lump in his mouth and smiled as he remembered the first time he ever cooked on an engine. "My grandad taught me when I was, oh, maybe twelve or so," he explained, wiping his hands on his coveralls and continuing on with his story. "We had been working on his old Chevy pickup. It was lime green and ugly as hell, but it was reliable and that's all grandad really cared about, so we kept it in good condition." He paused, taking a drink from his water bottle to wash down the rest of his food and the lump of emotion that always formed in his throat at the thought of his late grandfather. "Anyway, we had been working on it all morning, so when lunch time rolls around, grandad heads inside the house and comes back with some steak cubes, two potatoes, and a packet of foil. Then he shows me how to prep the food, cook it, and check it to see if it's done. Now, you fellas are reaping the benefits."

"That's awesome." Crumbs flew as Roe muttered around the end of his second dog, the earnestness in his voice making up for any lack of manners. "My granddad only ever taught me how to write a check. Not exactly something that comes in handy these days."

"Hey, you never know when you'll need to bust out a checkbook," Cooper mused. He had never owned a checkbook himself, and while he remembered practicing writing them out in school, he wasn't sure he could perform the same act again if pressed to do so today. "Pretty sure my gran still writes checks to pay her bills. She can text message with the best of them, but when I showed her how she could pay for things from her phone, she practically accused me of witchcraft."

They all shared a chuckle when an aqua colored, 1967 Mustang convertible pulled up to the shop. The vintage car was beautiful, but it wasn't what had all the guys at the table with him wagging their tongues out like a group of puppies. The driver's door opened and a long, slender leg appeared before the rest of the professionally dressed woman exited the vehicle. Jo, Bob's daughter, shook out her blonde curls and waved over to the table. "Hello, boys."

Cooper just shook his head and tried not to laugh. The flirtatious tone and sway of her hips did nothing for him, but the other three men were practically climbing over one another to get to her first. He could admit that Jo was an attractive gal, he had eyes after all, but even if she weren't the boss's daughter and all kinds of trouble, she just wasn't his type. His gaze flicked across the street to the tearoom where the one woman to get his blood stirring over the last few years currently was, probably serving some kind of fancy finger foods and hobnobbing with the more respectable members of society.

Cooper was so lost in thinking of what Virginia was doing that he didn't notice Jo approach until he heard her speaking from right next to him. "You should ask her out."

He slowly turned his head and peered down slightly to face her. There was mischief in her eyes and she was currently sporting what could only be described as a shit-eating grin on her face. Normally that spelled trouble and he wasn't in the mood for any of that today. "Ask who out?" he said dumbly, knowing full well he had just been caught gazing longingly across the way.

Jo rolled her eyes and nodded at the tea shop. "Gigi. Owner and proprietor of The Happy Kettle," she explained slowly. Cooper was used to people talking to him like he was slow, but at least he knew Jo wasn't doing it with any real malice, only attitude. "She also happens to be one of my very best friends and I know for a fact that she is single and ready to mingle." She waggled her eyebrows suggestively and Cooper stifled a laugh.

"No one under the age of seventy uses that phrase anymore." He was fairly certain even his gran didn't use it, but the tease was more about distracting Jo as he ducked his head to try and hide the smile that threatened to come out. Gigi. That seemed a much more appropriate name for the petite woman with auburn hair and bright smile. Not that he'd ever seen that smile up close, but one could see a lot when they looked over to the patio of the tearoom, and Miss Gigi Davenport always came out to greet her customers with a smile that could light up even the darkest of spaces.

"No matter what you call it, she's on the market, and I think you should go for it." Jo leaned in a little closer and lowered her voice conspiratorially. "Don't think I haven't seen you checking her out when she pops outside every now and then." His wide-eyed gaze met hers and she started to chuckle. "Oh, my god. That was a total shot in the dark, but it's true isn't it?"

Cooper shuffled his feet, annoyed that he'd given himself away. He may not be the best at expressing his emotions, but sometimes it seemed to be written all over his face. "I don't know what you're talking about," he lied and started to gather the trash from the picnic table. Feeling like a dumb teenager again had his mood heading south rather quickly, and he wanted nothing more than to end the conversation and get back to work. "Doesn't matter anyway. Woman like that wouldn't go for a guy like me." No matter how much he wished that weren't true or how often he heard his own words from the other day ringing in his ears, *love is enough,* he couldn't seem to get past other people past judgements and his own insecurities.

Jo looked over toward the tearoom and smiled. "Oh, I don't know about that." She turned her head back to look at Cooper, the same mischief in her eyes tempered slightly by a look of authenticity. "I think she might just surprise you." Jo raised her hand and started waving across the street.

Cooper followed her gaze and saw Gigi standing on her patio. She looked gorgeous in her long-sleeve, floral dress, her hair down and blowing slightly in the breeze. She smiled happily in their direction and waved back to her friend enthusiastically. He watched as her gaze met his and her smiled turned a little shy, but it was still there. They just stood there, eyes locked for what felt like the longest, most emotionally charged moment of his life. Then someone called Gigi's name and the spell was broken. She gave him another small wave and nodded as she turned around and went inside. "Interesting," he said to himself. Maybe he was more her type than he originally thought. The way her eyes always seemed to be drawn to him certainly spoke to that.

"Isn't it just," Jo replied. Cooper had honestly forgotten all about her once he had laid eyes on her friend, and even as he tried to give her his attention, he found it difficult to wrench his gaze from where it had been. "So, you going to make a move, gearhead?"

He leveled her with a glare. "I'll let that slide since you're as much of a gearhead as any of us," he told her, heading back toward the bay. Jo had also worked in the auto shop and while their time hadn't overlapped much, Cooper had witnessed enough to know was more skilled than pretty much anyone else he'd ever worked with. "I need to get back to work."

"Fine, fine. Avoid the question." Her complaint trailed behind him as she followed him into the bay, her heels clacking on the cement. "I wouldn't wait too long, though. Gigi won't be on the market for long." Cooper glanced over his shoulder, watching as Jo walked backwards toward the office where her father was working away at his computer.

Cooper merely grunted in reply, not sure what to do with all of this new information he had. Gigi was in fact single, and if the staring contest they had just participated in was any indication, she might actually be interested in him, too, but would it be for the long term, or was she just looking for a bit of fun? She definitely didn't seem like the type to have one night stands or want to be friends with benefits, but he didn't really know her that well.

He looked over through the glass window of the office to see Jo having lunch with her dad. Cooper could go ask her more about it, but he didn't want to come off as obvious or desperate, even though desperate was what he was starting to feel. Desperate for more Gigi. He shook his head and started organizing his tools. He suddenly felt like he was back in high school, nervous as he felt over this woman. Cooper hadn't felt butterflies in his stomach in at least a decade, but they were flitting around in droves right now.

Cooper felt a presence at his side and looked over to see all three of his coworkers gathered around him. "Hey," Roe started, "were you and Jo ever a thing?"

Cooper barked a laugh at anyone thinking he and Jo would ever be inclined to do more than bust each other's balls. "Hell, no. Even if she wouldn't eat me up and spit me out, I would never even try to date Bob's daughter. I like being gainfully employed, thank you very much."

Roe looked over at the other two and looked back at Cooper, his expression hopeful. "Do you think she might ever go out with one of us?"

Cooper chuckled until he realized that they were serious. It wasn't his place to speak for the woman, but he knew well enough to not give them any false hope. He shook his head solemnly. Poor kids. "Afraid not, fellas. From what I can tell, that woman does not shit where she eats, and even though she doesn't work here, her daddy does. I would do your best to move on."

"Figures," Justin muttered sadly and the men dispersed around the garage. He felt a little bad for dashing the hopes of those guys so thoroughly, but there was no way Jolene Farrow would date a guy that worked with her dad.

Cooper chuckled to himself at their hangdog expressions and got back to his business when his phone pinged. Knowing there was only one person who would text him in the middle of the day, he reached into his back pocket and checked the notification, a smile already plastered on his face.

Mags: **I need a ride home. Can you come pick me up?**

Cooper needed less than half a second to ready himself to do as she asked. He looked around the empty garage and trotted over to the office, knocking lightly on the open door while peeking inside. "Hey, Bob. My grandma needs a lift. Mind if I take off for a bit to go get her?"

Bob leaned back in his chair and took in the sight of the empty shop. "Go for it. I don't think we'll be getting more than we can handle anytime soon." He gazed over at his daughter proudly. "Besides, I can always tag Jo in if needs be."

Jo dropped her sandwich on her plate and shook her head. "I don't think so. I'm already pushing things today by having lunch with you when I should be at the office."

The typically jovial man's expression fell as he studied his daughter. "You work too hard," Bob grumbled at her before turning to Cooper. "Go head, kid. I'll see you back here later."

"Thanks, Bob." Rapping his knuckles on the door, Cooper left the office, thankful he had an employer that was not only friendly and competent, but flexible. Pulling out his phone, he typed a reply to his gran as he walked toward his house to grab the keys to his truck.

Cooper: **Sure thing, Mags. Where am I picking you up from?**

He watched the three dots bounce for a moment,

knowing that with her almost supernatural technical skills, very little time would pass before her reply came in.

Mags: **The Happy Kettle. Do you know it? It's right across from you.**

Cooper stopped dead in his tracks and looked over his shoulder. He couldn't see the tearoom from back here, but he tried to, nonetheless. Glancing down at his current state of dress, he swore under his breath. Gigi had only ever seen him in his coveralls, and while she still seemed to like what she saw, he had hoped that he could make a better impression when he actually met her for the first time. Cooper thought for a moment, deciding he could take an extra five minutes at home to stash his coveralls and wash his hands.

Cooper: **I'll be there in ten.**

Cooper strode into his house, ignoring Shep as he trotted over, already begging for scratches. He looked down at his dog and patted his head, only slightly regretful at not being able to give him any attention. "Sorry, boy. I need to get cleaned up so I can make a good impression on a pretty lady." He walked back toward his bathroom, shouting at his canine companion along the way. "I'll make it up to you later."

Cooper stripped off his coveralls and inspected the clothes he wore underneath. He decided that the dark wash jeans and white t-shirt were as good as his closet had to offer at the moment and started scrubbing his hands, taking extra care to remove as much grease and grime as possible. It was no small undertaking, and when he was finished, he looked up into the mirror and noticed that his hair and beard were a bit shaggy. There wasn't much he could do about that now, so he just ran his hands through both to tame them a bit and reapplied some deodorant, feeling a bit more presentable as he walked back through his house and out to his truck.

It seemed a bit silly to drive across the street, but Cooper didn't want his gran to have to walk further than necessary. He parked in the small lot between the tearoom and the hardware store and headed toward the small cottage. It was a cute shop. The pistachio green exterior was bright and fresh looking, and the flagstone walkway was lined with all kinds of vegetation from small flowers and clover to larger trees and shrubs. The place looked perfectly put together but also had a sense of whimsy and charm, just like the owner seemed to.

Cooper nodded to a few patrons who dined on the patio as he passed toward the front door. After one last once over in the reflection of the glass, he took a deep breath and pulled it open, stepping inside and immediately noticing the smell of tea, fresh bread, and sweet cakes. He glanced around the shop, taking in the pale pink walls, lavender tablecloths and white chairs. He couldn't spot his grandma, but his eyes did eventually land on the beautiful shop owner that had occupied almost every one of his thoughts over the last few weeks.

Gigi was busy packing up some tea boxes for a couple and didn't notice him right away, so he took a moment to admire the view. Her hair was the color of red maple leaves in the fall, and it played nicely off the ivory skin on her heart-shaped face. Her eyes shined with mirth as she laughed with her customers, the rich, musical tone of her voice causing goosebumps to erupt up and down his arms. As she bid the couple farewell, her gaze slid sideways over to him.

When her hazel eyes met his, Cooper could swear he felt rooted to the spot, more grounded than he'd ever felt in his entire life. Something about her eyes that weren't quite brown, blue, or green, but a wonderful mix of all three had him mesmerized and unable to move. He watched as she walked out from behind her small counter and toward him, her hips swaying hypnotically as she approached. He took in the sculpted calves exposed under the hem of her dress and tried to think of anything other than how good she would look naked.

A small smile pulled across her rosy lips, and it was so inviting that he fell a little bit in love with her on the spot. How could he not become immediately enamored with someone so warm and welcoming? "Can I help you?"

Her voice was rich, and just husky enough to get the attention of certain body parts that really didn't need to be making an appearance at the moment. Not only did he not want to startle her, but he also didn't need the town's more talkative citizens as witnesses to any of his humiliations. Cooper swallowed the lump that had formed in his throat and tried his best to act like a normal human being. "Yes," he started, his voice a little higher than usual. He shook his head and cleared his throat, trying once again for normal when he felt anything but. "I'm actually here to pick up my gran. Maggie Ellis."

Gigi's eyes widened, as did her smile. "Mags is your grandma?" He nodded and she clasped her hands together, the affection she held for his kin plain as day on her face. "Oh, I just love her to pieces. She and her friends come in here every Wednesday, and I so look forward to their visits." Her arm extended toward his as she stuck her hand out for him to shake, but it felt less like a perfunctory greeting and more like a lifeline. Something about her told Cooper she was going to save him, hopefully from a lifetime of loneliness. "I'm Gigi, by the way."

Cooper took her hand, the soft feel of her against his work-roughened skin causing sparks to crackle almost visibly on his skin the moment their fingers touched. The tingling seemed to zip all the way up his arm, and by the look of surprise on Gigi's face, she felt it too. He pulled out his best smile for her, trying to dazzle her the same way she had him. "Nice to meet you, Gigi. I'm Cooper."

"Cooper." She'd spoken his name quietly to herself, almost as if she were in a dream state, before shaking her head. "How about I take you to your gran?"

She didn't wait for a reply and slipped her arm through his, the two of them slotting together perfectly as she steered him around the tearoom. The tables they passed were occupied by patrons sipping tea, eating small sandwiches, or enjoying a slice of cake, chatter and laughter filling the air as they enjoyed their time there. The place was obviously very successful, so she must be doing quite well for herself in the money department. Thinking of their class disparity had his confidence wavering, so he tried to distract himself with conversation.

"You have a lovely shop." It was a true reflection of the woman next to him, only she was far lovelier than any building he'd ever been in. They passed pictures that hung on the wall, older photos from years past that showed the history of the shop they were in. Eventually, they were walking into another small room, a whole new set of eyes peering over at the two of them curiously.

Cooper ignored the lookie-loos and concentrated on the woman on his arm, a woman who was currently beaming the most stunning smile he had ever seen up at him. Gigi's head needed to tilt back a good amount for her eyes to meet his, and he couldn't help but think about how good it would feel to pick her up in his arms and hold her there so he could come face to face with her for a kiss. "Thank you." She spoke with sincerity, not a trace of false friendliness or arrogance he'd come to expect of the upper class. It was refreshing, and it endeared her to him even more. "It was my grandma's and I took it over after she passed."

Cooper set aside his current line of thinking and stopped walking, looking at her with a sympathetic expression, wanting, *needing*, to offer her even some small measure of comfort. "I'm sorry for your loss." No matter how much time passes, some things like the death of a beloved relative never seem to feel much lighter. He knew that well enough with his granddad.

She smiled sadly. "Thanks. It was a few years back," she explained, looking around the room, her eyes shining as they roamed the walls. "At least I have this place. It's filled with so many memories of her. Anytime I miss my grandmother, I just sit here and look around, and it's like she's right back here with me."

Cooper returned her smile, sliding his free hand into his pocket lest he was tempted to reach over and tuck the loose strand of hair that was cradling her cheek behind her ear. Now that he'd met Gigi, he wasn't going to screw anything up by jumping the gun. "I know what you mean. I think of my granddad anytime I work on a car or fix up something around my house."

"He's the one that taught you about cars?" she asked sweetly. Cooper nodded and she smiled wistfully. Each new type of smile she tossed his way was one he planned on keeping on file in his memory banks to think about the next time he was even the slightest bit down. "I guess that makes both of us legacies of some sort, carrying on our grandparents' traditions and skills."

Cooper hadn't ever really thought of his life in those terms, but it was nice to imagine that he was carrying on for his granddad in some manner. It was also pretty cool that the two of them had something in common despite their very different backgrounds and upbringings, a solid foundation to build a relationship on.

"I like that. Thanks, Gigi." She stumbled a little as she walked and he steadied her with a hand on her elbow. "You all right?"

"Uh huh." Her voice was soft as she blinked up at him with her doe eyes before they were moving again. They stopped at a large table in the corner of a brightly lit room where Mags and four other silver haired women sat and drank tea while playing cards. Gigi lightly touched a hand to his grandma's shoulder, alerting her to their presence. "Mags, you didn't tell me you had your own personal shuttle service. That's some fancy business. Here I've been giving you the senior discount for years when clearly you are fairly well off. Have you been holding out on me?"

Mags patted Gigi's hand and smiled up at her. "Ha! The only extra cash I get is when I clean up while playing poker with these four." Mags then swept her hands into the center of the table and gathered up what looked to be a good amount of loose change and some paper bills. She stowed the cash in her small purse and pushed up from the table. "Ladies. It was a pleasure stealing your retirement money. I will see you next week."

A chorus of grumbled goodbyes rang out from around the table and Cooper tipped his head to the older women. He held his arm out for his grandma and she took it, holding onto Gigi with her other hand. Mags smiled up at him as they steered their way back to the front of the shop. "Thanks for picking me up, son. Those ladies wanted to make a day of it and go shopping, but I just don't have it in me today."

Concern furrowed his brow and he noticed a similar look on Gigi, his heart warming at her thoughtfulness toward someone that was important to him. "You feeling okay, Mags?" he asked, slowing his pace for her.

She waved off his concern and blew a raspberry between her lips. "I'm fine. I just didn't feel like trying to twist and contort these old bones into a bunch of lingerie. Who needs fancy underwear at this age I ask you?"

Cooper shook his head and he glanced over at Gigi, who was covering up her giggling with her hand. It was said that the elderly had no filter when it came to conversation, but that had always been true of his grandma. "That's a little more information than I needed, Mags"

She swat as his chest, the contact feeling barely stronger than a stiff breeze. "Oh, please. You kids nowadays talk about all sorts of things." She stopped at the front counter and pulled out her winnings from earlier, thumbing through the thick wad and picking out a few twenties. "Isn't that right, Gigi? Why just the other week I thought I heard you and a friend talking about waxing or peeling or something like that."

Cooper raised an eyebrow at the woman in question and her face turned bright red as she stuttered a response. "I-I'm not sure what we were talking about, Mags." She took the money from his grandma and turned around and opened the register. When she faced them again her face looked less like a beet and more like a strawberry, but her embarrassment was still clear as day. Gigi passed some change to his grandma and managed a polite smile. "Either way, that's probably not something your grandson needs to hear about."

"I don't know about that," Mags snorted as she pocketed her change. "If it involved waxing, he should ask some questions. Maybe he can get rid of the shag carpet he's stapled to his face."

Cooper looked over at his grandma with a blank expression and sighed. It seemed as though his grandma was determined to embarrass both he and Gigi today. "Not with the facial hair again, please." He ran a hand over his beard self-consciously.

"I like your beard." Gigi's confession was quickly followed by her eyes going wide and her cheeks flaming once again. "Makes you look rugged," she mumbled, straightening some merchandise on top of the counter.

"Thank you, ma'am." Cooper let his southern charm speak for itself while he tucked the compliment away for later review. If she liked her men rugged, he would don some flannel and take up chopping wood as a hobby just to please her.

Gigi looked up at him with a smirk. "Ma'am, huh? How old do I look?" Gigi's eyebrow raised in challenge, but he knew better than to step into that trap.

Cooper smiled back, hands raised in surrender. "I meant it as a term of respect, Miss Gigi, and I may not know much about women, but I know enough not to answer your question." He winked at the woman and held out his arm for his grandma. "Shall we?"

His grandma smiled at Gigi. "Have a nice day, dear."

"You, too, Mags," Gigi replied to his gran, flashing a smile at him. "Cooper."

He was so busy enjoying the way his name rolled off her tongue that he barely managed to nod his head. "Ma'am." Cooper watched as she narrowed her eyes at him, but a smile played at the corners of her mouth.

Cooper steered his grandma out to his truck and helped her up onto the bench seat. When he slid into his own side, he felt the sting of her purse as it whacked him in the chest. "Hey, what was that for?" he asked as he rubbed the sore spot. He'd done plenty in the past to warrant such behavior, but for the last decade, he'd practically been a boy scout.

"You really don't know much about women, do you?" Mags huffed, clearly annoyed as he pulled out of the lot and into traffic, pointing the car toward her apartment. "That girl was giving you just about every signal there is and you left without asking her out on a date."

Cooper scoffed. "I don't think she was giving off every signal." His voice sounded unconvincing, even to himself. He could definitely feel something between the two of them, and she did seem pretty interested, but what was he supposed to do? Ask her out in front of his grandma and all her customers? He didn't need that kind of audience for his possible rejection.

"Gigi was practically begging you with her eyes to ask her out, and you flubbed it." His grandma crossed her arms in frustration. "And after all the work I put in to get you over here."

The truck screeched to a halt at a red light, and he couldn't stop himself from glaring at his grandma. If meddling in other people's business was an Olympic sport, Mags would win the gold every time. "Are you telling me you set this up? Did you even need a ride home?"

"Of course I didn't need a ride home." Mags held up her phone and shook it. "I know how to order a ride service." She sighed and looked over at him, her expression softer. "Every time I've been in that tearoom I've watched her looking out to the auto shop, hoping she'll see you. And I've seen you across the street, looking over at her. I thought I could play cupid, but I didn't take your total lack of game into account."

Cooper smiled, ignoring the slight on his dating skills because she had a very valid point. "How do you know we weren't looking at other people?"

Mags scoffed at his obvious attempt at subterfuge.

"I'm old, I'm not blind or stupid. I can tell when two people are looking at each other with hearts in their eyes." His grandma sighed dreamily for a moment before slapping his chest with her purse again. "So get it together."

"Okay, okay. Just stop hitting me with your purse." The light turned green and he started driving again, trying not to laugh at the comedy of errors he'd been unwittingly drawn into.

Cooper did want to get it together and ask out the pretty tearoom owner, he just wasn't sure exactly how to go about doing that. He thought about it some more during the drive to his gran's place and the whole way back to the garage, but he was no closer to figuring anything out by the time he arrived back there. There were still a few hours of work left, so after going back to his house and putting on his coveralls once more, he went back to the garage where he spent the rest of the day trying and failing to take his mind off of Gigi.

Chapter Seven

Gigi

Gigi locked up the tearoom promptly at 4:00 and ran into the kitchen to say goodnight to Stella, the head chef, and the rest of the kitchen and wait staff before she went into the back office and did her end of the day audit. She counted cash and receipts, making sure that everything on her count matched what was in the computer. When she was satisfied with her numbers, she placed the cash in the banker's envelope and put it into the small safe that was stashed in the back of the office, feeling as though she could finally relax after another day's work. The safe was the same one that had been there since her grandma opened the shop, and after Gigi secured the money and spun the lock, she kissed the tips of her fingers and pressed them to the picture of her grandma that hung on the wall above it.

"Love you, Granny Mae." Gigi spoke to the picture of the smiling woman at the grand opening of her tearoom every day as a way of keeping her close. Mae had always believed in her, and that meant more to Gigi than she had probably ever expressed while the woman was alive, so she made sure to do it now.

When she was finished, it was a little past 5:30, and Gigi was looking forward to a warm soak in the tub. Her feet ached from being in heels all day, and she considered for probably the hundredth time that day if she shouldn't be a little more practical with her footwear. The heels did add to her five foot four inches of height, and they made her legs look amazing, something she was pretty sure didn't go unnoticed by the handsome mechanic from across the way. Cooper Ellis. The name seemed the perfect fit for the sexy, muscular man, and

Gigi wondered if cars and home repair were the only areas in which he was good with his hands.

Gigi blushed at the thought as well as the memory of their interactions from earlier, and despite Mags's ability to embarrass the crap out of her, she had enjoyed the time spent with him immensely. There was a thoughtfulness about Cooper that spoke to her. He felt like a kindred spirit of sorts, something that had been made all the more apparent as she listened to him speak so reverently about his grandfather. It was the same way Gigi felt about her grandmother, and she was happy to know that at the very least, they had that one thing in common.

Gigi sighed dreamily as she thought of Cooper, grabbing her purse and coat before heading out the back. The keypad beeped cheerily as she set the alarm on her way out. Crime in Willow Creek was almost nonexistent, but the Happy Kettle was too precious to her to take any chances. The lot wasn't completely deserted, but there weren't a ton of customers at the hardware store. At least there was still a bit of light left in the sky, ensuring she felt safe as she approached her little blue car.

Opening the door, she slid inside, the cool leather causing a shiver to run up her spine. Gigi looked forward to the warmer months ahead, her mind working quickly to come up with images of what her mechanic would look like in a swimsuit. She pictured the two of them dancing under the water in the river, limbs tangling and laughter filling the air. She would bet good money that Cooper looked mighty fine in nothing but a pair of swim trunks. She laughed at herself and her meanderings. If he was interested, he probably would have asked her out, but since that hadn't happened, Gigi could only guess that her little infatuation was one sided.

Shrugging off the disappointment at that thought

as best she could, Gigi slipped her keys into the ignition and started the car. She put it in REVERSE, but the engine sputtered and shut down. She put her car back in PARK and tried turning it on and off again, but the car did nothing. No indicator lights had gone on, so she had no idea what could be wrong with her car. Truthfully, Gigi wouldn't have known anyway. Her dad always handled her car maintenance, paying someone to come by her place and look over the car, so she never really had to worry about it.

Pulling out her phone, Gigi considered calling her dad, but she didn't really want to deal with him or how pathetic she felt every time she went running to him or used her family's social connections to solve a problem. Relying a little less on her parents for these kinds of things needed to be a bigger priority. She was an adult, and her acting like it was long overdue. A minor inconvenience like this was something she could handle on her own, or at the very least, without calling her daddy at the first sign of trouble. If Gigi was going to start standing up for herself, she needed to begin somewhere, so why not start with something small like fixing her car.

Gigi found the latch that popped open the hood and she stepped outside. She propped open the front of her car and looked inside for a few minutes, nothing standing out other than the fact that the labyrinth of metal tubes and wires all looked rather dirty. "Yeah, I have no idea what I'm doing," she muttered to herself, pulling out her phone to call Jo.

"Ms. Farrow's office. Can you hold please?" A familiar voice rang through the speaker.

Gigi rolled her eyes at her friend's play acting. "Shut up, Jo. You know it's me." Jo never passed up an opportunity to bust someone's chops, but Gigi wasn't in the mood. She wanted to get home, get in the tub with a pint of butter pecan ice cream, and turn off her brain for a while.

Chuckling sounded on the other end. "Just practicing for when I'm a big shot at the office and you have to get through three personal assistants to get to me."

Gigi smiled at the thought, hoping that her friend eventually did reach that level of success. "I called your personal cell, silly. Anyway, I need your help." Even to her own ears, her voice was whiny, but at least she was complaining to a friend and not her dad. "My car won't start and I have no idea what I'm even looking at in here." Seriously. Gigi knew where the engine and battery were, but anything else was just a poorly educated guess. Maybe she should have taken auto shop in high school instead of choir.

Gigi heard some papers shuffle before Jo started talking. "And how do you suppose I am going to help you from over the phone?"

Gigi shuffled her feet on the asphalt, more uncertain of her self-rescue plan with each passing second. "I don't know. Can't you just tell me what to look for? I'm sure I can figure it out from there." There wasn't even a remote possibility of that happening, but Gigi was sure once she got Jo talking, her friend would be too intrigued to stop helping her. Jo loved cars and couldn't pass up the opportunity to solve a problem with one if she could.

Jo laughed for a little too long at her statement and finally sighed. "Oh, Gi. You slay me." More papers shuffling and a snap of her fingers followed her declaration. "I would love to spend the five or six hours it would take for me to walk you through every possible reason why your car isn't working, but I have to run into a meeting. Wait, are you at work?"

Gigi glanced around the parking lot, hoping a Good Samaritan would pass by and save her. Becoming more self-reliant turned out to be more difficult than she thought, and while she would definitely continue to pursue it, right now she just wanted things to be easy for her once again. "Yes, but no one else is around." Why couldn't her car have broken down on a Friday or weekend when more people were about?

"It's too bad there isn't an auto shop across the street from you where you could go get someone to help you out," Jo said sarcastically.

Gigi bit her lower lip, her eyes flicking across the street toward the garage. "Isn't the shop closed?"

Jo sighed. "I mean, yeah, but if my dad is still there, he'll take care of it for you. Or … I'm sure Coop is available. He lives behind the shop after all." The thought of seeing Cooper again had her heart racing, but she tried to calm it immediately, reminding herself that he might not even be interested in her.

Gigi's eyes wandered over to the shop again, and while most of it was dark, there was a small light on in the bay giving her the encouragement she needed. "I guess I could give it a shot."

Applause rang through the speaker. "Atta girl. Report back later with anything interesting, realizing of course that anything less than sex on a workbench will not be interesting to me." Unsurprisingly, Jo promptly ended the call.

Gigi grumbled at her phone, slipping it into the small pocket of her dress. Thanks to Jo, she was now thinking about sex when she should be thinking about her car. With a shake of her head, she grabbed her purse from the car and checked traffic before heading across the street. Gigi approached the bay that had the light on, peeking through the smudged glass to let her eyes wander around the shop. There wasn't a lot of light, just enough to see that there wasn't anyone inside.

With a sigh, Gigi turned to walk back to her car and screamed when she realized there was a person directly in front of her. The shrill sound bounced off the door, making her wince. Once her ears stopped ringing, she tilted her head up to see Cooper looking at her with concern in her eyes. "You okay?"

Gigi clutched a hand to her chest, trying to catch her breath after the scare while swatting at him with her purse. "God, you scared the crap out of me." She looked from left to right, seeing nothing but empty space on either side. He'd appeared like an apparition on Halloween night, and if it weren't for open expression on his face, she might have taken a step back. "Where did you even come from?"

"I was taking the trash out to the dumpster when I saw you." He hooked a thumb over his shoulder toward the dumpsters that were overflowing with black garbage bags. "What is it with women and their purses today," he murmured quietly, rubbing at the arm she hit while shaking his head at her.

She looked down at her large leather handbag and gave him a contrite expression. "Sorry about that. I get a little violent when I'm spooked." Probably a result of listening to too many true crime podcasts, but they were too entertaining for her to consider stopping.

"Good to know." Cooper smiled at her, his eyes traveling over her face as though he was studying a beautiful work of art. Her stomach fluttered at the soft look in his eyes, reconsidering her earlier position on him not being interested. "So, to what do I owe the pleasure?"

Gigi's mind was snagged on the word pleasure and how it fell from his full lips like honey off the dipper. "Hmm?" She stared at him dumbly for a long moment, cataloging his handsome features as she registered the rest of his question. "Oh. Um, my car won't start and I was hoping someone would still be around to maybe take a look at it for me."

A wide grin pulled across his face and he gestured for him to follow her. "Let me just grab some tools and we'll head over."

"Thank you, thank you, thank you." His offer of help had buoyed her spirits and she couldn't help espousing her gratitude as she followed him into the shop. "I'm at a total loss when it comes to cars, so I really appreciate you taking the time."

Gigi's eyes followed Cooper as he moved over to a clean and organized workbench and he reached underneath, grabbing for something. She watched with rapt attention as his coveralls tightened over his firm, round ass as he bent down to retrieve a toolbox. She'd never considered coveralls to be a particularly provocative outfit, but the way he wore them was so effortlessly sexy that Gigi wondered if he'd just unearthed a new kink for her. "Happy to do it." She was so lost in images of him bending her over the hood of a car that she didn't notice Cooper looking at her over his shoulder and totally catching her checking out his backside. He winked and stood up, walking back toward the open garage door.

She felt her cheeks flame once again and was thankful that it was dark enough now to not show against her skin as badly as it probably had earlier. Gigi followed him and when they made it to the main road, she slipped her arm in the one he had offered her. Cooper was every bit the gentleman, even though she didn't deserve such service after she had so blatantly ogled him. He didn't seem to mind all that much and even looked a bit pleased, so she tried not to beat herself up about it.

They crossed over and walked into the parking lot where her car stood, the hood still propped open. "I'm assuming this is you." He gestured to her Volkswagen with his toolbox, his mouth turned down slightly at the corners.

"Yeah, that's me." She walked up to the car with him, putting her hands on her hips as he placed his toolbox down on the ground.

Cooper looked over at her, his blue eyes sparkling in the fading evening light. They were the same color as the river, a bright blue that shone from the water when it was calm and peaceful. His eyes crinkled at the corners and he smiled at her. "Just a word to the wise, Miss Gigi. You should always shut your hood when you're away from the vehicle."

Her head bobbed as she rushed to agree with him. "Right. Someone might mess with it when I'm gone." She should have known better than to leave her car open like that. Apparently those true crime podcasts hadn't drilled street smarts into her brain quite as much as she thought.

He shrugged a shoulder. "Sure, that's always a possibility, but I meant it more because squirrels will climb in here and chew through wires and things like that. Nasty little buggers can mess your car up good."

"Oh." Gigi's body slumped. She felt a little silly for not knowing something like that was even a possibility. "Is that what happened to my car? Squirrels?"

Cooper shook his head slowly, a bemused expression on his face. "No. That's just a friendly warning. I wouldn't want you to run into any more trouble." He scratched his beard and his eyes raked up and down her body appreciatively, her body shivering as though it had been a physical caress. "Although, if it means you come knocking at my door again, maybe I should toss a few acorns in there and leave the rest up to the squirrels."

She chuckled and smiled coyly at him, her body swaying toward his. "You know, there are easier ways to get me to come knocking on your door." Gigi loved that he was flirting with her, but she wanted more than that from him. All those lingering looks across the street had sparked her near obsession with the man, and now she finally had him in front of her in relative privacy. Oh, the things her body longed to do with him.

Cooper stepped closer to her and she caught a bit of his scent. He smelled like worn leather and motor oil, not a combination she would have thought would work for her, but, boy, was it getting her libido up and running right now. "That so?" His voice was low and a little gravelly, his warm breath fanning across her cheek.

Gigi nodded and licked her lips, hoping that the two of them were going to kiss. She barely knew anything about Cooper, but what she did know was that she wanted him to kiss her, badly. You could tell a lot from a kiss, and she had the gut feeling that one from him would flip her world upside-down, something she'd been longing for. His eyes flicked to her lips and she tilted her head up when a loud voice boomed across the way. "You having car trouble, Gigi?"

Gigi blinked away the lust in her eyes, sighed, and turned to the owner of the neighboring business. "I am, Mr. Grady, but I've got someone here to help me with it." She looked over at Cooper who had an amused expression on his face before turning back to the older man across the way. "Thanks for your concern."

"Let me know if you need a jump. I've got cables," he said excitedly, turning and heading back into his hardware store.

Cooper chuckled as he leaned into her space a

little more. "What do you say, Miss Gigi? Do you need a jump from old man Grady?" He waggled his eyebrows and smirked and she slapped his arm for the second time that night.

"Don't be crass." Her scolding meant very little, especially when she couldn't hide her giggle or her smile.

"Just checking." He winked again and peered under the hood of her car. He pulled out a flashlight and proceeded to poke around for a few minutes. She stared in awe as his strong hands moved around so adeptly. They looked far rougher than any on the men she'd dated before, but she didn't want those soft men anymore. She wanted someone with a little more edge to them, someone whose hands would feel masculine, like rough sandpaper against her skin. She may want to be more independent, but she also liked feeling delicate. Cooper had already accomplished that just in the way he looked at her like she was something to be treasured. "What exactly happened when you tried to turn your car on?"

Gigi tried to switch gears and explain it as accurately as possible. For someone who knew next to nothing about cars, she was still confident she could do that much. "Well, I got it started, the engine turned over and everything, but as soon as I began backing out, it started making this sputtering sound. Kind of like, whooga wheeeee," she said, doing her best to imitate the sound her car made.

Copper tapped his lip. "Interesting. Can you make the sound again?" he asked, his brow furrowed in concentration.

Gigi nodded, happy to comply with any request he made. "Oh, sure. It was whooga whooga wheeeee, with the wheezing part kind of ending with a loud cough."

"Hmm. Once more." The additional request

seemed unnecessary, so she glanced over at him, seeing him trying and failing to keep his mouth from pulling into a smile. "Not sure I got it the first two times."

Gigi placed her hands on her hips and glared at him, though there was no malice in her stare because he looked so damn good when he was joking around. His eyes crinkled at the corners and his mouth ticked up on the left side, the lopsided smirk as endearing as it was alluring. She could stare at him all evening. "That's not funny, Cooper."

Cooper smiled apologetically, but it didn't hold for long. "C'mon. It was a little funny." He bumped her shoulder with his arm and smiled at her affectionately. "Besides, I couldn't resist. You're too cute when you're making your little car sounds."

"Whatever." Gigi turned, failing to hide her own wide grin. Forget her being cute, Cooper was the one that was far too sexy. Even when he was teasing her, she wanted him, and she was pretty certain she had a permanent blush on her cheeks whenever this man was around. Gigi tried to ignore the butterflies that were fluttering rapidly around her stomach and gestured toward her vehicle. "So what does that sound mean?"

Cooper's head bounced from side to side thoughtfully. "Well, it could mean a lot of things, but I'm pretty sure I know what your problem is." He walked over to the back of her car and reached down, his face scrunching with effort for a second before he popped back up, holding a very charred looking croissant. "Looks like someone stuffed this in your tailpipe."

He walked back over and showed her the offending pastry that looked like one of the world's worst baking fails. "Who would stuff a croissant in part of my car?" As far as malicious acts went, it was pretty tame, and as far as she knew, Gigi didn't have any enemies.

Still, the thought of someone messing with her car was a little unsettling.

Cooper rubbed his beard in thought. As she watched the move, Gigi felt her fingers itching to take their own run through the course hair. "It could have been some kids who were bored, just wanting to prank someone. Whoever did it just wanted to make sure your car wouldn't start, nothing more than that it seems."

Gigi grabbed the bread and looked at it thoroughly. "Yeah, but I'm the only shop around here that sells these, unless someone made a special trip to the bakery or the store just to inconvenience me." Shrugging, she tossed the croissant in the nearby trash can and dusted off her fingers. "Seems like a waste of a good pastry to me."

Cooper smiled and stepped closer to her once more. "I don't know if I would call it a waste. I kind of want to send whoever did it a thank you and a big ole gift basket." He grabbed her hand in his, rubbing his thumb over her knuckles lightly. Her arm tingled at the contact just like it had earlier in the tearoom, and if that wasn't a sign for her to make a move, she wasn't sure what would be. "Sure brightened up my evening."

A shaky smile pulled across Gigi's face, the butterflies in her stomach spreading their wings and going absolutely bonkers. "Mine, too, actually." She swayed toward him as if she was being pulled by some unknown force when suddenly, she heard Mr. Grady start shouting across the lot again.

"You get your car taken care of, Gigi?" the older man boomed at the two of them, breaking the romantic mood instantly.

Gigi sighed once more and dropped her hand from Cooper's grasp in order to wave over to her neighbor. "Sure did, Mr. Grady. Thank you so much for checking in on me."

"You're welcome. Have a good night, dear." He nodded curtly, squatting down in his rocking chair and pulling out a pipe.

Gigi smiled at the white haired man with the horrible sense of timing before looking over at Cooper. From the slight scowl he was pointing across the street, he was just as put out with Mr. Grady as she was. "How much do I owe you?" She wasn't exactly sure what the protocol was for after-hours work, but she wanted to give him something for helping her out of a jam.

"On the house, Miss Gigi." Cooper reached over and shut the hood of her car, leaning down and grabbing his toolbox. He stepped back over to her and tucked a strand of her hair behind her ear, the brush of his fingertips causing goosebumps to erupt across her skin. "Why don't you hop in and give it another try for me?"

"Okay." Gigi had been robbed of breath in his presence, her body singing at even the slightest of touches from this man. Everything Cooper did and said seemed to turn her on, and she was enjoying every minute of it.

"Good girl," he praised, and Gigi felt her knees go weak. She had no idea two words could turn her into a pile of mush, but when she heard them in his deep, honeyed voice, she was in danger of melting like butter in a hot pan right then and there.

Nodding, she slid into her car, and this time when she turned the keys in the ignition, the engine roared to life. The initial excitement she felt was tempered by the knowledge that it meant an end to her time with Cooper. Smiling to cover up her disappointment, she rolled down the window, taking another hit of his personal cologne when he stepped over to her and leaned down, resting his arms on the door. "Thank you for all your help. I owe you one."

"You don't own me a thing, Peach." He stared at her a moment longer, finally breaking out his own beautiful smile. "Drive safe, now."

"I will," she promised. Gigi would promise him anything as long as he kept looking at her with hearts in his eyes and called her Peach again. She wasn't sure what she had done to earn the nickname, but she didn't much care. All she wanted was to hear him call her that again and again as often as he could.

"Good girl." The second round of praise came as he leaned in and kissed her cheek. Her eyes fluttered closed as she tried to memorize the feel of his warm lips on her skin. When Cooper tapped the hood of her car and nodded to her, the spell was broken, but she knew the tingly feeling that lit up her whole being would last much longer. Gigi watched as he stepped back onto the sidewalk so that she could drive off and waved shyly at him, smiling once more as she pulled out of her spot and made the turn onto the main road, heading toward her apartment. When Gigi stepped into her home fifteen minutes later and caught a glimpse of herself in her entryway mirror, she wasn't at all surprised to see that the smile hadn't left her face the entire drive home.

Chapter Eight

Cooper

The smile hadn't left Cooper's face the entire rest of the evening prior, and he felt the corners of his mouth threatening to pull up again as he thought of Gigi and the time they spent together the night before. He couldn't stop thinking about how adorable she was while making her little car noises, how good she looked in her dress and heels, and how she smelled like peaches and cream. Cooper was tempted to go down to the closest drugstore and sniff out every lotion and shampoo on the shelves just to get another hit of the sweet scent.

Between her sweet smell, husky voice, and beautiful smile, he had no chance of not giving her that little goodnight kiss on the cheek. He had wanted to try for more, but it seemed like old man Grady was determined to block his every attempt. Cooper couldn't be certain, but he was pretty sure the old man had done it on purpose, probably in some ill-conceived attempt to protect Miss Gigi from riffraff like him. No matter. Next time he got his chance, he would make sure he and Gigi were far away from the prying eyes of the nosy old coot, and there would be a next time. He just had to come up with a plan to make it happen.

Shaking his head, Cooper pressed the pedal for the hydraulics system, raising up the sedan he was currently working on so he could get a better look at the undercarriage. He knew cars, but he didn't really know women. At least, not a woman like Gigi Davenport. She was flirtatious and open to his attentions, that much had been obvious. He just wasn't sure how to go about engaging a woman like her beyond the flirty banter. She was probably used to fancy dinners, country clubs, and rides in designer vehicles. Cooper couldn't offer her any of those things. All he could offer her was himself, and he wasn't so sure that would be enough. Gigi was as strait-laced as they come, and while he was no reprobate, he was definitely a little more bad-boy than the guys she likely had dated in the past. Maybe he could make that work for him.

Cooper smirked when he recalled how she had shivered at his touch, and how her eyes would light up every time he looked her way, and how she seemed to go weak in the knees whenever he told her she was a *good girl*. Gigi seemed like she'd spent most of her life doing what was expected of her, and maybe he could show her that she was perfect, just as she was. No expectations needing to be met with him. As far as he could tell, she checked every one of his boxes and then some. Gigi was sweet, kind, beautiful, and just the right amount of feisty to keep him on his toes. Cooper could help her cut loose and enjoy all of life's little pleasures, and at the same time, he could show her that he was worthy of her time and attention.

A plan started to form in his mind and he wondered when best to put it into action. He scanned the calendar and saw that Valentine's Day was just a little over a week away. It was a little presumptuous to ask her out for such a romantic holiday, but Jo had mentioned that she was single, and Cooper would bet his motorcycle that Gigi was a woman who loved Valentine's Day. He could buy some flowers and head over to the tearoom to ask her out on a date. Cooper had no idea what they would do on that date, but he had time to figure it out. First, he had to go get the girl, and as soon as he was done with this sedan and had a free minute, he would walk over to The Happy Kettle and make his move.

Four hours later, he was no closer to getting that

free minute than he had been when he first started his day. A steady stream of customers had come through the shop, not giving him a moment to spare for even another thought of the woman across the way. He was finally finishing ringing up his last customer when the shop bell rang, alerting him to the presence of another one. Cooper seriously considered telling whoever it was that they were closed, but that was both bad for business and his employment status. Bob might treat him like a son, but he would fire him faster than you could say "unemployment line" if he caught Cooper turning away a customer.

Cooper handed the keys over to the man whose car he had just finished tuning up and put on his best customer service smile for whoever was next in line, trying not to let his irritation show through it. As soon as Mister White Subaru Forester stepped out of the way, Cooper was greeted by the beautiful smile of one Miss Gigi Davenport, and his own smile went from perfunctory to genuine in not time.

"Well, well, well. My day just got a whole lot better." His eyes followed her as she stepped up to the counter, appreciating the way her dress hugged her curves before fanning out and fluttering at her knees.

"Flatterer." Her cheeks turned pink as they did every time he'd paid her a compliment. Her ivory skin stained with a rosy hue was his new favorite color, and he was going to make it his mission in life to get her to blush as often as he could. As he continued to admire her, Gigi held up a white bakery box for him to take. "I know you said I didn't owe you anything, but I wanted to do something as a way to say thank you for last night."

Cooper opened the lid of the box, the smell of fresh bread and sugar hitting his nose as he peeked inside. The thank you gift contained a few small sandwiches, a couple of biscuits, and two slices of what looked like coconut cake. It was certainly fancier and more indulgent than his normal lunches, and his stomach growled appreciatively at the prospect of a break from the usual. "Thanks, Peach." Cooper smiled in gratitude, not at all surprised at her thoughtfulness. "You didn't have to do this."

"I know." She rubbed her lips together and looked around for a moment before meeting his gaze once more. "I wanted to do something nice for you," she admitted sweetly.

Cooper stepped out from behind the service counter, leaning down to kiss her cheek. "This is very nice," he remarked, brushing his cheek against hers as he pulled back and inhaling her sweet scent into his nose. He enjoyed the way she smelled far more than the motor oil and exhaust smell he was used to, but even if he'd surrounded himself with the most beautiful scents in the world, none of them would compare to hers. "I appreciate it. Thank you again."

Gigi leaned into him and when he met her eyes, they were hooded and a little hazy. "You're welcome." Her voice was barely above a whisper as she swayed toward him. The thought of finally getting to taste her had his body temperature rising, but before he could do anything about it, the door between the office and the front banged open. Cooper straightened up, peering over his shoulder to see his boss headed their way. It seemed that the older men in this town were determined to prolong his sexual frustration.

"Gigi, my girl. I thought I saw you out here," Bob exclaimed as he came around to them and wrapped Gigi up in a big bear hug. He pulled back and pouted his lower lip. "Now that Jo's in her own place, I don't see you nearly enough. You need to come around more often."

Gigi looked guilty and pulled her lips inward.

"Sorry, Mr. Farrow. I just get busy with work and everything." She looked genuinely distressed at having disappointed the man, finally perking up and grabbing the bakery box from Cooper's hands. "Here. I brought you some lunch. I know how much you love coconut cake."

Cooper's brow furrowed as he watched Bob dig into the box, pull out a slice of the aforementioned cake, and took a large bite, his stomach protesting at the loss of such a delicious lunch. "Oh, my. This is just as good as I remembered. Your gran taught you well, dear." Bob raised his slice in salute and walked back toward his office. "Don't be a stranger."

"Have a nice day, Bob." Gigi waved off the older man, reluctantly turning her gaze at him. Cooper leaned against the service counter and crossed his arms over his chest, raising a brow at Gigi as he waited for her to explain herself. She looked all over the front room before throwing her hands up in frustration. "I'm sorry, okay? I didn't want to give away your thank you gift, but you saw him pouting at me. I felt awful for not having come around much." Cooper kept staring at her and she sighed, stepping up to him, crowding into his space. "How can I make it up to you?" She was being sincere and not at all suggestive, though he certainly wouldn't have turned *that* down.

"You want to make it up to me?" he asked, reaching his arms behind her and pulling her close. She had nothing to make up for because he was happy enough with just her visit, but she'd also opened up the door for him to secure that date he'd been wanting. Gigi nodded, peeking up at him with her hazel eyes. Flashes of her looking up at him like that wearing a white dress and in a much more official context went through his mind, but that was putting the cart before the horse just a bit. Setting thoughts of marriage aside for later, Cooper focused on the present as he leaned down closer to her ear. "Good girl," he whispered and felt her body tremble against his as she shivered once more. This one definitely liked to be praised, an observation he tucked away for later use. He ran his hand up and down her arm, the soft hairs feeling like the fuzz on the fruit she always smelled like. "I know how you can make it up to me."

Gigi closed her eyes and exhaled slowly. "How?" Her voice was barely audible, but it was also laced with desire.

He brushed his lips against the shell of her ear, enjoying the feel of her body next to his. "Go out on a date with me."

Gigi leaned back and blinked up at him, her expression one of confusion. What did she think he was going to say? While he was one hundred percent on board with exploring a more physical relationship with her, he wanted so much more than that, and this wasn't the type of woman you simply messed around with. "You want to take me out on a date?" she asked with disbelief, a smile pulling at her lips.

Cooper nodded, a bit taken aback by how shocked she seemed. Who wouldn't want to go out on a date with this woman? "I absolutely do." He stated his intentions firmly, skimming his hand down her arm again, grabbing her hand and threading their fingers together.

"Okay." She spoke the words while squeezing his hand and smiling, and Cooper took a mental picture for when he wanted to remember everything about the day his life changed for the better. "When?"

"Valentine's Day?" He hoped the idea of a first date on the love-centric holiday wouldn't scare her off. When it came to a day filled with hearts and love, he could only think of spending it with her. He could make it special, he just needed some time.

Her eyes sparkled and her smile widened, faltering soon after. "Shoot. I promised my mom I would go to a charity function for her friend on Valentine's." She scrunched up her face, the obvious annoyance not dimming her beauty in the slightest. "I can't get out of it. I gave my word."

Cooper was disappointed, but he tried not to let that show. He understood how important keeping a promise could be. After all, he'd promised himself to always look after Mags and fulfilling that is what had gotten him in front of Gigi to begin with. "No problem. How about the day after then?"

Gigi's smile returned and she nodded enthusiastically. "I would like that very much."

"Me, too," he agreed, escorting her over to the front door. Now that Cooper had a date lined up, he needed a solid plan in place for it and that wouldn't happen as long as she was in his proximity. Whenever Gigi was around, his mind kind of blanked on just about everything else. He pulled his phone out of his back pocket and handed it to her. "Why don't you go ahead and give me your number? You know, for planning purposes."

She hummed as she entered her number in his phone and hit CALL. Her own phone vibrated once before she hung up and handed his phone back. "Now I have yours, too, for planning purposes of course."

Cooper smiled and pocketed the device, opening the front door for her. "Maybe I'll call and we can talk more about planning later on tonight."

Gigi walked through the door and turned, giving him a once over. The look wasn't as heated as it could have been, but it had the same effect as if she'd been stripping him with her eyes. Cooper shifted on his feet, hiding the rapidly growing evidence of his arousal. "I might be able to make that work." With a wink, she strolled across the street and into her tearoom.

Cooper watched her the entire way and turned back into the shop with a smile. Gigi was perfect for him, he just knew it. Tonight's little planning session couldn't come soon enough.

****

The last week of Cooper's life had flown by. The days blurred together in a stream of car repairs, but the nights were much more interesting and filled with his new obsession—Gigi. He couldn't go more than an hour without thinking of her, and he made sure she knew it. If he wasn't texting her between customers at the shop, he was calling her every night or stopping by the tearoom just to hear her sweet voice and see her bright smile. After they had exchanged numbers, Cooper made sure to call her that night and they spent the better part of three hours talking to one another about everything and nothing at all.

It turned out that they had a lot more in common than a fondness for their grandparents and the ability to put in a hard day's work. They both enjoyed reading historical fiction, though she admitted that hers leaned a little bit more toward the romantic than his war epics did. Gigi also enjoyed a good war movie, though his favorite was *Inglorious Bastards* while hers was *The Last of the Mohicans*. Yup, she definitely had a soft spot for romance, something he hoped would come in handy today as he walked toward the front door of the tearoom.

It was finally Valentine's Day, and even though he wouldn't be able to take her out tonight, he still wanted to make her feel special. After taking the afternoon off, he went by the local flower shop to grab a bouquet to present to Gigi. Cooper wasn't sure what her favorite blooms were yet, so he just asked the florist to put together an assortment in shades of peach and pink, the two colors that reminded him of her the most. He lifted the flowers to his nose, inhaling their sweet scent as he opened the door to The Happy Kettle, eager to exchange the smell of the blossoms in his hand for once of peaches on soft skin.

Cooper stepped inside and saw that only a few patrons remained. He had come toward the end of her workday, hoping to have as much of her attention as he could possibly get while she was dealing with a busy holiday crowd, and lucky for him, it looked like his plan just might have worked. Gigi was cradling a phone on her shoulder as she scribbled something down in a planner. When she looked up at him, that bright, beautiful smile that he had been dreaming about appeared on her face. Cooper sighed, feeling like he was able to breathe easily again for the first time since he last saw her. The infatuation he had with Gigi seemed to grow with each passing day, threatening to consume him unless he was able to quell his need by at least laying eyes on her.

Gigi looked over at the flowers he held and placed a hand on her chest as she continued to talk on the phone. Once she hung up, she walked out from behind the counter and bounced in front of him. "Are those for me?" Her smile was infectious, but he managed to hold his back to draw out the suspense just a little.

Cooper shrugged nonchalantly. "Maybe," he said with a smirk. "That all depends on what you got for me." He tapped his cheek and she rolled her eyes playfully, standing up on her tiptoes, placing her hands against his chest, and kissing his cheek. It wasn't the first time she had kissed him there, but each time felt just as nice as that first one. Cooper felt his own cheeks blush a little in response and was grateful that his beard probably hid most of it. "Thanks, Peach."

"You're welcome." Her own cheeks were blushing as well, the look becoming almost permanent in his presence. Cooper could only imagine the picture they painted for her remaining customers, acting like a couple of school kids with crushes, but that was kind of what this felt like. He hadn't gotten to take her out yet, so he very much felt like his teenage self, just waiting until he could take the girl of his dreams out for a proper date.

"For you." He presented her with the bouquet, his chest filling with a sense of pride and accomplishment when she smiled and stuck her nose in the flowers, inhaling deeply and never taking her eyes off of him. "Happy Valentine's Day."

"Thank you. They're beautiful. Happy Valentine's Day." She walked back toward what he guessed was the kitchen, beckoning him with her free hand. "Come with me. I just want to put these in some water."

"Sure thing." Cooper followed like a love-struck pup, nodding a greeting to people as he passed, noting that a few of them looked a little too curious at what the two of them were up to. He supposed the town princess walking around with a mechanic was ripe fodder for the rumor mill of Willow Creek, but he ignored the irritation that caused and followed Gigi into the back where a group of people were cleaning up at the end of a busy shift. He nodded in greeting and watched a few of them giggle to one another before they turned back to washing dishes and mopping the floor. Yes, small town gossip was alive and well it seemed, but he ignored the way the thought of people judging him rankled in lieu of watching Gigi.

Gigi reached up to a high shelf to grab a vase, but he stopped her with a hand on her lower back. "Let me grab that for you, Peach." He took the vase down and handed to her, loving the graciousness that shined in her eyes at even the simplest gesture. "I don't want you getting hurt or anything."

"Thanks." Cooper located a nearby sink and filled the vase with water for her, grinning when she slipped the flowers in and arranged them just so, moving the blooms around until it met her high standards. "I'm going to put these in the front where I can look at them all day," she confessed, bustling back out of the kitchen.

Cooper followed her, trying to not be obvious about the way he couldn't stop staring at her ass as it swayed back and forth in front of him. He couldn't help himself. She looked amazing and her skirt hugged all her curves in just the right way, enticing him to try and get a peek of what was underneath. Once they were back up front, she placed her vase on the counter and leaned her elbows next to it, giving him the perfect view of her cleavage. He made a concerted effort not to stare and thought he did admirably considering just how badly he wanted this woman.

"So, Peach." His voice was thick with want for her, so he coughed to clear it and adjusted himself as discreetly as possible. "What's this charity event you've got going on? It better be for some sad puppies or lost unicorns because I'm going to miss spending Valentine's Day with my woman."

One auburn eyebrow shot up at his words. "Your woman?" She stood up and crossed her arms over her chest, not helping him with the whole avoiding her cleavage thing. "I think we skipped over a few steps here."

Cooper reached over and ran a lock of her hair through his fingers. "I don't think so. I'm pretty certain that the amount of time I spend thinking about you makes you mine." If she wanted him to pump the brakes, he would do so, but the thought of having to miss any more time with her made his chest ache. Leaning closer to her, he whispered in her ear. "And I think about you quite often, Peach." He heard what sounded like a whimper and he brushed his lips against her cheek as he pulled back. "So what do you think? Are you mine?" When she nodded slowly, a sly smile played across his face. "Good girl."

Heat flared in her eyes at those two little words, and she licked her lips, his eyes tracking the path of her pretty pink tongue as she did. "Does that mean you're mine too?"

Cooper ran his hand to the back of her neck and tilted her head up to face his. "I was yours the first time I laid eyes on you." He kissed her forehead, not wanting to risk more than that in front of her gossipy customers.

As if on cue, he heard a throat clear and he stepped back as a pair of older women came up to the register. He bowed his head slightly as he did with all older ladies and smiled, moving to the side as Gigi did her thing, ringing up their sale and settling their bill. One woman smiled at Gigi, but it wasn't altogether friendly. Cooper felt his hackles rising up on her behalf. No one should be looking down on his woman like that. She was lovelier than a spring day, so warm and welcoming, and anyone who thought otherwise probably had more than a few screws loose. "You have such a lovely space here, Virginia. Your grandmother would be quite proud."

"Thank you so much, Mrs. Bowman. That means a lot." Gigi passed a receipt to the woman, a genuine smile lighting up her face. Cooper knew how much Gigi's grandmother meant to her and any comparison to the woman seemed to always put her in a good mood.

The other woman with a pinched face glanced over to him dismissively, turning back to Gigi. "I'll see you tonight at the speed dating event, right? Your mama told us all how you'd be there looking for your next beau."

Cooper's eyes shot to Gigi's just in time to see her wince slightly. They would definitely be having a talk after these two old biddies made their exit. After they just declared themselves to one another, there was no way his woman was going to some speed dating event where a bunch of posh idiots would be wagging their tongues in her direction. Gigi smiled politely at the other woman and nodded. "I'll be there, Ms. Townsend." She gave the women a weak wave and watched them leave the shop. As soon as they were gone, she rushed out from behind the counter and came up to him, grabbing onto his arms. "I can explain."

Cooper crossed his arms over his chest and raised a brow at her, feeling put out. He wasn't upset with her but more at himself for dragging his feet when it came to making a move on her. "Go ahead, Peach."

Her arms fell with a sigh, and she started twisting her fingers together in front of her stomach before shaking them out quickly. "It's just … I promised my mom that I would go weeks ago. It was before we even met." She blushed, her mouth pulling at the corners as if she was hiding a smile. "Officially, I mean."

"Well, can you call her and tell her you have to cancel?" It seemed like a simple enough solution to him. They'd just discussed how they already felt like they belonged to one another, so why was she insisting on going?

Gigi bounced nervously in her spot. "I can't," she groaned. She seemed genuinely distressed at the thought of having to go or disappointing him, and the last thing he wanted was to upset her. "You don't understand how much my mother bugs me about my dating, and she said if I attend this one event that she would leave me alone about it. I really, really need her to leave me alone. She's been on me about my personal life since puberty and I'm starting to lose my mind."

Cooper turned away from the pained look on her face to stare out the window. He didn't have a nagging mom of his own for comparison, but he did have his Gran. Over the past week, he had also listened to Gigi talk about how much pressure her parents put on her, and he could imagine that held true for all aspects of her life, including dating. "Can't you tell her you're with someone?"

Gigi bit her lower lip and shook her head. "That will only make her more inquisitive and she'll demand to know everything about you and want me to drag you to Sunday dinner." She reached up and grabbed the sides of his leather jacket and pulled him down to her, her hazel eyes burning with intensity. "We still haven't gotten to go out on a date yet, and I would kind of like to get to know you more and have you all to myself for a while before I have to share you with *her.*" She leaned back and took his arms from his chest to wrap them around her waist. "Please try to understand. Besides, I'm not trying to make a match with anyone, and I'll be thinking about you the entire time. I promise."

He twisted his lips to the side in doubt, but he wrapped his arms more tightly around her anyway. She felt too good to resist the contact. Family was important to both of them, and as much as he wished he could force her to stand up for herself and him, he wasn't going to butt into something that could cause a disruption to the balance she was seeking to find with her parents. "The whole time?" he asked, voice dubious.

"The whole time." She made the promise and leaned her body into his, stirring up his desire for her once again. "And probably for the rest of the night, too." Screw it. There was no way he couldn't kiss her properly after a confession like that. Cooper leaned down and brushed his lips against hers, keeping it chaste while making sure to mark her for everyone to see, branding her as his before she had to go spend the night with a bunch of other men. He pulled back and watched as she slowly blinked her eyes open, a smile pulling across her face. The kiss hadn't lasted more than two seconds, but it was enough for him to feel like he'd just tethered himself to her permanently. If this was how he felt in the beginning, he could only imagine how much deeper his feelings would get as their relationship progressed. "Does that mean you forgive me?"

Cooper kissed the tip of her nose and smiled at her. "Nothing to forgive, Peach. You're keeping a promise to your mom and that means you'll keep yours to me when it comes to that date." He stepped back, his chest feeling slightly hollow as he was already missing her. "Think of me while you're out there getting hit on by God knows who."

"The whole time," she replied, holding up her palm. "I swear it."

Cooper grabbed her palm and kissed it, delaying his inevitable departure. "Will you call me when you're done? I at least want to know you got home safely." Cooper tried to keep the neediness in his voice to a minimum, but he wasn't sure he pulled it off. Gigi was right after all. They hadn't even gone out on a single date yet, and she didn't owe him anything, but he still hated the idea of losing her just when things had just started to get interesting.

"I will." Reaching into her flower vase, she plucked out a pink rose and handed it over to him with an adoring smile. "So you'll know I'm thinking of you."

Cooper lifted the rose to his nose and inhaled the scent, looking into her eyes the entire time. "I'll be thinking of you, too, Peach. Just so we're on the same page."

"Good," she said with a smirk and moved back behind the counter to help another set of customers check out.

Cooper walked out of the tearoom and blew out a slow breath, still not quite believing that his girl was going to be spending Valentine's Day of all days out with a bunch of random guys, and there was nothing he could do about it. He walked across the street toward his house and frowned. There had to be something he could do, but he didn't want to mess things up between Gigi and her mom. Things between the two of them were turning out to be a lot more complicated than he thought, but it wasn't a deterrent. If anything, it meant he had his work cut out for him, but he was up for the challenge.

Cooper opened the door to his house and stepped inside, scratching Shep's ears as soon as the dog wandered up to him. "Hey, boy. Looks like it's just you and me tonight," he grumbled, plopping down in one of his leather armchairs.

Cooper eyed the rose he still held in his hand and smiled at Gigi's sweet gesture, but he really wanted to be spending time with the woman who gave it to him. He suddenly got an idea in his head, and it could either go really well or really poorly, but Gigi was definitely worth the risk. He slipped his phone out of his jacket pocket and dialed his gran, smiling when she picked up on the second ring, her hazy voice sounding impatient immediately. "Yes?"

"Well, a Happy Valentine's Day to you, too, Mags." Cooper knew her cantankerous mood had nothing to do with him and everything to do with her being too old and tired for nonsense.

"Bah. I'm too old for romance. Now tell me what you want so I can get back to my shuffleboard game." Cooper chuckled at her moxie and cleared his throat.

"You wouldn't happen to know the location of a charity speed dating event that is taking place tonight, do you?" he asked, pleased when his grandma was able to give him all the necessary details. Small town gossip may not be something he enjoyed being the subject of, but it sure did come in handy sometimes.

Chapter Nine

Gigi

The event hall where the speed dating event was taking place was ritzy enough that even Gigi felt a little frumpy in her strapless, tea length cocktail dress. She chose the pink outfit because it was Valentine's Day after all, and it was one of the few dresses she owned that covered a good amount of leg. Between that and the short sweater she had over her shoulders, she felt sufficiently modest. She wanted to look cute, but Gigi wasn't trying to entice anyone tonight. She had a handsome, charming, funny, and sexy-as-hell man waiting for her at his house, and she kicked herself for the millionth time since he had come by and delivered her the most beautiful flowers she had ever received. She should have found some way to get out of the promise to her mom. The woman wasn't even here, but Gigi knew she had her little spies everywhere and if she hadn't shown up, she would have heard about it the next day if not sooner.

"I can't believe you dragged me to this," Millie groaned next to her. Millie was wearing a red, long sleeve sweater and a pink, rosette skirt. She looked amazing, like an adorably sexy cupid, and Gigi wouldn't be surprised if she got at least a dozen matches based on looks alone. Millie pushed her black frame glasses up on her nose and peered around the room. When she spotted the bar she smiled over at Gigi. "Are drinks free? I think I might need a little something to settle my nerves."

Gigi smiled fondly at her childhood friend. "You have nothing to be nervous about," she told Millie with all sincerity. "But, yes. Drinks are free." She happily looped their arms together and steered her friend over to the bar. If she was going to make it through the night,

Gigi was going to need a little liquid fortification as well.

After they ordered a couple of cosmopolitans and were given their drinks, they moved over to the side of the area where a grouping of small tables and chairs had been set up in a large square. There were heart and cupid decorations all over the walls and just about every other available surface. The whole place looked a little bit like the holiday section at Target threw up all over the place, a tacky juxtaposition to the overall glamour of the large room, but it was a themed event and she would expect nothing less than in your face branding from the organizers.

Millie found a spot up against a wall, and Gigi joined her friend. They sipped their drinks and watched on like a couple of seasoned wallflowers as more singles filed into the area and grabbed their own glass of complimentary alcohol. Gigi looked around at the men in the room, not for herself of course, but for her friend. When she spotted a decent looking guy over near one of the charity workers, she poked Millie's side to get her attention. "Hey. What do you think of that guy?" she asked as she discretely pointed out the man with jet black hair and expensive looking gray suit.

Millie looked at him and grimaced. "Eh." She shrugged, taking another sip of her drink.

"Eh? That's all you have to say?" Gigi chuckled and shook her head. For a librarian who consumed books like they were essential to her staying alive, she was not very good with words this evening. "I hope you make better conversation with your potential matches than you're making with me."

Millie sighed and lowered her glass. "Sorry, Gi." She looked around the room, her eyes widening and looking increasingly nervous as she took a deep breath. "I'll try to get more into the spirit of it, but putting myself out there is difficult for me."

Gigi rubbed her hand up and down her friend's arm soothingly. The romance novels Millie favored since she was young had given her a lot of ideas on how dating should be, but the reality was that dating apps and your friends forcing you to attend singles events were how people met these days. "I know, sweetie. I'm really proud of you, though." She beamed at her friend. Even by agreeing to come, Millie had taken a huge step in pushing her boundaries. "You're already killing this whole birthday challenge thing."

Millie rolled her eyes, but she returned Gigi's smile. "I think you're giving me a little too much credit."

"And I don't think you are giving yourself nearly enough," Gigi insisted. She knew how hard it must be for her shy friend to get out there and look for love, especially knowing that she had to give up the crush she had on Ford at the same time. "You're pretty amazing, Millicent Louise."

Millie's smile widened a bit. "You're pretty amazing yourself, Virginia Mae." They clinked their glasses together and polished off their drinks, Millie looking at the bottom of her empty glass with concern. "It's a good thing we ordered a car tonight. I'm already feeling the effects of this one and I still feel like I need another."

Gigi eyed her friend dubiously. Millie didn't drink often and when she did it was normally limited to one glass. "Are you sure? I don't want you getting sick."

Millie shrugged, a few strands of her long hair falling off her shoulder. "Maybe if I get sick, a handsome doctor will come to my rescue and we'll fall madly in love." Her eyes went a little dreamy and Gigi was sure her friend was already envisioning the exact scenario she had just presented.

Gigi loved how Millie always seem to find the most romantic spin on just about every situation, hoping that she was able to maintain that ability throughout the event. "Sure, that could happen. Or, you'll puke on his shoes and he'll never ask you out on a date."

"Maybe I'll stick to water then." Millie frowned at the thought as Gigi chuckled adoringly at the sour look on her face.

A chime sounded at the 7:00 hour and an older woman with gray streaks in her black hair stepped into the center of the room. She held a microphone in her hand and she waved everyone toward her with her arm as she spoke. "Welcome, welcome, welcome to the First Annual Hungry for Love Speed Dating Event, sponsored by the Feeding Families Fund headed up by me, Beverly Duncan, and my lovely husband, Hank. Hank, take a bow for the people." Gigi watched as an older man bent meekly at the waist and smiled at his wife. *So those were her parents' friends.* They looked vaguely familiar, but her parents had introduced her to so many people over the years that they all kind of blended together in a mash of fine cloth and pungent perfume. "Now, before we get started, we have a small video that shows you exactly where all of your donation money will be spent. So empty those wallets and give as much as you can to help the families of Willow Creek and the surrounding area that are experiencing food insecurity."

The lights dimmed and a video appeared on a large screen at the front of the room. Gigi absently watched the presentation and placed a couple of hundred dollar bills into the collection box that was being paraded around by a volunteer. Millie took out her wallet and bit her lip for a moment, ultimately slipping in a fifty dollar bill. Her friend didn't make much money as a librarian, but she was always generous with what she did earn, especially when it was for a cause she knew a little something about. Gigi had tried her best to make sure her friend never went hungry when they were growing up, but she knew that despite her efforts, there were still some nights Millie went to bed with an empty stomach.

The video ended and the lights came back up, causing Gigi to blink her eyes a few times to readjust them. Everyone clapped politely and Beverly Duncan made her way back to the center of the room, smiling at the gathered crowd of singles and raising the microphone to her mouth. "Thank you all for your generosity. Now, let's get this party started, shall we?" She walked to one of the small tables and pulled out a chair that faced the center of the room. "Here's how this will work. The ladies will take a seat on a chair that is in the center of the square, and the gentleman will take a seat at a chair on the outside. You will have five minutes to get to know one another, and then the bell will chime and the men will move to their left while the woman stay in their seats. You'll also have these nifty little passes to write down the names of anyone you would like to match with." She held up a white piece of paper as another volunteer walked around passing them out to everyone along with a pen. "At the end of the night, you'll turn in your pass and we'll contact you with the names of anyone you matched with. Any questions?"

Gigi felt the soft wool of Millie's sweater brush her arm. "I have a question. When will I wake from this nightmare?" Gigi stifled a laugh at Millie's whispered joke lest they be called out for being too disruptive.

"You'll do great," Gigi promised and they moved to take a seat.

Millie shook her head, unconvinced by Gigi's declaration. "Easy for you to say," her friend griped as she pulled out a chair at the table next to Gigi's. "You already made a match."

Gigi felt bad that her friend was so disheartened, but she couldn't help but smile at the truth of Millie's statement. She had made a match with a good man she should be with right now instead of wasting time at this event. "True, but maybe you'll meet a sexy mechanic of your very own." Most of the guys milling about looked more like the type of guy Gigi usually dated, all buttoned up and clean cut, but you never knew. Maybe Millie would find her special someone tonight.

Millie held up crossed fingers as the men moved to join them at the tables. A bell chimed to signal the start of the first five minutes, and Gigi looked across to the person in front of her. It was the black haired, gray suit wearing guy she had pointed out to Millie earlier, and while he wasn't bad looking, he was no Cooper Ellis. He held his hand out across the table for her to shake. "I'm Giles Duncan. It's a pleasure to meet you."

Gigi took his hand and shook it, appreciating his firm grip while also feeling nothing from his touch. "Gigi Davenport," she replied politely. So, this was the man her mother had wanted to set her up with. From the outside, he looked well-dressed in expensive clothes and his hair was styled neatly. Everything about him screamed success, but again, it did nothing for her.

"Oh, I know who you are." He smirked, his eyes twinkling with merriment. "I think our moms may have conspired to get us both here this evening. They seem pretty keen on the idea of the two of us dating."

Gigi chuckled, knowing the man was speaking the truth. "I think keen is a bit of an understatement. My mom bribed me to come and has name dropped you every time she's called me the last couple of weeks."

"Same." He laughed jovially, the sound rich and soothing, and leaned in toward her. "It will never work out between us, though, so I'm afraid they're destined to be disappointed."

Gigi tilted her head, wondering exactly what he meant. "Not that I'm complaining because there is someone else I'm interested in, but just out of curiosity, why wouldn't it work out between us?"

Giles clucked is tongue and lowered his voice. "I'm very, very gay, and as pretty as you are, you're still missing a very essential piece of equipment." Gigi clapped a hand over her mouth to cover her bark of a laugh, glancing around to make sure no one noticed too much.

Once she had her delight at his declaration under control, she addressed his abrupt confession. "True." She looked across the room at Beverly Duncan who was watching the two of them like a hawk. "Does your mom not know?"

Giles leaned back and shook his head, his expression more entertained than sad. "Oh, she knows. She just thinks that throwing beautiful women at me will change my mind. I keep telling her that's not how it works, but she's a determined old gal."

Even though it didn't seem to bother him too much, a frown pulled across Gigi's face. "That's awful." It was one thing for her mom to set her up constantly, but it was another thing entirely for his mom to deny his identity.

"I'm used to it," he said with a shrug. Gigi was in awe of how little Giles let his mother bother him and wondered if she would ever be able to do the same. "My boyfriend actually thinks it's pretty funny." Giles turned around and waved to a tall, blond man who was wearing a chauffeur's uniform and hat. Blond guy smiled at Giles and winked at her. Giles turned back to her and grinned, clearly very in love with the man who'd just paid him some attention. "My mom thinks he's my driver and personal valet."

Gigi giggled at their attempts at maintaining an obvious lie for his mother. "And he doesn't mind that she thinks that?"

"Not at all," he scoffed. "It was actually his idea. This way he gets to travel with me and we get to sleep in the same room." He glanced over at his mom and smiled. "She'll have to get used to him sooner rather than later anyway because I'm asking him to marry me tonight."

"Aww," she cooed. She may not be as sappy as Millie when it came to love, but even she could appreciate the romance of a marriage proposal. "Congratulations." Gigi wanted something like that for herself. The marriage, not the hiding who she was or who she was with for years on end. That seemed way more complicated and unpleasant.

"Thanks." The bell chimed, bringing their time together to an end. "Hey, you own The Happy Kettle, right?" She nodded to him as he stood up from the table. "I'll be in touch. Kevin and I want to rent out your shop for our engagement party."

"That would be amazing. Definitely call me." Gigi rifled through her purse, handing him a business card and waving him off. "Have a great evening and good luck with your proposal." He smiled at her and instead of heading over to Millie's table, he walked over to his boyfriend and pulled him in for a kiss. Beverly Duncan looked like she might faint and started to wave one of the event tickets in front of her face, the scene almost too comical for words.

"What was that all about?" Millie leaned over and asked. Her eyes were bright with curiosity, but the story would have to wait until Gigi had more time to give her all the details.

"I'll tell you about it later." After assuring her friend that she would eventually spill the tea, she looked over to see who her next table mate would be. A stocky gentleman with thinning hair approached and Gigi smiled cordially at him, but before he could take the seat across from her, the chair was being whipped away and Cooper plopped into it instead. Gigi looked around the room before meeting his gaze again. "What are you doing here?" She was more than happy to see him, but she was worried this might get back to her mom.

"What do you think I'm doing, Peach? I'm speed dating." He looked over at the man whose seat he stole and shrugged. "Onto the next one, pal."

Gigi smiled apologetically at the man before she addressed Cooper. "I appreciate the sentiment, but you can't do that." Her head scanned the room to see if anyone noticed the disruption, but everyone seemed blissfully unaware.

"Yea, you can't do that," the other man chimed in. Gigi appreciated the solidarity, but she also would rather have Cooper in front of her anyway.

Cooper looked over to the empty seat in front of Millie and gestured for the other man to take it. "Will you look at that? Another chair opened up just for you." He gave the man a pointed look and it didn't take more than a second for him to cave and take the seat Cooper was offering.

"Sorry about that." Gigi always felt the need to be polite, even to strangers, and apologized to the gentleman before whipping her head back over to Cooper. "You can't be here." There was little force in her voice because being able to see him again had already made her night. He looked really good, too. Cooper's black jeans, black leather jacket and boots made him seem like the quintessential bad boy, and it worked for him. It worked for her, too, if the dampness in her panties was any indication.

"Why not? You said you had to come to this event and that you couldn't get out of it, but you never said I couldn't join you." He reached across the table and took her match card, smiling when he saw it was blank. "No luck so far, huh?"

Gigi snatched the slip of paper back and put it down in front of her. "I wouldn't say that. I had a very nice conversation with a man just before you got here." She wasn't sure if she was trying to make him jealous or what, but as happy as she was to see him, his presence had thrown her for a bit of a loop and she wasn't sure what to do.

Cooper smirked and grabbed her hand from across the table. "You mean the guy that's over by the door making out with another man?" He nodded to where Giles and his boyfriend were still playing tonsil hockey, their display turning enough heads that Gigi no longer worried about anyone paying attention to her. "Well, I guess you do have one thing in common. You both go for handsome blond fellas." He brought her hand up to his mouth and kissed her knuckles, the hair of his beard brushing her skin and sending tingles up her arm.

"That's true." The quiet words seemed to float from her mouth without her permission, her mind going blank the minute he had put his lips on her hand. She wanted to feel those lips everywhere, but they shouldn't do this here. Her mom's little minions were always watching and taking notes, even with Giles and his future fiancé providing a distraction. Gigi had already clocked nosy Ms. Townsend giving them the eye from her table on the other side of the room, and that did not bode well for her mom staying in the dark about Cooper. She wasn't ashamed to be with him, but her mother was so toxic, she wanted to protect him and her feelings for him from that. Gigi shook her head to clear the haze that she always seemed to slip into whenever Cooper was around. "You have to leave."

His smile slipped and he frowned, hurt swimming in the pools of his baby blues. "I'll leave when you decide you've had enough of this farce and come with me."

She snorted and crossed her arms. Gigi wanted to leave just as much as he wanted her to, but she was also stubborn and didn't enjoy being told what to do. The bell chimed and she smiled over at him triumphantly. "Your time's up."

Cooper narrowed his eyes at her before he dropped her hand and wrapped his arms and legs around the sides of his chair. "I've told you, Peach. I'm not going anywhere without you."

Gigi huffed, only the teeniest bit irritated and more turned on at his forcefulness, as she looked over at Millie. Her friend was watching the two of them with rapt attention, her chin propped on her fist. "Can you believe this?" Gigi asked her, feigning annoyance. Truthfully, she kind of liked that he was fighting so hard for her attention. Most guys she went out with just assumed she'd be falling all over herself because of their status and didn't try much to win her at all.

Millie smiled at Cooper. "I can, and I applaud his tenacity." Her eyes went dreamy again as they often did. "I think it's romantic."

"Why, thank you, ma'am." He smiled back at Millie, shooting a smug look at Gigi.

Gigi sighed and introduced the two of them. "Millie, this is Cooper. Cooper, this is my friend, Millie. The traitor."

Millie just kept smiling despite her new moniker.

"It's nice to meet you, Cooper. I'd shake your hand, but…" she trailed off, gesturing to where he had entangled himself in the seat, his limbs acting like tentacles as they wound through the wooden slats.

"Don't you have your own table to manage?" Millie wasn't helping Gigi's will to stay at the event, not that she had much of one to begin with. The longer Cooper sat across from her the more she wanted to drag him out of there and spend some quality time together.

Millie's eyes widened and she turned to the man across from her who she had essentially been ignoring for the last two minutes. "Sorry about that." She smiled contritely at her potential match, leaving Gigi and Cooper to themselves.

Gigi sat back in her seat and took in the sight in front of her. Cooper sat there looking all kinds of sexy, and here she was trying to get him to leave. Well, screw that. She held up her end of the bargain with her mom by showing up here, and now she was leaving to go spend time with the one man she was actually interested in. Cooper must have seen her resolve crumble because his smug expression got about ten times worse. "What's it going to be, Peach?"

Gigi sighed and gathered her things, looking over at Millie who seemed to be struggling to make conversation with her table mate. "Are you going to be okay if I take off?"

"I'll survive." Millie nodded, but her smile was strained. Gigi felt bad for dragging her out to this event only to abandon her, but maybe it would be good for Millie to be there on her own. Kind of like taking the training wheels off a bike or a trial by fire. Millie was a sweetheart, but she was stronger than anyone, especially herself, gave her credit for. "Have fun, you two," Millie said, turning back to her stilted conversation.

"Thanks, Mills." Gigi pushed out her chair and stood up, startling slightly when Cooper was already next to her, his arm out for her to take. She slipped her arm through his and they walked toward the exit, nodding to Giles and his boyfriend on their way out. The cool night air hit her skin and she wished she had more than her small shrug sweater to cover her shoulders. Cooper stopped just outside the venue and took off his jacket, slipping it over her and zipping it up once her arms were all tucked inside. She felt a bit silly in the oversized jacket, but breathing in the woodsy scent it carried calmed any embarrassment she felt, and she looked up at him with a smile. "What shall we do now?"

Cooper smirked and steered her toward the parking lot. He wore a charcoal gray sweater that clung to all his bulging muscles in a most appealing manner. The sight of him made her knees wobble at the same time her heart thumped happily in her chest. She nearly tripped, too concentrated on him and not the asphalt under her feet, but Cooper was there to steady her when she faltered. "Well, I can think of all kinds of trouble the two of us could get up to." He winked at her and kept walking. "For starters, though, I thought I could take you out on that date I've been begging for."

"I like the sound of that." No matter where they went on their date, she would be happy to just be spending some one-on-one time with him. After a moment of walking through the lot, they came to a stop in front of a vintage motorcycle. Gigi gasped, looking between the bike and her dress, trying to figure out how she was going to ride on the back of it without flashing her goods at every car they passed. "I'm not really dressed for that," she gulped.

Cooper smiled and grabbed a helmet from the side of the bike, strapping it onto her head with great care.

"I'll help you." When he was satisfied that the helmet was in place, he tapped the top of it lightly. "You ever been on a motorcycle, Peach?" She shook her head from side to side and a wide grin appeared on his face. "You're in for a real treat then." The words held quite a bit of promise that she was sure applied to more than just the bike ride, but she set that aside as he helped her swing her leg over the bike while keeping all her parts covered. It turned out that she didn't really show much since her dress was kind of wrapped around her legs and her bottom was holding it down.

"Thanks." It seemed like she was always thanking him for something, and as much as he looked like a bad boy, he was all polite manners, handling her with the kind of care she had longed for all her life. Growing up she had been given everything she needed except for the one thing she wanted most—attention that didn't come with strings attached, so to be looked after like she was something precious with no expectation of much more than her company in return was a nice change of pace.

Cooper took a long look at her and smiled. "You look real good on the back of my bike." He winked, swinging his own leg over, sitting down in front of her and putting his own helmet on. Cooper kick started the engine and Gigi laughed as it rumbled to life, the vibrations shooting through her body as she wrapped her arms around his torso and tried her best to concentrate on holding on tight and not feeling him up. He placed a hand over the spot where both of hers were laced together on his stomach, the heat of his hand branding her as his. "Lean when I lean, and don't let go," he explained as he throttled the engine and peeled out of the parking lot.

Gigi held in a scream of both fright and delight as they sped down the street, the cold wind whipping though the ends of her hair and the streetlights passing by in a blur. She'd never felt more scared, more excited, or more alive than she did at that moment. While some of it was due to the thrill of being on a motorcycle for the first time, most of it was because she was with a guy she truly liked. A guy she had picked for herself. A guy she really, really hoped she had a future with.

Chapter Ten

Cooper

The cold wind hitting Cooper's face was a welcome distraction from the warm body plastered up against his. Driving a motorcycle required a fair amount of concentration, but that was hard to do when he could feel the softness of Gigi's curves against his back, her hands snaked under his arms, gripping him tightly around the waist. Every now and then, he'd speed up just enough to get her to squeeze him a little tighter so he could enjoy the feel of her front pressed to his back just a bit more. Cooper had never taken a girl out on his motorcycle before, he'd never wanted to, preferring to use his time on the bike for reflection and relaxation. He was glad he was sharing this with her, though. Gigi was special, and he wanted to treat her as such. He might not be able to take her out for a fancy meal or bring her pretty flowers as often as she deserved, but he could share the parts of himself that he had kept hidden from anyone else.

When they pulled up to a red light, Cooper reached down and grabbed onto the smooth fabric covering her leg to get her attention, wishing he could be touching her creamy skin instead. "How you doing, Peach?" he called back to her over the rumble of the engine.

Cooper peeked over his shoulder and saw her smiling as brightly as ever. "This is wild. I love it!" She snuggled closer to him on the bike and laid the side of her helmet against the wool of his sweater, the sentimental move making his heart swell. He squeezed her leg one last time and they took off again once the light changed.

Cooper knew exactly where he had wanted to take her the moment she hopped onto his bike, but he was enjoying the ride far too much to head straight there. He loved the feel of her arms around him, the way she held on firmly but with care making him feel safe and protected. Cooper was a bigger guy and didn't often feel like he needed protecting, but with Gigi next to him, he felt more comfortable in his own skin, felt like he could really be himself and take on the world if he needed to. It was a heady feeling, and he wanted it to last for as long as possible. He took his time weaving them through the city, passing through the main drag downtown and out into the suburbs before heading back to their original destination.

Cooper pulled the bike into a space in front of The Tap House bar and grill and cut the engine, pulled off his helmet, and hopped off the bike. He held out a hand for Gigi and she took it, eyeing the bar dubiously, but there was more curiosity than judgement in her gaze. It definitely wasn't the type of place she was probably used to, but it was somewhere he had come for a beer every now and then, and while the décor may leave something to be desired, the service and food were as good as any in Willow Creek.

Once Gigi was standing in front of him, he smiled down at her and unstrapped her helmet, placing it on the bike near his own. "What do you think, Peach? Are you a motorcycle gal now?"

She smiled and ran her fingers through her mussed hair, attempting to smooth out the tangles. "I really liked it," she gushed, excitement shining in her eyes. "Though next time I think I'll opt for pants to make things a little easier."

Cooper grinned and removed his leather jacket from her shoulders, draping it over one arm while offering her the other. "As long as there's a next time, I'm good with you wearing whatever you want." Cooper wanted her to always feel comfortable around him whether she was in one of her frilly dresses, sweatpants, or nothing at all.

Gigi slid her arm through his and he walked them through the large wooden door and into the bar. The entrance was dimly lit, but it was much lighter near the dance floor, so Cooper steered them over to a table in that area. Gigi looked stunning in her pink dress, and while a dark corner would have worked better for keeping such a beautiful woman all to himself, he needed the light to able to stare at her all night long. He pulled a chair out for her and she removed the small sweater from over her shoulders, sitting down in the chair. Cooper tried not to get distracted by the sight of all that smooth, luscious skin as he stumbled over to his chair next to her, watching her head swivel around like it was on a stick as she took in all the sights of the bar and smiling at her curiosity.

The dark wood floor was bare while the walls were covered in various pictures and posters advertising beers and other alcohol, illuminated by the exposed light bulbs that provided the whole place with a warm glow. It was fairly crowded, but not so much that they were elbow to elbow with the other patrons. Most people probably didn't think to bring their Valentine's date to a dive bar, but he wasn't most people, and if he and Gigi were really going to make a go of this thing, they needed to see just how well they fit in each other's worlds. Cooper was already one hundred percent on board with trying to have a relationship with this woman, but he wasn't positive she was on the same page.

Gigi's eyes met his and she smiled awkwardly. "I feel a little overdressed." Her shoulders seemed to turn in slightly as she waved a hand up and down her body self-consciously.

Cooper snagged that hand and kissed the back of it, wanting to assuage her worries. "You look amazing. You could wear a potato sack or a ball gown and you would be the most beautiful person in the room, so don't even think twice about it."

That blush he loved so much colored her cheeks as she smiled shyly over at him. "Thanks," Gigi said sweetly as she moved her eyes up and down his body. "You look really good, too."

Cooper leaned over and brushed her hair over her shoulder, nuzzling the skin there. "Thanks, Peach." He'd purred near her ear, smiling as his beard tickling her skin made her tremble. She leaned into him and he felt like maybe they should have skipped dinner and gone straight to dessert, but he wanted to treat her right, and that meant wining and dining and not hopping straight into bed, as much as part of him might want to. He kissed her shoulder and pulled back, grabbing the two menus that sat on the table and handing her one. "We need to order some food or I'm going to end up spending the whole night nibbling on you."

Gigi smirked and opened her menu. "I don't see a downside to that plan." The boldness of her admittance had a strange, almost primal need to claim her come over him. A low rumbling sound came from his chest, and she simply winked at him, slipping her gaze back to the menu in front of her, not realizing that she was a gazelle who'd just given permission to a lion to chase her. "What's good here?"

"I'll tell you what's good," Cooper hinted as he stroked his fingers over her bare shoulder, wishing they weren't in public so he could feel the smooth skin under his tongue. Just when he thought he might dare to try, they were interrupted by the waitress coming over to their table, giving him a chance to reel in his inner caveman.

"Sorry for the wait, folks," the middle aged redhead said. Gum snapped between her teeth as she gave them both a cursory glance. "It's been slammed tonight. Do ya'll know what you want to eat or drink?"

Cooper gestured for Gigi to go ahead, wanting to hear the husky tone of her voice again. It did things to him, amazing, wonderful, deliciously dirty things, and he was grateful for the table over his lap to hide the proof of that. "Do you know what you want, Peach?" He moved his eyes up and down her body, not bothering to disguise the heat in his gaze. Just because he wasn't clubbing her over the head and dragging her back to his cave just yet didn't mean he couldn't still let her know how badly he wanted her in other ways.

Gigi's eyes widened and she started to fan herself with her menu. She pulled her hooded eyes away from him and pointed them at their server. "Um, do you have any specials?"

The woman snorted. "You mean like happy hour or our two for twenty wing baskets?" The redhead took in Gigi's attire and grimaced. "That's about as special as we get here, Princess."

Cooper didn't like the way the woman was looking at or talking to his woman, and he slid his arm around Gigi's shoulders protectively, pulling her closer to him. For her part, Gigi just smiled politely at the woman, either ignoring or oblivious to the veiled sarcasm in her tone. "You know what, I think I will have the cheese fries and a cosmopolitan, please."

The waitress looked over her shoulder toward the bar before turning back to Gigi, her expression uncertain. "Not sure if we can do a cosmo."

Gigi tapped her chin for a moment, nodding at the woman. "Then I'll take your bartender's best approximation of one," she said with a smile, not seeming to care that she would probably end up with the worst cocktail ever. "Oh, and a glass of water, too, please."

The waitress scribbled down her order with a roll of her eyes. "And for you?"

Cooper stared daggers at the woman. She was definitely eating into her tip money with her bad attitude and obvious judgement. Maybe she was just run down from a busy night, but he still didn't like the way she was treating Gigi. "I'll have a burger and onion rings, please. And a water as well, thank you."

The waitress finished her scribbling and shoved the pad in her apron pocket. "I'll be back with your drinks in a minute," she said curtly, turning on her heel and leaving.

"Sorry about that." Cooper frowned at the server, returning his attention to his date and running his hand over Gigi's shoulder. "Normally the service here is pretty top notch."

She shrugged a shoulder. "Oh, that's okay. It was probably a little silly of me to order a cocktail, but I don't really enjoy beer." That tracked, but their having different preferences in alcoholic beverage was definitely not a deal breaker. She could drink champagne, wine coolers, or only water and he wouldn't care. "I'm sure whatever they make me will be just fine."

Cooper stared down at Gigi in awe. She was the sweetest little thing, and he admired her ability to rise above the pettiness and judgement of other people, especially given that she'd been born into quite a bit of privilege. That could breed arrogance, but he could see that there wasn't a pretentious bone in her body. "I know you might not come to this type of place regularly, but I'm glad you're here with me tonight." He glanced around the room, taking in the sights that had become familiar to him over the years before meeting her eyes again. "I like to come here sometimes to unwind at the end of a long week. It's a great place to people watch and the food is pretty good considering what the rest of the place looks like."

Gigi scrunched her face up a little. "I think it looks fine," she told him. Again, there was no judgement in her tone. If anything she was giving him a small look about his own comments. "Besides, I go to a lot of different places with my friends all the time." The waitress came by with their drinks and dropped them at the table without a word. "This place is pretty nice compared to some of the bars I went to when I was in college. Dollar drink nights didn't often take place at the nicest bars in town." Gigi chuckled and grabbed her glass, eyeing the reddish-pink liquid with trepidation for a moment, taking a sip. When she immediately began coughing, Cooper reached over and rubbed her back with his palm and pushed her water glass in front of her. She sputtered for another minute and took a long drink from her water glass, coughing one last time and wiping a tear from her eye. "Whoa. That is definitely not a cosmo."

Cooper took the cocktail glass and sniffed it, the fumes practically singing his nostrils as he looked over at the bar to glare at whoever mixed her drink. There were too many people around for him to know exactly who made it, but whoever was responsible either made a colossal mistake or was being an asshole. "Sorry, Peach." Cooper pushed the glass as far away from her as possible, taking her hand in his and stroking her knuckles. "Looks like they got a little mixed up and gave you some Fireball mixed with grenadine."

"Honest mistake." Gigi sighed and leaned over to rest her head on his shoulder, position that had his protective instincts flaring up. She was a strong woman, but he couldn't help but want to protect her from everything, even something as trivial as a bad cocktail. "I should have asked for a less fussy drink. They're really busy, and I know how crazy things can get when you've got a full house."

Cooper smiled at her ability to be so understanding and rubbed her shoulder some more. "Throw a lot of ragers down at the tearoom, do you?"

She snorted and shoved him lightly with her body. "You're poking fun at me, but it can get pretty busy. No one's swinging from the chandeliers or anything, but when there are rooms filled with people all making a bunch of different demands, it can get a little overwhelming." She peered up at him, her hazel eyes twinkling at their banter. "I bet it gets the same way down at Bob's sometimes."

Cooper smiled down at her, glad she was taking as much an interest in him as he was in her. "It can, but the best thing about my job is that no matter how busy it gets, I still have enough time in the day to sneak over and see you." The times he had managed to do so over the last week were some of the best he'd had in a very long time. Cooper couldn't imagine going more than the few hours he did between seeing her.

Gigi's eyes crinkled in the corners as her smile widened. "I like that about your job, too." She moved their hands and started running her fingers over his now, skimming his knuckles, flipping it over, and running them up and down his palm. "I also like that you use your hands. They feel strong and capable, but also like they're still soft enough to hold onto something precious without crushing it."

Cooper was pretty sure Gigi was referring to how he would treat her heart, and she was one hundred percent correct. Each moment that he spent in her presence drove home just how special she was, and he wanted to do everything in his power to keep her by his side. It was a lot to feel for someone he was still getting to know, but her caring nature and openness felt familiar, like he'd known her longer than he actually had. "I take care of things that are precious to me," he vowed, tipping her chin up so her gaze met his. "That includes you, Peach."

Cooper leaned down and ran his lips over hers in a feather light kiss, a spark like static shock bursting between them. He could have turned it into something deeper. Hell, half this bar had probably witnessed more than their fair share of public make-out sessions, but this wasn't the time or place for the two of them. Cooper wanted her to know he was serious about her, and that started with keeping what they did with one another as private as possible. When he pulled back, Gigi had a dreamy look on her face, so he figured he was doing something right. She sighed and leaned into him some more, and they sat in silence, enjoying the feel of just being next to one another for a while.

A few minutes later, the waitress dropped off their food. "Here you go. Anything else?"

The interruption did little to draw his attention away from the woman in his arms. "Thanks, but we're good," he muttered at the woman and turned back to his girl. Cooper tipped his head at Gigi's large plate of cheese fries. "You going to be able to manage all that on your own?"

She scoffed and lifted a gooey fry with the tips of her delicate fingers. "Please. I may be little, but I can put away more food than most grown men," she revealed, popping the fry into her mouth with a flourish.

Cooper chuckled as he imagined the petite woman next to him chowing down on hot dogs with the tenacity of the guys at the garage. "Well, as long as you don't turn into a grown man, we're good." She slapped his arm and he stole one of her fries in retaliation, the saltiness of the potato and cheese not erasing the sweet flavor that lingered on his lips from their kiss. "Sorry, Peach," he said unapologetically.

Gigi got some pay back of her one as she snatched one of his onion rings. She munched on it daintily for a moment, her expression thoughtful. "Why do you call me Peach? I haven't been able to figure it out."

Cooper had to wrench his eyes from her lips that were now glossy from her fried food as he tried to concentrate on her question. While he formulated his response, he ran his fingers up and down her arm. "Your skin is soft and velvety, spending time with you is refreshing," he said with a bright smile. "It's like summer all the time whenever I'm with you."

"That's really sweet," she confessed, her cheeks blooming.

A smirk came across his face, and he leaned in toward her, running his nose along her neck. As he moved his head up and down, he inhaled deeply, causing her to shiver. Cooper finally made it up to her ear and whispered in it. "But I call you Peach because that's what you smell like. Peaches and cream, and I have to tell you, I can't get enough of it." He kissed the spot just below her ear and pulled back to grab a bite of his burger.

When he looked over to Gigi, she had a shy smile on her face and the flush on her cheeks and chest grew hotter. "Good to know," she rasped, grabbing another fry.

Eating required they be much less touchy feely, but it was a nice trade for them having time to talk about their various interests. They compared notes on the books they'd both read and the movies they'd seen. Gigi asked him all about his dog, Shep, and expressed a strong desire to meet him. Cooper had always been well aware of their differences—how could he not be when she was so obviously from a higher class—but by the time the check was delivered, he felt a lot better about that fact. The more they shared about themselves, the more he discovered that they were a lot more alike than they were different.

"I can't believe you're the reason why I had to wait months to read *The Man in the High Castle*," Gigi ranted as he dropped some bills on the table. "Millie told me someone lost the only copy and I had to wait forever for them to order a new one."

"Sorry about that." Cooper apologized with a light laugh and stood up, smiling when he saw that Gigi already had her hand out for him to take and help her up, like she knew he would be there to help her even though she didn't need it. "It wasn't lost so much as I accidentally dropped it in an oil pan. It was kind of ruined after that."

"I can imagine." Putting on her sweater, she turned and let him help her back into his leather jacket, his fingers skimming along her neck as he did.

Cooper glanced over at the dance floor, noting all the cozy couples that swayed there. "Are you sure you don't want to dance?" He wanted her in his arms as much as possible, and dancing was a great way to accomplish that.

She shook her head and patted her stomach. "I think I overdid it with the fries. Dancing doesn't sound too appealing at the moment."

"Definitely next time then," he insisted as he escorted her out of the building. He added dancing to the mental list of activities he wanted to do with Gigi, a list that was getting longer by the minute.

"As long as there is a next time," she quipped,

echoing his sentiment from earlier.

Cooper stopped at his motorcycle and grabbed onto her shoulders, giving them a light squeeze. "Peach, I get the feeling that with you, there will always be a next time." He helped her onto the bike and put on her helmet before strapping on his own. As soon as he was sitting down, her arms automatically wound around him, and Cooper couldn't keep the dopey grin off his face no matter how hard he tried, though he wasn't trying all that much. At this point, he was pretty sure it would be a permanent fixture on his face whenever she was around. "Hang on to me."

"Oh, I plan on it," she bragged, leaning her body against his as they took off. Gigi gave him her address and he pulled the bike out onto the main street to head that way. It was almost 10:00, so traffic was light and they made it to her place in less than fifteen minutes. He would have liked to prolong their night out, but they both had a full day of work ahead of them the next day. Beyond that, she had already been out for a while, so he wanted to take her home and let her get some rest. Cooper felt the need to take care of her as much as he did anyone else in his life growing, but instead of feeling like another item on his to-do list, it felt as if he'd been given the key to unlock something beautiful, meaningful.

That feeling resonated as Cooper pulled up to the curb in front of a modern looking, white two-story, complete with white picket fence and lush garden in the front. The house was palatial and his eyes nearly fell out of his head at the sight of it. Cutting the engine, he spun back to her, struggling to keep his jaw from dropping to the floor. "This is your house?" There was no way he could bring her back to his little converted garage home if she was used to a place like this. The home could have been the centerfold of one of his gran's southern lifestyle magazines.

Gigi smiled and removed her helmet, shaking her long auburn locks out once she had. "No, this is my landlord's home." She nodded to a path toward the side of the house. "I rent out their guest house in the back."

Cooper hopped off the bike and stowed his helmet. He reached for her hand and helped her off the bike, but he didn't let go of her. Instead, he interlaced their fingers together and walked with her along the path to her place. The side of the house was nothing special, but it opened up into a huge backyard with dark green grass, a swing set, and a treehouse. He let out a low whistle. She may not live in the palace of a home, but she lived adjacent to it. He suddenly felt very stupid for taking her to a dive bar for their first date.

His eyes continued to widen as they took in more of the professionally landscaped backyard. "Pretty nice place."

"Eh, it's okay," she said unimpressed. Cooper stopped walking and pulled her back to him. When she met his eyes, they were filled with laughter from her teasing. "Oh, my god, your face. Do you really think I'm that much of a snob?"

The longer he stayed silent, the more her eyes dimmed. He grimaced at his jerk behavior. "No," he insisted. He didn't think she was a snob, but she was from a rich, prominent family, and her upbringing would color her perception just as his had his own. "I know what you're used to, though, so you not being impressed by this place wouldn't be that surprising."

Gigi's smile slipped and she looked a little hurt by his comment. Seeing her disappointment felt like a physical blow, and he was already wishing he could pull his foot from his mouth. Cooper could be a bit of a dick sometimes, and right now he wanted to kick himself for making her feel even the slightest bit badly. Before he could start to make it right, Gigi stared walking again. "I'm used to big houses, nice clothes, and new cars," she explained, stopping at the front door of a tiny house near the back of the property. She turned to face him, and the sad expression on her face gutted him like a fish. "I'm also used to being told what to do, when to do it, and am constantly reminded of when I fail to live up to expectations." She unzipped his leather jacket and handed it back to him, raising her chin at him defiantly at the same time. "Just because you know where I come from doesn't mean you know who I am."

Gigi whipped around and unlocked her front door. She went to step inside, but he stopped her with a hand on her arm. "Don't go," he pleaded. She slowly spun back around, but she wasn't meeting his gaze. With one of his fingers under her chin, he raised her face up to his. When her eyes finally connected with his, he could see the hurt he caused and he knew he needed to fix things or this would be over before it even started. "Gigi, I'm sorry." She nodded, but he could tell she didn't fully believe him. He ran a hand through his hair and groaned in frustration. "I really am sorry for what I said. I do know you, and you are kind, caring, smart, funny, and sexy as hell. I just get into my own head sometimes, and it's hard to not wonder what an amazing woman such as yourself is doing with a bum like me."

Her lips twitched. "Maybe I like bums," she mumbled, her voice still holding a trace of sadness.

"Well, then I guess I have that going for me." He cupped her cheek and sighed when she leaned into his touch. At least she wasn't trying to run away anymore.

She looked up at him, her brow creased. "You're not really a bum. You have a lot going for you, Cooper." Her body swayed closer and she placed her hands on his chest. "You're smart." She raised herself up, and he leaned down to meet her as she kissed the hollow of his throat. "You're funny," she purred, kissing underneath his jaw. "You treat me better than anyone ever has." Another kiss landed on his cheek and she moved over to the side of his head. "And you're the sexiest man I've ever laid eyes on," she whispered huskily, grazing his ear with her teeth.

Cooper shivered and placed his arms on her shoulders, pulling her back in front of him before diving down and taking her lips in a deep kiss. He poured every bit of longing and desire for her that had been building over the last week, hell, the last couple of months, into the kiss. Cooper licked the seam of her lips and when she gasped, he drove his tongue inside, tangling it with hers. She tasted salty and sweet, which seemed fitting at the moment seeing as how she had gone from mad to kissing him in no time at all. A warmth burned through his chest as his hands slid down her arms, and he rested them on her lower back, pulling her even closer to him. Cooper wanted their bodies plastered together until it looked like they were one person, wanted to be able to feel her heartbeat next to his, and wanted to pull her inside him so that he could always protect her.

As they continued to kiss, she moaned and the sound went straight to his groin. There was no way she wouldn't be able to tell what she was doing to him, and it took all his willpower not to start grinding himself against her hot little body. Gigi's hands slipped from his chest to his back, and she lowered them all the way until she was gripping his ass like her life depended on it, kneading the tight muscles with her hands. Cooper was wound up so tight he was sure he would snap at any moment. His mind worked to stave off his release as he mentally took apart a car engine just to keep from going off in his pants. He was getting way too turned on and needed to break this up before he pushed them both through that open doorway and onto her bed. He wanted to go there, but more than that, he wanted to build something lasting with her. There was no guarantee that sex would derail his plans, but he wanted to play it safe just in case and especially after his slip up just now.

Cooper finally pulled back, breaking the kiss. He rested their foreheads together as they both tried to catch their breath, the warm air leaving their lungs causing puffs of steam to appear in the cold night air. Gigi shivered, and while he would like to think it was because of him, he knew it was more likely because of the weather and the fact that she wasn't wearing enough clothing. Kissing the tip of her nose, he smiled at her as he warmed her arms with his hands. "That was one hell of a goodnight kiss, Peach. Thank you."

Gigi licked her lips and smiled. "You're welcome" Squeezing his ass with her hands one more time, she backed into her place, leaning against the door jamb and crossing her arms over her chest. "Anytime you're having doubts about whether or not we're a good fit, I want you to think about that kiss." She winked at him and walked backwards into her apartment, shutting the door.

Cooper waited to hear a lock click, and when he didn't, he knocked on the door. Gigi opened it, peeking out at him with a confused look on her face. "Yes?"

He stepped closer to the opening and looked down at her, hoping she could see just how important her safety was to him. "Lock the door, please. I'll worry about you all night if you don't." He brushed some hair back behind her ear. "Can you do that for me?" She nodded and he leaned in to kiss her forehead. "Good girl." Gigi's eyes went hazy as she shut and locked the door, and he reluctantly walked back down the path to his motorcycle.

Cooper put his jacket and helmet on, got the engine going, and started the drive back to his place. He thought back about what she said, and any time he had doubts about them, he would think about that kiss. He wasn't going to have to do that because it would probably occupy his thoughts every other free minute of his day until they got to do it again.

Chapter Eleven

Gigi

The wine had been flowing freely for the last hour, and Gigi was really feeling the buzz as she and her two best friends gathered in her apartment to recap their Valentine's Days. Deep down, she knew that the thrumming in her veins was only half due to the alcohol. The other reason she was so excited that she could barely stay still was because of how she just couldn't stop thinking about Cooper and the date they had shared the night before. The bar had been a nice switch from the usual places she was taken on a date, and while the little mix up with her drink had left her feeling like her throat was on fire, she had been able to move past that quickly, focusing on the wonderful conversation with the man next to her.

Gigi had been surprised to learn that in addition to books and movies, they also both really enjoyed hiking and fishing. Her dad used to take her and Ford fishing when they were younger, and while he hadn't made the time to do it in a long while, it was still something she enjoyed. Fishing was a great way to relax and enjoy the outdoors, and Gigi was excited to try it with Cooper sometime soon.

The thought of spending more time with Cooper, and potentially getting more kisses, had a smile spreading across her face. The kiss at the end of the night had her toes curling in her heels and she had been so tempted to invite him in, but she didn't want to move things too far too fast, and he seemed to be on the same page. There was also the little matter of what had happened before the kiss. For as cool and confident as Cooper seemed, it turned out he was still a little unsure of himself when it came to her. Gigi was used to being judged based solely on her last name, but usually it was people instantly thinking the best of her because of her family connections, not the opposite. That he thought she might be as snobbish and stuck-up as her parents and most of their social circle had hurt her feelings, but she also couldn't really blame him for thinking that way when they came from such different backgrounds.

Cooper had told her all about growing up with his grandparents and how they didn't have much, but they had a lot of love and that's all he ever really needed. She tried to express that that was all she needed, too, but she wasn't sure if the message got across in between the kissing and him insisting she lock up once she was inside. Gigi liked that he was protective of her, and she felt the same way about him, even messaging him the moment she got inside, asking him to text her when he got home safely. He had done just that about fifteen minutes later, and they texted for a bit before saying goodnight. Gigi felt warm and tingly inside at the memory of their short messages to each other, little blurbs that did nothing other than prolong their time connecting with one another. Cooper had asked her to go out again tonight, but when she explained that it was girl's night, he told her he understood and that he would miss her while she was having fun with her friends.

Gigi took another sip of her wine, looking down at the empty glass. It was Saturday night, and she was happy that the tearoom was closed the next day because she had a feeling she might be a little hungover tomorrow if she didn't stop getting distracted with thoughts of Cooper while she drank. Needing to get something in her belly, she grabbed a slice of cheese and a cracker from the tray Jo had brought with her, munching on the small snack as she watched Jo and Millie argue about which of them had a worse evening the night before.

"I sat through five minute interviews with twenty different men and I didn't get a single match," Millie proclaimed sadly. She shook her head and polished off the wine from her glass. "I'm so pathetic that the charity organizer even offered to refund me the price of my admission ticket as well as any donations I made. Can you believe that?" She grabbed a cracker and waved it around the air in front of her dramatically. "They thought I would pull money from hungry families. I'm not a monster," she said emphatically. "Just unlovable." Millie's mouth pulled into a deep frown before she tossed the cracker into her mouth and chewed on it angrily.

"You aren't unlovable, Mills," Jo stated firmly. "You didn't match up with a room full of men you probably had zero real interest in anyway." She flicked a crumb off of her pajama pants and poured Millie some more wine. "Tell me I'm wrong."

Millie sighed and brought her now full glass into her chest, clutching it like a comfort item. "You're not wrong," she breathed out slowly. "But how am I supposed to date around if I can't match with anyone at a speed dating event?"

Jo snorted, grabbing a handful of buttered popcorn and stuffing it into her mouth. "Easy. You go on Tinder, hook-up with a few dudes to get your nerves out, then you can try for an actual date," she mumbled around her mouthful, washing it down with some wine. "You're too nervous about all this stuff and I think a good," she made a circle with one hand and poked her other finger through it a few times, "could be good for you."

Gigi tried not to laugh at Jo's crass gesture, but she was pretty sure she failed because Millie shot her a look as her cheeks flushed with embarrassment. "I don't think that will solve my problem. I'd be even more nervous about a hook-up than I would a date."

Jo, the resident hook-up expert in their group, rolled her eyes. "Then I guess it's time to join a convent. May I suggest Our Sisters of Perpetual Sexual Frustration? Because that's where you're headed, babe."

Jo grabbed some more popcorn and leaned back on her elbows. The three of them were currently spread out on the floor of Gigi's living room in their pajamas. They did their girl's night in a variety of different ways. Sometimes they got dressed up and went out, sometimes they picked out outfits for each other and hit a bar, but tonight they opted for pajamas and snacks, having had enough of going out after last night.

"I'm not sexually frustrated," Millie insisted. "You don't need another person to get off."

Jo snickered and smiled wickedly. "No, but it's so much more fun with another person," she insisted, waggling her eyebrows. She and Millie laughed, and Jo turned her head toward Gigi, her eyes narrowed. "Speaking of getting off with another person… How are things with your mechanic friend? Have you given Coop a ticket to ride the Gigi Express yet?"

Gigi snorted and tried to keep herself from spitting out her wine. "Why are we referring to sex with me as a train ride?"

"You guys never understand my sports metaphors, so I was trying something new," Jo explained with a shrug of her shoulder. "And don't think I don't see you trying to change the subject, Miss Davenport."

Gigi brushed some non-existent lint off of her cotton camisole to buy some time and looked at her friends. "A lady doesn't kiss and tell," she said primly. There was no way she was going to get out of the evening without dishing the dirt, but she didn't have to make it easy on her friends.

"A lady might not, but you always do," Millie shot back and Jo held up her hand to high five her. Gigi made a grab for Millie's wine glass and missed when the woman hugged it close to her once again. "Hey, now. No stealing my comfort wine."

Gigi speared her with a look, but withdrew her hand. "Fine, but let's keep the sass to a minimum, Miss Millie. I have the feeling you'll be a bit of a mean drunk."

"Yes, mother," Millie mumbled, then snickered at her own joke as a hiccup erupted from her throat. She covered her mouth and looked down at her glass. "Yeah, maybe I've had enough." Millie put her glass on the coffee table and pushed it away from her, Gigi shaking her head at her friend as she did. Millie wasn't a big drinker, so when she did imbibe, it tended to hit her pretty hard.

"Anyway." Jo nudged Gigi with her bare foot, obviously eager to get back to the good stuff. "Spill the beans, babe. We want to know all about your date with the motorcycle man."

Gigi couldn't stop the dreamy smile from coming across her face and she proceeded to tell them all about her date with Cooper, from the ride on his bike, to their dinner at the bar, and finally to the goodnight kiss they shared on her doorstep less than twenty-four hours earlier. "It was so great, you guys. He was a perfect gentleman the whole night, always helping me and opening doors and pulling my chair out. And our goodnight kiss." She fanned herself with her hand while pretending to swoon. "Let's just say that my vibrator basically paid for itself last night after he left."

While Millie's face turned a little red at the mention of the sex toy, Jo hooted and slapped Gigi on the knee, her smile smug. "I knew you two would have a great time together. Coop is the nicest guy in the shop and you are the nicest person I know," she glanced over at Millie. "Well, maybe second nicest. Anyway, I'm so glad the two of you are getting together."

Gigi smiled, but something nagged at her and it had for a while, so she decided to just bite the bullet and ask the question. "You and Cooper never..." she trailed off and Jo raised a brow at her.

"Never..." her friend mimicked, raising her brow in question. Jo was going to make her spell it out for her, a quality Gigi appreciated at times when it wasn't directed at her.

Gigi sighed and made the same crude gesture that Jo had earlier, frowning when Jo's face reared back in disgust. "Ew. God, no," she said emphatically, causing Gigi's eyes to widen. Jo sat up and waved her hands around. "Not that there's anything wrong with him, but you guys know I don't hook up with my dad's shop guys. I spend enough time around them that it would be like hooking up with one of my brothers."

"You don't have any brothers," Millie added.

"Yes, Millie. I remember," Jo replied with an eye roll. "My point was that, no, I have not ever hooked up with or even thought about hooking up with Cooper, so feel free to go ahead and squash that worry right now."

"Okay, good." Gigi felt her body sag with relief. The last thing she wanted to do was get into anything messy with a guy and one of her friends. Lord knew the situation was messy enough with her parents being overinvolved in her love life. Luckily, Gigi hadn't heard from her mom, so she hoped that she had gotten away with the whole ditching the charity event to hop on the back of a motorcycle thing, but she could be wrong. For all she knew, her mom was just sitting on the information to use against her at the most inconvenient time. Gigi boxed up that worry and put in on the shelf for later and turned back to her friends. "So we know how my night went, and we know how Millie's night went. Sorry again about dragging you into that." She touched a hand to Millie's knee, truly regretful after hearing how poorly it went. "But I'm still a little fuzzy on the details of your night, Miss Jolene."

Jo sipped her wine and lolled her head. "Not many details to share. I worked until 7:00 and then had to attend a dinner with a potential client until almost 10:00. The whole night was a bit of a wash really."

Gigi watched as Millie looked at Jo and Jo looked back at her. They seemed to be having some sort of silent conversation and it was bugging Gigi that she wasn't a part of it. "What's going on right there?" She pointed back and forth between her two friends who continued to speak to one another with only their eyes.

Millie continued to glare at Jo, giving her fiercest "this is a library and you need to act appropriately" look. Finally Jo caved and sighed. "Ugh, fine. The dinner with the client included drinks and one of the guys had a little too much and got a little too hands-on with his ideas about what working with them would be like."

The wine soured in Gigi's stomach as she processed the words and saw the sullen expression on Jo's face. "What do you mean a little too hands-on?" Jo picked up her wine glass and covered her mouth when she spoke, making nothing but low mumbling noises. "I didn't catch that."

Jo sighed and dropped her wine glass back down. "I said he grabbed my butt."

Gigi's mouth hit the floor at the audacity and the inappropriateness. "What? Are you okay? What did you do about it?"

Jo winced. "Um, nothing. I'm fine." She looked a little embarrassed which was unusual for Jo. Normally her strong friend owned every feeling and didn't shy away from sharing anything.

"Are you really? What that guy did was not okay. Can't you at least report him to your boss or something?" Gigi couldn't believe that her badass friend got mauled and the guy was apparently still walking around with all of his appendages intact.

"I can't," Jo started. She looked exasperated but so very tired, and Gigi wondered just how much longer Jo could keep pulling her long hours at a job she hated. "I mean, technically I can, but you don't know the culture at that place. I'm pretty much the only woman left standing at this point and if I make waves I'm pretty sure I'll get fired. I need this job."

"So then we sue their asses for sexual harassment," Gigi demanded, Millie nodding along with her in agreement.

"You don't get it because you are your own boss and you have a safety net in the form of rich parents." Jo pinched the bridge of her nose. "I've been with this place since I got my degree and if I get fired, I have no other references except a couple of internships from college and that was years ago. Between a lack of other prospects and the fact that my dad needs me around more and more to check up on him, I can't afford to lose this job."

"What's wrong with Pops?" The thought of her friend's dad being in trouble quelled her anger on Jo's behalf slightly, and she reached over to grab Jo's hand to offer her comfort. Pops was one of the sweetest men she had ever met, and him not being around anymore was just untenable.

"Nothing major yet, but since I'm not living there anymore, he's been living off of frozen food and beer." She laughed without humor, her body slumping closer to the floor. "I'm pretty sure the only time he eats anything green is when I stop by for lunch and force him to eat a salad."

"I'm sorry, sweetie." Millie scoot closer to her and rubbed her hand up and down her arm. "What can we do to help?"

Jo smiled sadly. "I don't know, but if I think of something, I'll let you know." She picked at a few kernels in the popcorn in the bowl, seeming to think better of going for more and gently shoving the whole thing away. "In the meantime, just maybe don't be too hard on me for not having the energy to fight the crap I deal with at work. I just need to stick with it long enough to get a promotion, then Pops can retire or I can hire a housekeeper or someone to hang around and make him eat his five fruits and veggies every day."

Gigi crawled over to Jo and wrapped her up in a hug. "Sure thing, Jojo. Just so you know, though, if I ever find out who that potential client was, I'm going to break his fingers," she promised as she squeezed her friend. The likelihood of her succeeding was slim, but she would try to break his fingers at least for hurting her friend.

"Thanks, Gi." Jo returned the hug fiercely while peeking over her shoulder to look at Millie. "What about you, Mills? Are you going to write a strongly worded letter to the guy's business?"

Millie shrugged. "I was going to offer to kick him in the junk, but if you want a letter instead, I'll be sure to use my best stationary."

Jo snorted a laugh and the three of them giggled. It was a welcome change in tone from the conversation they had just been having. "I'll take the former. Thank you." With Jo in better spirits, they spent the rest of the evening on lighter topics, but Gigi's mind kept wandering back to her date with Cooper, and while she had been happy to have spent an evening with her best friends, she couldn't help but miss the man who she couldn't stop thinking about.

Chapter Twelve

Cooper

The air was thick with the humidity that poured off the mass of sweaty bodies that were currently moving around at the Willow Creek Fitness Club. This wasn't normally Cooper's scene, but when his gran texted asking for him to act as her workout buddy, he couldn't say no and now here he was, standing at the front of the gym by himself. Cooper looked around the modern fitness center and searched for his grandmother. The place was packed with people getting in their daily cardio or strength training, and there was even some kind of dance fitness class going on in a room near the back. He preferred to work out at home with the set of weights he had and take his dog for a run every day, enjoying the solitude more than anything, but to each their own.

His eyes roamed around the large warehouse like structure until he finally spotted Mags on a treadmill, not a single bead of sweat on her as she walked along at a snail's pace. "Working hard, Mags?" he asked as soon as he was next to her.

Cooper's grandmother huffed and shook her head. "This darn thing doesn't seem to go above one mile an hour." Her complaint was punctuated by a rapid pressing of her finger on the machine display at random.

Cooper reached over and pointed at the up arrow under the speed heading. "How you can order food and a ride from your phone and not know how to work a treadmill is beyond me," he told the elderly woman with a smile.

"They just need to make these buttons bigger. Ageism is what it is." Mags slammed her hand down on the big red button marked "stop," and with a hand from

Cooper, she stepped off the machine and the two of them walked over to a bench press.

Cooper hummed noncommittally as she laid down under the ten pound bar and reached her arms up to grab it. "What's with the new health kick, Gran? And don't they have exercise facilities at your apartment?"

"They do." Her frail arms started pumping the small weight up and down a few times. Cooper doubted she would drop it, but he spotted her, nonetheless. Better safe than sorry, he told himself. "But I'm tired of being ogled by the sharks over there while I try to get in my daily movement. I can't concentrate on my health with all those eyes on me all the time, and I want to be around to meet those great grandbabies you promised me."

Cooper scoffed. "I don't remember making any such promise." Though the idea of having a few auburn haired little ones running around didn't sound all that bad. *Cart before the horse, Coop.* It was a good reminder not to go too fast, but the way he was feeling about Gigi had him wanting to slip their relationship into fifth gear.

"You may not have said it, but you made it the minute you were born. Besides, you're older now and I want to see a chubby baby face before I shuffle off this mortal coil."

Copper didn't like the idea of his gran not being around, though he knew that would happen eventually. She was spry, but she was older and with that came the inevitable shuffle she referred to. Still, it wasn't something he wanted to be reminded of all the time. "Come on, Mags. I have plenty of time. You're going to live forever."

"Maybe," she mused, huffing a breath and sitting up on the bench seat. "So, how are things going with your lady friend anyway?"

"Lady friend?" Cooper asked with a smile. Gigi

was a lady, but he hoped she was more than a friend. He liked her, more than liked her actually, but he didn't want to talk much about it. It felt like talking about their relationship too much was tempting fate, and after his slip up the other night when he had hurt her feelings, he wasn't taking any chances. He didn't want to lose her. "Gigi's amazing, Mags. I can really see myself with this one long term." When his grandmother eyed him for more information, he shook his head. "I'm not saying anything else. It's private business."

"Private business." She snorted as she walked toward the drinking fountain, her feet shuffling along the tiles. "I just have to wait twelve hours and ask some of the ladies at the complex to get all the details."

Cooper sighed, knowing that might be true, but he was pretty sure Gigi was keeping things as down low as he was, so at least the more personal details would be just for them. After a quick drink, Cooper and his gran were walking through the front door and out into the crisp, outside air. It would have felt a lot more refreshing had he done anything to work up a sweat, but it seemed that being Mags's work out buddy consisted mainly of coming to pick her up and take her home. While he was more than happy to be her shuttle service, the whole fitness club thing seemed like a waste of time and money for her. "You plan on getting a membership to this place, Mags? I'm pretty sure you can get as good a workout at home by lifting a couple of soup cans and walking to your mailbox."

Mags swatted his arm, but he saw the smile pulling at the corners of her mouth. "Nah," she said, shaking her head as they walked to his truck. "Too many young people showing too much skin for my taste. Thanks for coming to give me a ride home, though."

"A ride? I thought you needed a workout buddy."

Cooper loved their ability to tease one another. With a light laugh, he opened the door for her, helping her up onto the passenger seat. "You don't need to make up lies to get me to shuttle you around, Mags."

"I know." His grandmother gave him a toothy smile that made her look younger than her years. "But it's more fun when I do. Besides, I know you don't want to take any time away from your lady friend."

Cooper chuckled and got into the car, heading toward his grandma's apartment. Mags wasn't wrong, though. He didn't want to take time away from Gigi unless he absolutely had to. He just hoped Gigi was feeling the same way.

****

As it turned out, Cooper had been away from Gigi a lot more than he wanted to, not having seen her for more than five minutes at a time the entire week since their date. The auto shop had been overrun with people needing all kinds of maintenance done, and as the senior mechanic, he was on call for almost all of it. Any time he did get a spare minute, he would slip out and head on over to the tearoom, but Gigi was just as busy as he was. A couple of her kitchen staff members came down with the flu, and she had to run around and make up for their absence.

By the end of the day, she looked so knackered that all she could manage was a goodnight kiss and a promise that they would spend more time together later. Cooper couldn't fault her for being exhausted at the end of the day. He hadn't been faring much better himself. Luckily, today had been far less busy than the rest of the week had been, and he had about ten minutes until his lunch break where he would hopefully have time to stop by and at least pull his girl into her office for a quick kiss or two before he had to be back.

Cooper ran a rag over his workbench, wiping up the dirt and grime that had gathered there from his earlier work. He heard Tommy and Roe gabbing nearby, but when their talk died down suddenly, Cooper looked over at them to see their eyes practically bugging out of their heads. He followed their gaze and smirked when he saw Gigi walking toward the open garage bay looking like a dream come true.

Her hair flowed behind her in waves as she walked, and her eyes sparkled in the sunshine, but it was her dress that most likely had the boys' attention. The weather was surprisingly warm for February, and it seemed like his girl was taking full advantage. She wore a white dress with pink roses all over it. The hem ended a few inches above her knees, so you got a nice view of her legs, and it was cut low enough to show a good amount of her ample cleavage as well. The thin straps that held the dress up tied at the top, and his fingers twitched with the need to undo those bows and open the best damn present he had ever seen.

"Hot damn." Roe was practically drooling as he checked her out, giving out a low whistle as he watched her approach.

"You can say that again," Tommy replied, his own eyes wide with interest. "Too bad a girl like that would never go for guys like us." Cooper may have thought that too at one time, but now he knew better.

As Gigi got closer, a smile pulled at her face and Cooper got an idea. He stowed his rag on the bench and walked over to his coworkers. "Twenty bucks says you're wrong. I bet I could convince her to take a chance on me."

Tommy snorted. "There's no way that's happening" His head bounced between Gigi and Cooper before he shook it in disbelief. "You're on, Coop."

"Right? Count me in," Roe added. "Easiest money I ever made."

"Get your wallets ready, fellas," Cooper said as he walked out of the bay door and up to Gigi. She stopped in front of him, but before she could say anything, he pulled her into his arms and swung her around. She gripped his shoulders and he bent her at the waist, dipping her low and planting a kiss on her full, rosy lips. She squeaked in surprise, moaned, and kissed him back with vigor. Gigi opened her mouth for him and he slipped his tongue inside, running it along hers and tasting tea and mint. Her hands moved from his shoulders to his upper back and she pulled her body closer to his. He was getting very aroused and was still technically on the clock, so he swung her back upright and broke the kiss.

Gigi looked shocked and delighted by the whole thing as she ran a hand over her hair and dress to smooth them out. "Hi, Peach."

"Hi yourself," she said breathlessly. She looked around and picked up the large handbag she had been carrying. He hadn't noticed it before, and she must have dropped it when he dipped her for that kiss. "I know we haven't gotten to spend a lot of time with one another much this week, so I thought we could have lunch together." Her gaze turned heated as her tongue ran over her bottom lip. "If I would have known that was the greeting that was waiting for me, I would have found a way to come by a whole lot sooner."

Cooper leaned down and kissed her cheek. "That greeting will always be ready for you, Peach. We can have lunch at my place." He grabbed onto her hand and threaded their fingers together as he walked her into the bay. She waved hello to his coworkers who just stood there, jaws on the floor as he walked her toward the back door. "I'm taking my lunch." Roe nodded in reply, but

Tommy was still dumbstruck and didn't acknowledge what he'd said.

Cooper opened the back door and led her across the small expanse toward his home. She took in the converted garage with wide eyes, looking impressed. "This is your place? And you said you did all the work yourself?"

Cooper smiled and nodded as they approached the front door, pride filling his chest. He was loving that she was impressed with his skills and hoped to continue to impress her in the future. "It is and I did. Well, I did most of it. I don't mess with electrical work." He turned the knob, but paused before pushing the door open, turning to Gigi. "Shep's likely to get very excited when you come in, so just be prepared for lots of doggie cuddles."

Gigi's eyes sparkled and she grinned, the prospect clearly more of an incentive than deterrent. "Yay! I love animals. My parents aren't big on pets, so we didn't have any growing up." She bounced on her heels excitedly and he had to pause for a moment just to take in how adorable this woman was.

"Well, now's your chance to make up for lost time." Cooper pushed open the door and let her walk past him. Right on cue, the sound of nails on hardwood clicked and Shep appeared from around the corner of the house where he barked once and jumped up onto Gigi, placing his paws directly onto her dress. "Shep, down," he scolded lightly.

"It's okay." Gigi leaned down and scratched behind the dog's ears, cooing at him as she did. "Aww. He's just a big cuddle bug, aren't you, boy?" Gigi kicked off her heels near the door and kneeled down to get even closer to his canine companion. Shep nuzzled her and she giggled, the bright sound quickly becoming one of his new favorite. "Oh, I absolutely love him."

"Pretty sure he loves you, too." Her eyes turned to his and when she smiled, he wasn't sure whether he had been talking about the dog or himself. Cooper had never been in love before, but he was pretty sure he was on a collision course with the emotion now, and it was coming up on him, fast.

Gigi gave Shep a few more scratches before she stood up and dusted off her dress. "Should we eat?".

Cooper shook his head to clear his mind so he could be present in the here and now. There was plenty of time to think about the future later. It was all he seemed to be able to think about lately, and that future included her. If he wanted to make that a reality, he needed to put in the work first. Cooper put his hand on the small of her back and steered her toward his kitchen and small dining area. "Right this way."

He watched as her eyes roamed around his apartment, and he wondered what she thought of his space. Once she had taken in just about everything except the bathroom, she turned to him with an awed expression. "This place is amazing, Cooper. It's beautiful." She ran her hands over the arm of one of his leather chairs fondly, stepping over to the table, placing the bag on top, and pulling out two containers. "I wasn't sure if you would want a ham or turkey sandwich, so I brought one of each."

"I'll take the ham, thanks." He stepped over to the sink to wash his hands. He always washed them after every customer, but he still didn't want to ruin her efforts by accidentally eating motor oil and making himself sick.

Gigi put the containers down, reaching in and pulling out two more, presenting them to him like a game show host. "Potato salad," she explained as she unloaded some waters and silverware, finally grabbing a seat. The moment her backside hit the wood, Shep crawled under the table and laid his head in her lap, the dog clearly as taken with Gigi as he was. "God, it feels nice to be off my feet"

Cooper watched as she lifted a forkful of potato to her pretty pink lips. "Come over later and I'll give you a foot rub." He took his seat next to her, adjusting himself slightly as he grabbed his sandwich. "I've been told I give amazing massages."

She raised a brow at him. "By whom?" Her eyes were narrowed slightly and her cheeks were a little pink, but not with a blush of shyness of embarrassment. Her cheeks might as well have been painted green from all the envy she was obviously feeling.

Cooper smirked. "Why? Are you jealous, Peach?"

She shifted in her seat. "No." Her voice was insistent, but from the way she avoided his gaze, he could tell she was lying. Truthfully, he kind of liked that she was a bit jealous. It meant that she was invested in what they were doing, maybe not as much as he was, but it was something.

Cooper scooted closer to her. "You know I only have eyes for you," he vowed, lightly kissing her lips. She had no reason to be jealous. He really did only have eyes for her and no one else and had for quite some time. "Besides, the only person I've given a massage to is my dog, so you can tuck that green-eyed monster away for the time being."

She raised her chin at him and took a bite of her potato salad. "Good." Her head gave a quick nod of approval as she chewed her food for a moment before putting her fork down. "I don't normally get jealous, just so you know. I don't want you to think I'm super possessive or anything."

Cooper smiled and hooked a foot around the leg of her chair, scooting it over until it bumped up against his. He wrapped his arm around her shoulder and leaned in, running his nose through her hair and getting another hit of her sweet fruity smell. "You can get as possessive of me as you want, Honey." He nibbled on her ear and cheered himself on when he heard her breath hitch. "You can brand me, tattoo your name on my chest, or do any damn thing you want to let the world know I belong to you."

Cooper turned her head toward him and took her mouth in a punishing kiss. He was hers, just like she was his. Everything about this woman drove him crazy with the need to shower her with affection and own her body and soul at the same time. He wanted to take care of her and let her know that she was safe with him, but he also wanted to hear her screaming his name from all the pleasure he would give her. She might not be on the same page as far as their relationship was concerned just yet, but he was sure she'd get there soon. If her moans and whimpers were anything to go by, at the very least, she enjoyed the physical side of things.

Nipping at her bottom lip one last time, Cooper broke the kiss and tried to focus on their meal. "Eat up now. I don't want you wasting away on me."

"Okay," she breathed out, smiling as she picked up her fork and speared a chunk of potato.

"Good girl." He'd whispered the words, smiling when she trembled in her seat. Gigi loved his praise and he loved to give it to her. If anyone was worthy of it, it was the beautiful, thoughtful woman beside him.

Finishing their meal and chatting about much lighter topics was difficult to do when all Cooper wanted was to pull her into his lap and kiss her. Keeping his hands off her was a trial, but he didn't want to start something he couldn't finish. When they were done, had cleaned up, and Gigi had given Shep a good ten minutes of her undivided attention, he walked her back out to the garage where he would reluctantly say goodbye. They passed through the garage, and luckily his coworkers were all too busy to gape at his woman again.

When they stopped at the edge of the lot. Cooper kissed her lips lightly, his stomach sinking at the thought of goodbye. "When am I taking you out again?"

Gigi smiled at him, the sunny expression on her face easing the pain of separation slightly. "I have the girls over tonight and a party for my dad tomorrow night, but I'm free on Sunday."

Cooper twisted is lips in thought. He had hoped they could get together sooner than that. "This party for your dad, is it the type of thing you would bring a date to? Or maybe even a boyfriend?" he asked hopefully.

Her eyes lit up and seemed to glaze over at the word boyfriend. The term seemed a bit inadequate for just how intense his feelings felt, but it was all he had right now. After a moment, the light in her eyes dimmed slightly and her brow furrowed as she pressed up against him and gazed up into his eyes, searching for something. "Would you be upset if I wanted to keep you all to myself a little bit longer?"

Cooper sighed and rested his forehead against hers. It wasn't the answer he'd been hoping for, but he would respect whatever boundaries she needed to keep with her parents in order to feel comfortable. "I'd never get upset with you for something like that, Peach." He wrapped his arms around her in a hug, hoping to imbue her with some of his own strength until they were together again. "I just want to spend as much time with you as possible."

"I know, and I want to spend time with you, too." Gigi bit her lower lip and pulled back slightly, looking over his shoulder. As she stared, she seemed to disappear to another time and place completely for a second. "I'm just not ready to deal with my parents yet."

"Sure." Cooper's agreement was always at the ready for her, even though that small voice that liked to think the worst was telling him that she was ashamed to be with him. He stamped that voice down as best he could and kissed her forehead, not wanting to let judgements from others in the past taint his present. "I'll call you later and we can make more definitive plans."

"I look forward to it." Gigi turned and walked across the street to her tearoom, but turned back to him and blew him a kiss before heading inside. Cooper nodded to her and once she was gone, he spun on his heel and got back to work. She wasn't ashamed of him, he told himself. She just needed time to figure out a game plan for dealing with her uppity parents which was totally understandable.

Cooper walked back to his bench and checked his schedule to see if he had anything on his docket for the afternoon. Other than a few tune ups and one oil change, nothing major was listed. He was just gathering up his tools when Roe walked over and slapped twenty dollars on the bench. Cooper snorted at the wrinkled bill. "Keep your money, Roe. I was messing with you two. I've been seeing Gigi for a couple of weeks now."

"Huh." Roe's voice was filled with skepticism as he stuffed his money in the pocket of his coveralls. "I wouldn't have guessed that."

Cooper took a deep breath and looked over at the younger man, already knowing the answer to his question. Having grown up just below middle class and never having gone to college, Roe was basically a younger version of Cooper. "Why is that?"

Roe shrugged a shoulder. "I don't know. I haven't seen her around at all, and she looks like one of those fancy southern girls, all prim and proper. I guess I just never pictured you with a woman like that."

Cooper turned to face Roe fully, feeling the need to defend himself and Gigi more than he ever had anything else in his life. "Well, she's special, and she'll be around a lot more often if I have anything to say about it." He was certain that Gigi would be in his life for a long time, hopefully forever.

"If you say so." Roe scratched the back of his head, his expression beyond dubious. "If it were me, I'd be thinking that this was just some walk on the wild side for her. You know, a way to mess with mommy and daddy." The younger man snickered and Cooper felt his skin bristle in irritation as he bit back the reply that was on the tip of his tongue.

Cooper didn't appreciate the input into his relationship, but he had invited it by messing with the kid earlier, so he supposed he deserved the other man's derision a bit. "Well, it's a good thing I'm not you then," he ground out, turning back to his work bench. "Let's get back to work so we can get out of here on time."

Roe raised his hands in surrender and backed away slowly. "Sounds good, Coop."

Cooper felt a little guilty for getting so upset with the man. It wasn't Roe's fault he was putting to words the very insecurities that had been eating at Cooper for a while. He had felt pretty confident in who he was as a person, and as much as being with Gigi made him feel like the luckiest guy on the planet, it had also stirred up some old feelings of inadequacy he clearly hadn't dealt with fully. Cooper took a deep breath and tried to exhale all the negative emotions that were running through his mind. He would focus on finishing up his workday, see if one of the guys wanted to grab a beer, and then call Gigi. Talking to her always made him feel better. He just hoped it was enough to drown out the voice that lingered in his mind. The one that wouldn't stop whispering, *not good enough.*

Chapter Thirteen

Gigi

The party for her dad's law firm was in full swing, but Gigi wasn't in a festive mood. The ballroom of the exclusive Fairmont Hotel downtown was decked out in shades of blue and gold, tables were scattered around the room for people to mill about and socialize at while they sipped champagne and ate hors d'oeuvres, and a band played classic swing music for anyone interested in dancing. The law firm of Davenport & Atwater was celebrating a particularly successful financial quarter, and every lawyer and client seemed to be in attendance at the swanky event. The Who's Who of Willow Creek had gathered there tonight, and everyone seemed to be having a great time. Gigi, however, had never been more bored in her entire life.

In lieu of faking her way through the evening, Gigi opted to sit at the edge of the ballroom to avoid having to mingle with the upper crust of her hometown. The bubbles from the champagne tickled her throat as she looked around the room for anything or anyone remotely interesting to her. She had already been cornered a few times by friends of her parents, and while she didn't mind talking about her business, everyone seemed far more interested in when she would settle down and if they could set her up with someone they knew. Gigi politely declined their offers, but she would have felt better if she could have just told them the truth. She was taken, seeing someone, and she wasn't interested in anyone else.

As she thought of Cooper, her stomach gave a telltale flutter of delight, but there was also a tightness in her chest. The guilt of not bringing him as her plus one was eating away at her, and Gigi wondered just how long it would take her to gather enough courage to tell her parents about him. Cooper was amazing, and he deserved to be as much a part of her life as possible, but she wasn't letting that happen. He tried to hide it well, but Gigi could tell it was bothering him, and she didn't want to lose a good guy because she was still afraid of her parents. She was twenty-eight years old, for heaven's sake, and it was time for her to act like it.

Fabric brushed her arm and she startled, dreading another stilted conversation, but her shoulders came down from up near her ears when she saw that it was only her brother. "Oh, it's just you," she sighed, relief coloring her tone.

Ford shot her a wry smile. "Good to see you, too, sis." He took a sip from his champagne glass and gazed around the room, sighing heavily, his defeated body language matching her own. "God, I am so bored."

Gigi snorted, nearly performing a spit-take with her drink. Her brother was turning out to be a lot more like her than she ever thought. "Same, but I have reason to be. I'm not even a member or client of the law firm." She gestured around the ballroom filled with expensive suits and even more expensive faces. Gigi wasn't against plastic surgery because she was all about bodily autonomy, she just had a hard time keeping up with everyone's ever changing looks. "These are your people, so what's your excuse?"

Ford's mouth flattened into a tight line. "These aren't my people," he muttered irritably, polishing off his drink and swapping it with a full one from a passing tray. "I don't have people."

Gigi looked at her brother more closely. He looked as perfectly put together as he always did without a hair out of place or wrinkle on his suit, but when she looked closer, she saw the shadows under his eyes and the wariness written on his face. "Are you okay, Ford?" Gigi and her brother weren't best friends, but she liked to think they were close enough for him to be able to talk to her about his troubles.

Ford tilted his head and looked down at her. "Haven't you heard? I scored a big client this quarter and I'm swimming in money. I'm fantastic." He chuckled, but Gigi didn't believe him for one second. Ford had a beautiful home, drove a luxury vehicle, and wore thousand dollar suits, but she knew he didn't really care about any of that stuff. It was all for show, and Gigi wasn't sure how much longer he could keep up the ruse. It looked like play acting as the perfect son to their parents was slowly eating away at him just as was her playing the dutiful daughter, and she didn't put in nearly as much effort as he did.

Gigi reached over and lightly touched her brother's forearm. "I know you're lying. What I can't figure out is why." Ford's eyes flicked over to where their parents stood in the middle of a circle of people, talking and laughing as though they hadn't a care in the world. They were definitely in their element while she and Ford grew more uncomfortable as the night went on. Gigi peered up at him, tugging on the sleeve of his suit jacket. "I think they'd understand if you wanted to leave the firm. Strike out on your own if that's what you're wanting to do."

Ford's expression was pained, his mind clearly stuck in some destructive loop she couldn't access. "It's a lot more complicated than that."

"How so? Explain it to me so I can help," she pleaded. She wanted to help her brother, but she couldn't even help herself, so what use was she, really?

"I appreciate the offer, Ginny, but I've made my choices. Now I have to live with them," he said, resigned.

"I don't think that's true," she protested. She hated seeing her big brother, the guy who always looked out for her growing up, look so defeated. Gigi wanted to fix things, but she struggled to think of what she could do about it, especially when she didn't know exactly what the problem was to begin with.

Gigi's phone pinged and she pulled it out of her green clutch purse, smiling at the name on her screen. Putting aside her worries about Ford for the moment, she swiped open her phone and read the message.

Cooper: **Missin' you, Peach.**

It was a simple note, but it still caused her heart to skip a beat. Gigi had been missing him, too, all day, in fact. The shop had been too busy for him to stop by the tearoom and she had to head home right after work to get ready for this party. Her thumbs flew across the screen as she typed out her reply.

Gigi: **I'm missing you too, Cuddle Bug. Oh, and you too, Coop.**

She smirked as she watched the three dots dance on her message screen, eager for his reply, eager for more of anything from him.

Cooper: **I see how it is. Just for that, I'm retracting my offer of a foot rub.**

She laughed to herself and replied.

Gigi: **That's too bad because I was going to reciprocate with a little rubbing of my own. ;)**

Cooper: **Wouldn't you know it, that foot rub is back on the menu.**

Gigi cackled at his reply, but quickly covered her mouth when she remembered where she was. Ford looked at her with his eyes narrowed. "Who are you texting?"

She thought about lying and telling him it was Jo or Millie, but this was Ford, and even though he might be resigned to his fate of doing the bidding of their parents, she wasn't and she needed to start acting like it. Gigi stood up a little taller and looked her brother straight in the eyes. "I'm texting my boyfriend."

Shock painted Ford's face. "Since when do you have a boyfriend?"

Gigi smiled as she thought about Cooper. "Well, technically he's been my boyfriend since yesterday, but we've been seeing each other for a couple of weeks and I think it's going pretty well."

Ford nodded and his gaze flicked over to their parents. "I'm guessing that because this is news to me, Mom and Dad don't know, and if they don't know I can only assume it's because this relationship is with someone they wouldn't approve of."

Gigi shrugged a shoulder, playing dumb when she knew the truth. "I don't know if they would approve or not." Their parents definitely wouldn't want her dating a blue collar worker, but she didn't care about any of that. Ford leveled her with a look that called "bullshit," so she gave up the ruse. "Fine, they probably wouldn't approve of Cooper because of his job, but he's really great and he treats me well, and that's all I care about."

Ford was silent for a good minute, probably processing this new information. "What's he do?"

Gigi hesitated telling him, but Ford wasn't a snob. She could consider this a practice run for when she eventually told her parents. "He's a mechanic at Bob's Auto Shop."

She braced herself for possible ridicule following that declaration, but none came. "You said he treats you well?" Ford asked and Gigi's nod was immediate. Cooper considered her needs and was supportive of her in a way she'd always longed for but never gotten. "And you really like him?"

Gigi's mouth pulled up at the corners until the apples of her cheeks hurt. "I really, really do." It was fast, but she was pretty sure she was already falling in love with Cooper. Being with him was like flying, only instead of being afraid of falling, you felt able to enjoy the floaty feelings that ran through your body because there was someone right there with you, holding your hand.

Ford pulled her in for a side hug and kissed the top of her head. "Then I'm happy for you, Ginny."

Gigi beamed at her brother and his support for her relationship, but that smile faltered when she saw that her parents were approaching. "What are we happy about?" her mom asked, and as she did, the high Gigi had gotten from telling her brother about Cooper immediately started to dissipate.

Gigi glanced at her bother, but he wasn't going to be able to help her out of this. She was going to have to do this all on her own and that was okay because it was high time she started taking control of her own life. After taking a deep breath, she looked at both of her parents directly and gathered all the strength she could. "We're happy about the fact that I have a boyfriend."

"Really?" A smile pulled across her dad's face. "Well, who's the lucky guy?" His eyes pinged around the room, probably assuming she was dating one of the many successful lawyers or businessmen in attendance.

Gigi glanced over to her mother, who looked far less curious. Her expression read a little like she already knew who Gigi was talking about. Damn that Ms. Bowman and her gossipy ways. She probably called her mother the minute Gigi left the charity event with Cooper last week. Gigi dug down deep, grounding herself as much as she could while holding on tight to the confidence she'd mustered up moments ago. She was a grown woman who could make her own decisions and her parents would just have to deal with it. "He's not here, Daddy. He's at home right now, relaxing after a long day of work."

Her dad nodded, but his brow furrowed. "Well, what does he do for work?"

Gigi raised her head and spoke proudly because that's what she felt when it came to Cooper. "He's a mechanic. He works with Jo's father at Bob's Auto." Cooper was one of the hardest working men she knew and she was proud to be with him, no matter what might come out of her parents' mouths in the next few minutes.

Her dad chuckled and glanced at her mom for a second, rolling his eyes before looking back at her. "Very funny, Virginia. What does he really do?"

"I already told you, Daddy." Gigi managed to keep her voice steady despite the fact that her insides were churning with fear at what her parents would say or do and the now bitter champagne she'd enjoyed earlier.

"Virginia Mae," her dad chided. Hearing her full name made her feel like her younger self, the girl always wanting to go her own way but pulled back with the need to garner her parents approval. "Please tell me this is a joke." Her father was whisper hissing his words, something he only did when he was upset. He also probably hadn't wanted anyone to hear about Gigi's new man or his chosen profession.

"She's telling the truth, Clifford." Her mom's voice and demeanor were eerily calm. The fear in Gigi's gut turned to dread at what the woman had in store for her. "She's been seeing this boy for at least a week."

Gigi scoffed at her mom's dismissive language. "He's hardly a boy. He's thirty-three, and I like him a lot. He's a gentleman, he's good to me, and we have a lot in common." That was all they should care about, but of

177

course it wouldn't be, not for Clifford and Theodora Davenport.

"What could you possibly have in common with a man like that?" His face was turning an alarming shade of purple, and Gigi hoped he wouldn't have a heart attack or stroke. She knew he wouldn't take the news well, but she didn't think it would literally kill him.

Gigi started to argue with him, but her mother held up a hand to stop her. "It's fine, Clifford."

Her head whipped around so that she was facing her mother, hope flickering in her chest that perhaps this once when she really needed it, her mother was going to support her. "It is?" she and Ford asked in unison, disbelief laced in both of their voices.

"Of course, dear." The now placating tone she used snuffed the flame of hope that Gigi had so stupidly lit. "This is your little act of rebellion, and we'll let it play out until it comes to its natural conclusion. Then you can get back to dating more appropriate men. So, have your fun, and we'll be here to listen when you're ready to get serious."

For a moment, Gigi wasn't sure she heard her mother correctly. When the words finally registered, Gigi fumed and tried her best to keep her temper under wraps. She may be angry with her parents, but she didn't want to cause a spectacle. "I'm already being serious," she insisted, her voice low and emphatic. "Cooper isn't an act of rebellion."

"Whatever you say, dear." The patronizing shot was fired, hitting Gigi square in the chest. That they thought so little of her own self will wasn't surprising given how often she'd caved in the past. "Come on, Cliff. Let's go find the Atwaters. I'm sure Reggie has a few stories that will calm you down." Gigi's dad gave her one last disappointed look and walked off in the other direction on the arm of her mom.

Gigi was still feeling enraged, but she was also second guessing herself as she often did after speaking with her so-called caregivers. This wasn't some kind of "sowing her wild oats situation." She really liked Cooper and could see herself loving him for a long time. She didn't think she was being naïve, but her mom had put doubts in her head and there was only one place she could go to get rid of them. Gigi turned to her brother who looked at her with sympathy. "I'm leaving. There's somewhere else I would rather be."

"Good for you, Ginny" There was a small spark in his eyes when he looked at her, and while she might not have good parents, she had a great brother. "I'm proud of you."

Gigi hugged her brother tightly. "Thanks, big brother." She pulled back and smiled at him. "It's not too late for you, too," she told him, hoping to see him do a little something for himself sooner rather than later.

Ford smiled sadly. "Not sure that's true, but I appreciate you saying it." He leaned down and kissed her cheek. "Goodnight, Ginny."

"Night." Turning on her heels, she made a bee line for the exit.

Gigi ditched her champagne glass on some random table, leaving the ballroom and the hotel, getting to her car as quickly as her feet would carry her. She hopped in and exited the parking lot, pointing it toward Cooper's place and pushing the speed limits the whole way there. When she finally pulled around to the back of the auto shop and parked near Cooper's truck, she gave herself a once over in her rearview mirror and approved of what she saw. She had gotten dressed to the nines for the party and had the hair and make-up to match, and she still looked pretty darn good.

Gigi got out of the car and approached the front door with determination. For a second, she wondered if maybe she should take a moment to calm her emotions a bit. Her parents had her worked up, and she wanted Cooper to know she had a clear head when she told him how much she wanted him. After a deep breath, she knocked on the door and Gigi stood there anxiously for a good minute. When no one came, she peeked around to glance at the large windows. There were still lights on inside, so she raised a fist to knock again, but there was still no answer. Maybe she should have texted first. Cooper could be out with a friend or with his Gran, though she doubted even the lively Mags was up past 8:00 on a Saturday night.

With a sigh, Gigi turned around to leave, but stopped when her eyes snagged on two shapes moving toward the home. It was Cooper and Shep jogging toward her. The dog saw her first and started running faster, but luckily he was on a leash and Cooper was able to wrangle him back. Gigi shuffled on her feet until they got up next to her, suddenly feeling a little silly for showing up out of the blue, but after the confrontation with her parents, she needed to see him, needed to prove to herself that this was more than some rebellious act. With all her heart, she knew that what they had was more than just some anomaly in her otherwise humdrum love life. It was something real.

Cooper slowed down and walked up to her, pulling out his ear buds as he walked and reining Shep in so that he wouldn't jump on her. "Hey, Peach." He was slightly out of breath, the sound getting her worked up as she took him in. He was covered in a fine sheen of sweat, his white t-shirt plastered to the hard muscles of his arms and torso and Gigi did her best to look him in the eyes, but it was hard with so much delicious man on display.

Cooper leaned down and kissed her cheek, shaking her slightly from her stupor as his masculine scent washing over her. "This is a nice surprise."

Gigi smiled at him, his words instantly buffing out the chinks her parents had put in her armor. Even sweaty from a long jog, he looked and smelled amazing, but even better was that he was still the same great person she knew he was. "Is it okay? I wanted to come see you, but I can take off if you're busy or want time to yourself."

Cooper scoffed and opened the door to his house, gesturing for her to enter. "Are you kidding? If I have a choice between anything and spending time with you, I pick you." He followed her in and shut the door, toeing off his running shoes and letting Shep off his leash. The dog came to her, but he didn't jump up and she rewarded him with lots of ear scratches and kisses. She stood up from the dog and saw that Cooper was leaning against his entry table, his eyes roaming up and down her body. "Damn, woman. You look absolutely magnificent."

Cooper held up a finger and twirled it in the air. She rolled her eyes slightly but complied with his request and spun around in a circle for him, showing off her green cocktail dress. It was a halter top, and the material was silky and hugged her entire body. "Like what you see?"

The table squeaked against the hardwood floors as Cooper shoved off of it and walked up to her. "I always like what I see when I look at you, Peach." He grabbed her hand and made to pull her close, but he stopped when she was halfway there, looking down at his disheveled appearance and chuckling. "I should probably go clean myself up."

He started to walk away, but Gigi tugged on his hand and pulled him back to her, shaking her head from side to side. "Nuh-uh." Without hesitation, she wrapped her arms around him, linking them behind his neck. "I like you like this."

"You do, huh?" He grabbed her hips and walked the two of them backwards until she was pressed up against the wall. "How much do you like it?"

Gigi trembled in his arms as a wildfire of desire burned throughout her body. Everything he did and every word he spoke in his low voice that reminded her of slow, sweet molasses always made her weak in the knees. She channeled some of that bravery from earlier and reached up on her tiptoes, licking a stripe up his neck and enjoying the salty taste of his skin. "I like it a lot," she whispered, tugging his earlobe into her mouth and nipping at it with her teeth.

A low grumbling sound came from Cooper's chest as he hoisted her up into his arms and walked her over to one of the leather sofas. He sat down, pulling her into his lap. "I like the way you think, Peach."

Cooper reached to the back of her neck, his hand hot against her skin, and pulled her down for a kiss. His lips were warm and supple, and she tugged one between her teeth, nipping at it lightly, diving back in, and running her tongue into his mouth. One of his hands gripped her waist while the other roamed up and down her legs causing her to shiver once more with desire for him. His rough hands felt amazing, and Gigi felt so good she thought she just might float away like a balloon off its string, so she gripped his damp shirt to ground herself. She cupped his cheek with her other hand and continued to kiss him like there was no tomorrow, wiggling her bottom in his lap, feeling his stiff length poking into her backside.

Cooper grunted and pulled back, the two of them breathing heavily after their little make-out session.

"While I would obviously love to take this further, I think we should chat first."

Gigi frowned and tried to stand up, but Cooper locked his arms around her waist and kept her where she was. "Did I do something wrong?" He seemed to be enjoying everything they were doing, and from the way her heart beat like a drum, she was too.

Cooper smiled wryly. "Honey, does it feel like you did something *wrong*?" he asked as he shifted her in his lap and she felt his erection again.

She whimpered at the feel of him beneath her. "Then why did you stop?" Gigi wanted to keep going. It was like all her intentions to come here and tell Cooper how she felt flew out the window the moment she touched him. Getting more of those touches was all she could think about.

Cooper sighed and rested his head on her shoulder. "I stopped because as much as I want to go there with you, I get the feeling something is on your mind, and I want to talk about it."

Gigi's brow furrowed. It was amazing how well he could read her after only a few weeks of really knowing one another. "How did you know?" Her sex-addled brain cleared up a bit more the longer they spoke, and she appreciated that at least one of them was able to keep a level head.

Cooper smiled at her. "You're pretty easy to read, Peach. I can tell when you're happy, and when you're not, and as happy as you are to see me, I can see something else lingering back there. When you're here with me, I want all of you here. Does that make sense?"

Gigi wanted to be all there with him, too. She rested her head against his and wrapped her arms around his shoulders, wanting to keep him close. "I told my parents about you," she stated calmly.

His breath hitched and his mouth twitched at the corners, but a smile didn't follow. "How did that go?"

"Not well." Gigi didn't want him to feel bad, but she wasn't going to be dishonest, not with him. "My dad was a little upset, and my mom said that this was just me acting out." Some of the anger from earlier reignited in her chest, fueling her determination to stay on the path she'd chosen for herself for once. "I'm not some teenager sneaking out of the house at night to piss off my parents. This isn't like that."

She felt Cooper's chest rise and fall as he took a deep breath. "What is it like then?"

Gigi skimmed her hands along his shoulders until she was cupping his jaw again, the soft tips of the hair of his beard tickling her palms. "I like you, Cooper. I know it's early days, but I can see a future with you." The confession came easily when she was staring into his eyes. The baby blues lit up, but he didn't say anything, making her feel slightly anxious. "If you don't feel the same…"

Cooper pressed one of his fingers to her mouth. "I'm going to stop you right there because I have felt that way since just about the moment I met you." He leaned in and lightly brushed his lips against hers. "I don't want to cause trouble for you with your family, though."

"You're not. They're causing trouble with me, not you." Her forehead fell against his, needing as much connection as possible. Life as Gigi knew it was changing, but with Cooper by her side, she knew she could handle it. "You're just an excuse for them to get on me about not being who they want me to be. If it wasn't you, it would be something else like how I dress, or how I run my business, or how I don't associate with the right people." She sighed sadly at the reality she'd ignored for too long. Family was important to her, but not to the point where she was willing to push aside what she wanted. Not anymore. "It's always been like this."

Cooper rubbed her back and ran his fingers through her hair. "I'm real sorry to hear that. You deserve the world, Honey. Hopefully, you'll let me be the one to give it to you."

Gigi smiled at the promise in his voice and kissed him. "I don't need the world," she told him honestly. "I just need you."

Cooper smiled against her lips. "Good." He shifted them on the chair and held her tightly, the warmth of his body soothing the rest of her frayed nerves, providing the comfort she'd needed and known he could give her. "Now, how about we sit here for another minute, then we can watch a World War II documentary while I give you that foot rub I mentioned earlier."

"That would be perfect." Gigi sighed happily and for the rest of the evening, everything was perfect, just like it was any time the two of them were together. Now, if only she could drown out the voices of her parents causing her to doubt herself, things would be even better.

Chapter Fourteen

Cooper

The last month of Cooper's life had been the best in recent memory. He spent his days working hard at the garage, and he spent most nights with Gigi. They would cuddle and watch movies at his place while Shep stood watch over the two of them or sometimes they would talk for hours on Gigi's couch while she ate butter pecan ice cream and he drank a beer. No matter what they did, the night would always devolve into the two of them tangled up together on one surface or another as they kissed each other silly. Cooper adjusted himself as he thought about last night when Gigi had come over wearing a pair of cut-off shorts and a tank top. There was so much smooth, ivory skin on display that Cooper couldn't help himself from exploring it.

They barely made it ten minutes into the movie they were watching before they were horizontal on the couch, their limbs tangling together like a pretzel. He was struggling to keep going at the slow pace, but after her revelation that her parents thought she was just going through a phase, Cooper felt hesitant about them moving things to the bedroom. It was probably still those old insecurities that he'd buried long ago digging their way up to the surface, but he wanted them to be more solid before they took that next step. Deep down, he knew once he made love to her, that would be it for him. Gigi already felt like she was his in every meaningful way but that one, and if she left after he'd experienced what he already knew would be the best he'd ever had, it would make losing her even more devastating.

Cooper shook the insecurities away as best he could and tried to focus on the evening ahead as he finished getting ready for his big date. He was taking Gigi to dinner at his Gran's. It was a big step, and even though Gigi and Mags already knew one another, it would be the first time his grandma would be interacting with Gigi as his girlfriend, not the owner of The Happy Kettle. He was hopeful that having his woman spend time with his family outside of the normal venue would help settle his nerves a little.

Giving himself a once over, Cooper looked down at his dog who had been sitting next to him almost the entire time. "What do you think, Shep?" His dog's head tilted as he seemed to take in his dark wash jeans, white t-shirt, blue button down, and brown boots. Shep barked and Cooper smiled, reaching down and scratching the canine behind the ears. "Thanks, boy. It's about as fancy as I get. I just hope it's good enough."

Cooper walked out of his bathroom and grabbed his phone, wallet, and keys before heading out to his truck. He'd considered taking the bike, but Gigi complained that it might mess up her hair and she wanted to make a good impression on his gran. He could respect that because even though they'd been together for about six weeks, he was still trying to make a good impression on her. Gigi didn't need it, but he needed it for himself.

After hopping in the truck and making it over to Gigi's in record time, Cooper walked back to her small house and knocked on the front door. When it opened, he had a hard time keeping his eyes in their sockets. This woman always looked like an absolute knockout, but tonight, she was something else. She wore a light blue dress covered in yellow flowers. One shoulder was exposed, and the other had ruffles along the edge that draped down toward a bow tied at her waist, and her shoes had straps that wrapped over her feet and up to her ankles. Her hair was curled a little more than usual, but it suited her perfectly, matching her entire look in a way that only she could pull off.

Gigi was the picture of grace and beauty, and once again he thought she deserved better than him, someone that completed that picture better than he could. "Hey, baby. You look really good." Gigi's compliment cut into his spiraling, and he tried to focus more on her than himself as she stepped out of her house and shut the door, leaning up to kiss his cheek.

Cooper grabbed her hand and laced their fingers together. "Thanks, Peach. You look stunning as always." He walked the two of them toward his truck and opened the door for her, jogging around to get in on his side.

When he was in, she looked over at him with curiosity. "Are you sure this is okay? I wasn't sure what to wear to a Pancake Breakfast and Bingo Night."

Cooper chuckled and started the truck, heading toward the senior living community. "I am one hundred percent certain that what you are wearing is more than okay." Grabbing her hand and resting it with his on the console between them, he smiled when his inner critic was silenced by the contact. "If anything, I'm a little worried that some geezer is going to have a heart attack when he sees you. Let's just hope everyone's taken their meds this evening."

Gigi slapped his arm playfully. "You're bad." Her scold was light, made even less impactful by the wide smile on her face.

"You love it," he teased. He loved to mess with her just to see her cheeks blush or that mega-watt smile come across her face.

"I do love it. Quite a bit, actually," she said seriously. Cooper's hand gripped the steering wheel tightly. Could she be talking about what he hoped she was talking about? Cooper was already certain that he was in love with her, but he hadn't said anything yet in case she wasn't there with him. It was scary, being with someone so colossally out of your league, and he was hesitant to make himself that vulnerable by saying it first.

"I'm glad." The reply didn't at all encapsulate how he felt, but his mind was still a bit of a mess. The number of people in his life who had loved him had been few, and wrapping his head around the possibility of Gigi being added to the list was difficult to reconcile. She smiled at him, but it didn't quite reach her eyes and he wondered if maybe he hadn't just screwed something up. There wasn't much time to think about that, though, because they were already pulling up to the apartments. He parked the truck and turned to his woman. "Gigi..." he started, but she was already opening the door and hopping out.

"We should get going." Her words were quick and she was avoiding his gaze. If he was needing confirmation that he did something wrong, he was pretty sure he just got it. *Damn it.*

Cooper hopped out of the truck and caught up with her, grabbing her hand and dragging her back to him. She spun around to face him, but her eyes landed everywhere but on his. He lifted her chin up so he could see her face. "Look at me, Peach." When her eyes did finally met his, he could see hurt and confusion. "Talk to me. What did I do?"

Gigi sighed, waving off his concern with a flick of her wrist. "You didn't do anything. I'm just having a hard time with things."

Cooper's brow furrowed with worry. He hated seeing her having to deal with anything troublesome and he wanted to ease her pain if he could. "What things?"

"Nothing. Just family stuff." She closed her eyes and exhaled slowly, and when she opened them again she looked different. Not better necessarily, but like she'd tucked away her feelings for another time. "Can we not talk about it right now? I want to just have fun with you and Mags."

Cooper nodded. He would respect her wishes, but he wasn't going to forget about it completely. "Will you tell me about it another time? I don't like seeing you upset."

She smiled more genuinely this time and hugged his arm, walking him back toward the dining hall where they were meeting his Gran. "I promise."

"Good girl." Keeping her close, Cooper opened the door for her, escorting her inside with a hand on her lower back. He looked around the room and spotted Mags at one of the smaller tables, using her purse, jacket, and whatever else she had on her to reserve the rest of the seats. When they walked up to her, she was busy scolding a couple of older gentleman. "Back away vultures. These seats are taken."

"Jeez, Mags. You don't have to be mean," one of them said, scratching at the back of his ear.

"Go on. Git." Her face held a deep frown as she shooed them away with her hands.

The men left promptly and Cooper couldn't help himself. He chuckled as he and Gigi approached the table. "I thought you said they were sharks, not vultures."

His gran spun in her seat, the frown immediately turning upside-down as he bent down and kissed her cheek. "They're whatever I want them to be and right now I want them to be gone," she cackled and looked over to Gigi. "Well, it's about time my grandson brought you here. I see you at the tearoom, but you're so busy we don't have a chance to chat."

"It's good to see you, Mags" Gigi leaned down to hug the frail woman. Seeing the two most important women in his life together tugged at his heart, and he couldn't help but picture a future where the three of them spent a whole lot more time together.

"It's good to see you, too, dear." Mags speared Cooper with a look, the same one he'd get whenever he came home later than he should have or flunked a test. "Glad you finally got your head out of your ass as far at this lady is concerned."

Cooper frowned. "Thanks, I guess?" He shoved aside his gran's things and pulled out a chair for Gigi, taking a seat next to her, letting his eyes roam around the room as he did. "So, Gran, what's tonight all about?"

Mags rubbed her hands together like she was plotting a bank heist, and a wide grin erupted once more on her wrinkled face. "Well, tonight we eat pancakes and play bingo," she leaned in closer to the two of them and lowered her voice, her eyes darting to the sides nervously. "I also have an in with the bingo caller, so I think our chances of winning are pretty high."

Cooper raised a brow. "How in the hell do you have an in with the bingo caller? What does that even mean?" He was certain that bingo was a tamper proof game, but if anyone could find a way to cheat, it was his gran.

"It means that they'll call the numbers on my bingo sheet and we split the winnings fifty-fifty." His grandma's eyes sparkled like she was winning the lottery and not a small pot of cash from her fellow community members.

Gigi giggled and Cooper just shook his head. "Don't they pass the bingo sheets out at random? How will the caller know which one you get?" The whole scheme seemed to have quite a few logistical holes in it, but he supposed he should just leave well enough alone and let her have her fun.

His gran scrunched up her face. "I don't know how it all works, son. I just know that it will," she huffed, crossing her arms over her chest.

Cooper held up his hands in surrender. Clearly his logic was no match for her confidence. "If you say so, Mags."

Gigi smiled at his grandma. "Well, I think it will work out just fine, and I, for one, am excited to see how it all goes down," she conceded, earning a nod of approval from Mags.

His gran looked over at him triumphantly, and Cooper just laughed. "I see how it is. Two against one now, is it?" He wasn't the least bit bothered by the idea of the two of them ganging up on him if it meant they were getting along well, in fact, he welcomed it.

"Afraid so," Gigi said with a wink. Suddenly, a group of employees descended from the kitchens and into the dining hall. Plates piled high with pancakes and berries were placed in front of them as well as some bingo cards before they were left alone again. Their table spent the next hour eating, marking their cards, and laughing when just about everyone in the place seemed to get a bingo except for Mags.

"I don't know what on Earth is going on, but you can be sure that Martha and I will be having a talk later." Mags grumbled as they stood up from their chairs, her salty attitude delighting him to no end.

Cooper helped his grandma up and offered her his arm, Gigi taking up the other side. "Go easy on her, Mags. Maybe she got a little confused. Bingo is a complicated game after all." He tipped his head at some of the other residents as they passed, wanting to earn as much goodwill for his grandma as he could before she inevitably went off on her bingo tirade and alienated half the community.

"Humph. I don't know how complicated it is." Mags continued her not-so-quiet griping as they walked back toward her apartment. "And from what I hear around the shuffleboard court, Martha is an expert at handling balls."

Gigi snorted and Cooper ducked his head to hide his smile, trying to stifle his laughter. "That's awful, Mags."

The older woman stopped, her eyes playful. "Oh, please. That's nothing. Why I heard that Mr. Biggins…"

"Stop, please," Gigi implored, wiping a tear form her eye. "I don't want or need to know this much about my customers." Cooper couldn't blame her. He had definitely started seeing at least a few of his old schoolteachers and coaches differently after some of the information Mags had revealed to him over the years.

Mags patted Gigi's hand and they stopped at her front door. "All right, but only because you asked so nicely." Gigi leaned down and kissed her cheek, causing Mags to blush and wave her off. "Save it for my grandson." Reaching up, she pat a hand against Cooper's cheek. It felt little more than a light breeze against his skin, but he knew his gran was still as strong as she ever was, at least mentally. "I'll see you next week. Both of you," she insisted, heading into her apartment.

After saying goodnight to Mags, Cooper wrapped his arm around Gigi's shoulders and led her back out to the truck. After he had her tucked safely in her seat, he rounded the hood and climbed in himself, turning to Gigi and frowning at her guarded expression. He didn't like it, and the need to know what was bothering her was quickly building up again. Cooper started the car and steered toward her house, feeling only slightly better when she reached across the console and grabbed his hand.

They drove in silence for a bit until he just

couldn't take it anymore. He squeezed her hand tightly and gazed at her out of the corner of his eye. "Can we talk about it now?"

He watched as Gigi bit her lip for a moment, but eventually, she nodded her head. "Okay," she said quietly.

Cooper exhaled slowly. "What's the family stuff you're dealing with?"

Gigi shrugged a shoulder, but Cooper had become such an expert in her body language that he could see the wobble in it. "It's nothing major. It's just that my parents aren't really talking to me all that much, and even though I hated how much they were involved in certain aspects of my life before, I guess I just hate feeling like such a disappointment." She turned in her seat to look at him, her eyes fiercely determined. "I don't want you to think I regret us being together because I don't. It's just that I've always felt like I was never living up to their expectations, but this is the first time I've had to deal with the repercussions for longer than a few days. I'm not used to it, and it's not a good feeling."

Cooper laced their fingers together and brought her hand up to his mouth to kiss the back of it. "I'm sorry you're having to deal with all that, Peach. Your family is important to you, and I get that." He wanted to say more to soothe her, so he divulged something he hadn't even told his gran. "I also know a thing or two about being a disappointment."

"What do you mean?" she asked, her tone soothing. He was supposed to be making her feel better, and he wanted to. Maybe his being vulnerable with her like she just had been with him would go a little ways toward doing that.

They had arrived at her place, so he parked the truck and unbuckled himself so he could face her more fully. "I mean that I know what it's like to feel like you aren't good enough for someone." He gazed out the window for a moment, feeling the pain of a rejection he wasn't even old enough at the time to remember before looking back at her. He'd mentioned little of his parents, focusing more on the two people who'd actually stuck around to raise him, but ignoring their existence never made the pain fully go away. "My mom left when I was born and I have no idea who my dad is."

Gigi frowned and rubbed her hand up and down his arm. "I'm so sorry, baby. That's all about them, though, not about you." He raised his brow in protest and she continued. "I'm not saying your feelings aren't valid because they are, but they left you because they couldn't handle parenthood, not because of anything you did. Some people aren't meant to be parents."

He smiled sadly at her. There was no better illustration of that fact than his parents. "That's true. It wasn't just them, though. I was never the smartest kid in school, and I was never a sports star. I'm not a creative type either. I mean, you've heard what I named my dog." Cooper swallowed the lump in his throat that thickened with each word he said. "I always worked hard, but that never seemed to matter to anyone but my grandparents. It used to bother me a lot, but I know my worth. I know my job isn't much, but I do it well." He reached over and stroked her cheek, hoping she understood. "Look, all I'm trying to say is that no matter what anyone else thinks, you have to know your worth. I don't always remember that, but I try, and it might not mean much, but I think you're worth a whole helluva lot, Peach."

Gigi's eyes shined and her lips formed a small smile. "It means a lot, Cooper." She scooted toward him, climbed into his lap, and gripped his face. She leaned in and brushed her lips against his. "It might not mean much to you, but I think you're worth a whole helluva lot, too."

Cooper kissed her deeply then, trying to let her know just how much those words meant to him. When he was done, he rested his forehead against hers. "That means everything, Honey." The proximity light above her landlord's garage lit up and shined through the windshield, dragging a sigh from Cooper's lungs. He didn't want to give the neighborhood a show, and he planned on giving her a proper goodnight kiss. "Let me walk you to your door."

They exited the truck and walked to her small home hand in hand, standing awkwardly for a moment as she unlocked her door. "Thanks for coming tonight. I know Mags was grateful for it and I want you to know that I am, too."

Gigi smiled up at him and walked through her door, stopping in the entryway. "You're welcome. I'm just sad Mags's little scheme didn't work out in her favor." She tossed her purse and keys on a small table and turned back to him. "Although, her not winning was just as entertaining."

"It was." He approached her slowly, heat in his gaze. Now that they were out of view, he couldn't wait to get his hands on her. "I don't want to talk about my grandma anymore, though."

Cooper kicked the door shut with his boot and crowded up against Gigi. He pulled her into his chest and kissed her forehead, the tip of her nose, and her cheek, finally taking her mouth in a punishing kiss. Their tongues collided and danced together as he slid his hands down to her hips, the softness he felt making him harder than he thought possible. When he squeezed them, she groaned and wound her arms around his middle, gripping his back hard, slipping her hands underneath his shirts, and rubbing his back with her smooth, cool hands. He trembled, something that had only ever happened when he was with her, and then she moved her hands south, slipping them into the back of his jeans and gripping his bare ass and urging him on.

Cooper's grip on her hips tightened and his breathing got shaky. "Don't start something you can't finish, Peach." He meant what he said, but boy did he ever want her to keep going.

Gigi continued to nip at his ear, kissing and licking the sensitive spots around it. "Oh, baby. With you, I'm pretty sure I can always finish." Her voice was husky and filled with lust, and it was driving him mad.

Whatever control he had been clinging to reached its breaking point. He slipped his hands under her legs and hoisted her up against the wall, pushing her dress up to her thighs in the process. Cooper ran his hands up and down the smooth expanse of her legs while he held her in place against the wall. "You want to finish?" he asked, pushing her dress up even higher and grinding his erection against her center. They'd both been working themselves up almost every night, never taking it further, but that seemed to be over now. Gigi nodded frantically at his question, but he didn't keep going. Instead, he ran one hand up her body, skimming the underside of her breast and coming to a stop on her shoulder, stroking the hollow of her throat with his thumb. "I need to hear you say it, Peach. What do you want?"

Gigi whimpered and took a deep breath. He wasn't sure what her previous experiences had been, and he honestly didn't want to think too much about it, but he wanted to give her exactly what she wanted. In order to do that, he needed to her words. "I want you to make this ache go away," she pleaded, rubbing herself against him like a cat in heat. "I want you to make me come. Please."

"Good girl," he whispered near her ear, nibbling

at the lobe. "How far do you want to take this? Do you want to do this here? Or over there?" He nodded to her bed that was on the other side of the small house. He saw a momentary flash of doubt in her eyes, so he kissed the tip of her nose and rested their foreheads together. They didn't have to go all the way tonight. Lord knew he was happy to have her in his arms any way he could. "We'll take it slow."

"Not too slow, I hope," she whined, gyrating her hips, creating a good amount of friction between their two bodies. If she kept this up they could probably start a fire from all the rubbing.

"I think my good girl likes to be a little bit bad sometimes, doesn't she?" Bunching up her dress for easy access, Cooper slipped a hand to her ass, palming and kneading the soft muscle.

"Uh-huh." Gigi continued to babble almost incoherently as his hand continued to explore the cheeks that were exposed to him. Every inch of her body was soft and supple, the opposite of just everything about him, and they fit together so perfectly it made his chest squeeze happily.

Cooper chuckled and ran his hand over to grab the thin material at the waist of her thong. He ran his calloused fingers underneath, hoping his hands weren't too rough for her as he grabbed the strap and twisted, ripping it from her body. Gigi gasped, but he just smirked at her, stuffing the ruined panties into his pocket as a keepsake. "I'll buy you another pair," he promised, slanting his mouth over hers in another brutal kiss. It was hard, full of hunger, and it revved his engine more than anything else ever had.

Cooper hooked one of her legs under his elbow and slipped his other hand between her legs, moving to her front. He ran his fingers up and down through her slick folds a few times, only barely grazing the bundle of nerves that he knew was begging for all his attention. She moaned into his mouth as his fingers continued to work, the sound making him smile against her lips. "I'll get there, don't you worry."

Cooper slid one finger into her channel, quickly followed by another, the feel of silk squeezing his digits making his dick leak. He stroked her inside with his long, thick fingers and just when she was getting nice and wound up, he reached his thumb up and started to circle her clit. He stroked and rubbed her until she was a whimpering, mewling mess. She was close, her eyes rolling up into her head and her breathing heavy, but it seemed she needed something more to push her over the edge. Cooper read her body's signals and slipped a third finger inside her, filling her up as much as he could while pressing down hard on her clit at the same time until Gigi cried out against his mouth. Her face was pure bliss, but seeing it once wasn't enough for him. He continued to stroke her and rub her small nub until her legs were shaking and she was crying out the sweetest song he'd ever heard for a second time.

Cooper slowed his movements, helping her come down from her high while peppering kisses along her warm, damp cheek. He gently placed her legs down on the floor and righted her dress, but before he could do anything else, Gigi dropped down on her knees, running her hands up the back of his legs over his jeans. His eyes widened and when he opened his mouth to insist that reciprocation wasn't necessary, she shushed him and reached her hands up further, grabbing his ass and pulling him toward her.

"Let me do this for you. I want it." Gigi's voice was slightly breathless from her orgasm as she removed her hands from his rear, unbuckled his belt, and pulled his jeans and trunks down to his thighs. He watched her eyes widen at his long, thick erection and for a moment he worried that he would be too much for a petite thing like her to take, but she just smiled up at him and licked her lips. Damn, this woman was a dream come true in just about every way. She wasted no time in wrapping one hand round his shaft, pumping it a few times while running her tongue up the underside and through the slit at the top, the warmth of hand and mouth feeling better than he'd imagined, and he'd imagined it *plenty*.

"Christ," he ground out, his shaft pulsing in her hand. His legs wobbled and the need to drive himself further into her mouth was there, but he held back. He may be a caveman in some ways, but he wouldn't take advantage of her like that unless she asked for it. "I'm pretty close already. Watching you come was enough to just about get me there."

Gigi was beautiful when she came and he had nearly lost it as he witnessed her pleasure, her eyes brightening and her skin flushing that beautiful shade of pink he loved so much. She hummed in reply, taking all of him into her mouth in one go. He hit the back of her throat and pulled back in a panic, but she just doubled down her efforts, bobbing up and down as she pumped her fist. Her free hand moved from where it had been cupping his ass to between his legs, and she played with his heavy sac, rolling his balls in her fingers.

He'd never felt this good from a blowjob, and he knew that in addition to his girl's skills, the fire in his belly was also due to the emotions between them. Sometimes sex was just sex, but with Gigi, everything they did felt more meaningful. "Damn, Peach." Cooper stroked her cheek lightly, running his fingers through her hair to show her how much he cared and loved her attentions. His balls drew up tightly as they readied themselves to empty, and Gigi worked him over for another minute as a strangled cry came from his mouth. "Gonna come."

Cooper tried to pull out, but she reached back and grabbed his ass just before he shot into her mouth, watching her swallow every drop. She popped off him and ran a finger over her lips, slipping it into her mouth and sucking it clean. Cooper's dick twitched at the sultry picture she painted, but he wasn't twenty anymore and another round would have to wait. Pulling his pants back up, he held out a hand for her. She took it and he raised her up, frowning when she groaned. He couldn't believe he let her go down on her knees on a hardwood floor for him. "I'm sorry, Honey. I shouldn't have let you do that. I don't like seeing you hurt."

Gigi rested her head against his chest as he rubbed his hand up and down her back. "I appreciate that, but I'm fine and I liked everything about what just happened."

"As I'm sure you noticed, I liked it, too." Cooper kissed her on the lips, tasting his own salty release and grabbed her hand, pulling her toward her couch. "If it's okay with you, I'd like a moment to cuddle before you kick me out for the night."

"That's more than okay with me, and you can stay if you like." The words had barely left her mouth when she yawned, contrasting what she'd just said. He was okay with prioritizing rest, especially after the fun they'd just had. When they plopped down together on her gray sofa, Gigi instantly snuggled into his chest as he relished the feel of her in his arms. Cooper always wanted her with him, but he wasn't sure when he should tell her that. Now could be good, but they'd also just messed around, and he didn't want her thinking it was some post orgasm declaration. He needed her to know he meant it with all his heart.

Cooper ran his hand through her hair, and he leaned his head against hers. "I want you to know something, Peach."

"Hmm," she hummed sleepily.

It seemed she was still in her post-orgasm haze, so he talked quickly before she fell asleep on him. "I care about you, and we'll figure out this stuff with your family. Just don't give up on us, okay?" When she didn't respond, he looked down at her face and saw she was already out. Smiling at her, he placed a gentle kiss atop her head. "I love you," he whispered, excited for the time when he could tell her and she would actually hear it.

Chapter Fifteen

Gigi

The tearoom was quiet this afternoon. Thursdays weren't usually very busy, but the rain outside probably had as much to do with her lack of customers as the day of the week did. It was no matter. The occasional slow day wasn't going to hurt her bottom line. Grandma Mae had created a successful business, all Gigi had to do was not ruin it and everything would be fine. What wasn't fine was the near constant ache in her core. After the other night when Cooper had brought her to orgasm, *twice*, and she had returned the favor, Gigi had been wanting a repeat and to maybe even take things further. She had only hesitated for a moment when Cooper asked her how far she wanted to go, but he was able to read her so well that they waited. It had only been a few days since then, but Gigi was done waiting.

"Uh-oh." Jo pointed an accusatory fork at Gigi, glancing at Millie before looking back over to her. "I'm pretty sure she's thinking about sex again."

Millie giggled into her teacup, but said nothing as Gigi glared at Jo. "How on Earth did you guess that?" The slow business day had afforded her time to have lunch with her friends, but after Jo's eagle-eyed observation, she wasn't sure that she wanted them around. It was one thing to constantly be thinking about sex with her boyfriend, but everyone else knowing that was what she was thinking about was another matter entirely.

Jo sighed heavily, spearing a chunk of her spinach and feta quiche. "I recognize the look. It's on my face just about every damn day since you guys made me stop hooking up," she grumbled, popping the bite of egg into her mouth and chewing savagely. "I'm so sexually frustrated that I've gone through like three vibrators already."

Millie gingerly put down her teacup. "They can wear out?" Her friend looked genuinely perplexed, and it caused Gigi to wonder how experienced Millie actually was when it came to sex. Before she could ponder that further, Jo interrupted her thoughts with a reply.

"They can, and have." She shrugged like the revelation was no big deal and poked at her plate for another moment, dropping her fork with a clang. "It doesn't help that the freaking new hire is always taking the good equipment in our gym. How am I supposed to work off my frustration during my lunch break if I can't hop on my favorite treadmill?"

"You could just use one of the other ones," Gigi suggested with a smirk, enjoying the knowledge that her friend was getting served a little of what she dished out on a daily basis. Jo was far too controlling for her own good, but Gigi would save that conversation for another day, preferably one where Jo wasn't so riled up.

Jo sighed, her frustration not dissipating in the least. "If I did that, he would win, and I can't have that." She picked up her fork and speared her quiche as though it had personally offended her, stuffing it into her mouth. "Besides," she mumbled around her mouthful. "I was there first."

"Ah, yes. The playground defense," Gigi countered, sharing an amused look with Millie. "You should check with my brother to see if that would hold up in court."

"Shut up," Jo said good-naturedly, waving off Gigi's remark. "I just need to get some from an actual man and not a machine, and I'll be good. I just haven't been able to find the time to try and make an actual match on an app. Finding a hook-up was so much easier."

"Speaking of." Gigi jumped at the segue Jo had provided, loving that the conversation no longer focused on her. Smiling, she slid her gaze over to Millie. "How goes the man hunt for you?" Millie had been mostly quiet about her dating life over the last month, and Gigi wanted to check in on her, make sure she was doing okay with what seemed to be a bit of a nerve-wracking experience for her.

Millie put down her teacup and rubbed her lips together, a nervous gesture Gigi recognized instantly and she would bet her business that she was also twisting her fingers together under the table. "Well, I actually have a date lined up for next weekend." She looked anxious, but Gigi couldn't tell if it was nerves or excitement. Probably a combination of the two, but some of it seemed to clear as Millie looked over at Gigi and smiled hesitantly. "Do you think I could come over sometime before then to maybe try on a dress or two? I don't have much in my closet and I don't want to spend a lot of money on a dress I might only wear once."

"Or maybe only for a few hours if things go really well," Jo remarked with a waggle of her eyebrows.

Millie's eyes widened to the size of her cup saucer. "I don't think that's going to happen." Millie was an adorable woman, and Gigi hoped she would start to believe that about herself soon or her friend just might end up talking herself out of going after something great like she deserved.

"Come on, Mills." Jo elbowed their friend in the arm, snickering at whatever joke she was about to make. "A vagina is like a classic car. It needs regular maintenance and the occasional drive around town to remain in good working condition."

Gigi barked a laugh, but she looked at Millie

apologetically when she caught the wounded look on her friend's face. "Sorry, Mills." She reached over and patted the woman's hand. "She's not wrong, though."

"That's easy to say for someone who has a boyfriend and is having sex on a regular basis," Millie muttered.

Gigi blushed and she quickly picked up her napkin to dab at the corners of her mouth to hide it. Unfortunately, Jo clocked the move right away and dropped her fork again. "Oh. My. God." She leaned over the table to inspect Gigi, her eyes narrowed in scrutiny as they traveled across her face. "You two haven't had sex yet."

"Um, well…" Gigi started, not sure where to go with the rest of her sentence. It really wasn't anyone's business but hers and Cooper's, but she and her friends had always had a pretty open border policy when it came to relationship talk.

"Why haven't you two done it yet? I mean, you're two very attractive people with all the working parts … unless Cooper's a little light in the pants department?" Jo asked, a grimace on her face.

Gigi snorted. "No, that's definitely not an issue." She remembered the heavy feel of him on her tongue and had to press her legs together to relieve the pressure building in her center and focus on the conversation to try and keep the memories of that night from flooding back to her. "We've messed around a little, but just haven't gone fully there yet. There's no specific reason."

"Well, as the only one of us in a committed relationship and who isn't under strict orders to stay away from fuckboys, I think you owe it to Millie and me to go get some." Jo polished off her quiche, checked her phone, and abruptly stood up. "Now, I have to go check on Pops before I head back to the office. Maybe I'll borrow some of my dad's tools and cause some car trouble for my new coworker," she divulged, her eyes lighting up with mischief.

"Leave the man alone, Jo," Millie scolded. She was definitely the mom of the group, always giving the kind of good advice that Jo probably wouldn't follow. "He probably doesn't even know that he's pissing you off."

"Oh, he knows." Jo's voice rang with certainty as she went around the table to give hugs to Gigi and Millie. "Bye, gals." With a curt wave, she breezed out the front door and across the street.

They waved off Jo and both stood up to clear the plates and glasses. "You don't have to help with this, Mills. You can just head back to the library." Gigi's friend was always a helper, always taking care of other people, but she so rarely looked after herself that it honestly was starting to concern Gigi a bit. She hoped that this dating endeavor brought Millie the prince she had always wanted because no one deserved to be treated more like a princess than her best friend.

"I don't mind." Millie gathered the teacups, walking them back to the kitchen with Gigi. They dropped the dirty dishes off with her dishwasher, and after chatting with the young woman for a few minutes, they both made their way out front, making a brief stop at the counter where Millie bought a couple of dinner mints. Gigi always tried to refuse money from the woman, but Millie always insisted on paying like a proper customer would. Gigi wondered if it had to do with her upbringing, something related to pride in being able to actually spend money now, but Millie didn't love talking about how things were for her growing up, so Gigi never pressed the issue. "Thanks for lunch, Gi. I'll call you later about the dress."

"Sounds good." She expected that to be the end of the conversation, but halfway toward the door, Millie turned around and looked back at Gigi.

"I think you should go for it." A sad smile was on Millie's face as she spoke and Gigi's brow furrowed in confusion at the appearance of it, but before she could ask for clarification, her friend continued. "With Cooper, I mean. Not because you're both attractive or because he's packing in the pants department," she said with a roll of her eyes and pink on her cheeks. "I think if you're ready, you shouldn't wait. When you love someone, and they love you, you shouldn't hold anything back." A deep sadness flashed through her friend's eyes, but it disappeared with a shake of her head and Millie was smiling again like it had never happened. "That's my two cents anyway." With a polite nod, Millie walked out the door, leaving Gigi alone with her thoughts.

Millie's words rang through her mind for the rest of the day. Gigi hadn't told her friends that she was in love with Cooper, but apparently it was obvious. What wasn't obvious was whether or not he was there with her, but did that mean she shouldn't tell him how she felt? Gigi wanted to tell Cooper that she loved him, but putting that out there was big and scary. It was something she had never done before, and while she had done a lot of big, scary things lately, like standing up to her parents and trying to coordinate this drag queen brunch for her tearoom, this seemed bigger than that. Like Millie, maybe Gigi wasn't giving herself enough credit and could handle one more leap from the cliff of the unknown. Her phone pinged and she took it out of her pocket, smiling at the perfect timing of the message.

Cooper: **I hope you have your dancing shoes on, Peach. I'm taking you out tonight. Come over after work?**

Gigi's smile widened as she typed out her reply.

Gigi: **I'll be there, dancing shoes on and everything.**

Cooper: **I can't wait.**

Gigi's mind spun with all the possibilities the night could offer, and she found that she could hardly wait either.

****

Three hours later, she and Cooper were spinning around the dance floor at Bumpkin's, a bar on the far side of town. They were weaving through the throngs of moving bodies that were crowded around them, Cooper holding onto her tightly as they twisted on the dancefloor, swinging along to the country music despite neither of them favoring the genre. Gigi liked pop and Cooper listened to classic rock, but you can't grow up in the south without at least having a minor appreciation for country music or having the ability to both two-step and line dance. Cooper reached their arms up and spun her around as Johnny Cash's "Ring of Fire" played from an old jukebox, a move that caused her to smile even more brightly than she already was. They had been having such a great time that the muscles in her cheeks were sore from smiling and laughing all night long.

The song ended and another rolled out right after, but Gigi needed a bit of a break to rehydrate. "I need some water," she called up to Cooper over the din. He nodded and grabbed her hand, pulling her back over to their two-top that was close enough to the dance floor to have easy access but far enough away to be able to carry on a conversation and not have to worry about drunken dancers crashing into one or both of them. Gigi pulled herself up onto her high stool and slammed back the water from her glass, the cool liquid refreshing her parched throat.

"Slow down there, Peach. Wouldn't want all that

water going to your head and impairing your judgement," Cooper winked at her, taking a sip of his beer. He had nursed the same bottle all night while she refrained from alcohol altogether, not wanting to risk it getting in the way of what she wanted to do tonight. Cooper was a gentleman, and if he thought she was even the slightest bit inebriated, he might not go through with what she had planned.

Gigi hadn't gone straight to his house after work, but instead she left work a smidge early and made a stop at her place, packing an overnight bag and changing into her sexiest bra and panty set, hoping to get to show them off to her man later and earn herself a sleepover invitation. She didn't normally put this much thought into spending the night with a guy, which was one more indicator of just how much she cared for Cooper Ellis. He was caring, hard-working, smart, and sexy. He was the total package, and after the buildup over the last month, she was hoping to get another shot at his other package later on that evening. Gigi looked across the small table to Cooper who was looking at her like he was trying to read her every thought, his wanton gaze making her flush with need.

Cooper's blue eyes blazed with heat, and the more he looked at her, the more fiery they looked. He took another sip of his beer, placing the half empty bottle on the table. "I think we should get out of here. What do you say, Peach?"

Gigi smiled and nodded. "I say take me back to your place," she said boldly. He held out his hand for her, and she took it without thinking, knowing she would always hold onto this man whenever he offered. They started to walk toward the door, but when the song changed to Dolly Parton's "I Will Always Love You," Cooper stared deeply into her eyes for a moment, steering them back over to the dance floor.

"One more dance?" He placed her hands behind his head and slid his own down her arms and her sides, letting them come to rest at her hips. Gigi blinked up at him, appreciating the strong lines of his face, but it was the expression there that really caught her attention. Cooper was looking at her like she was the single greatest thing that existed in this world, and when she caught the sight of the love and affection looking back at her from his eyes, she felt like it just might be true.

Gigi leaned her head against Cooper's chest, letting the steady beat of his heart calm her own as she listened to Dolly sing about bittersweet memories of love being all she had left, the lyrics triggering a memory of Millie's words from earlier about not holding anything back. The song slowly came to an end, and Cooper leaned down to brush his lips against hers before they were back on their way out to his motorcycle.

The night air was cool, not cold, but Gigi shivered anyway, the excitement and anticipation of what she was about to tell him making her feel like she could vibrate right out of her own skin. They got to his bike and he pulled out a helmet for her, but she stopped him before he could place it on her head. Cooper's brow furrowed with concern. "Everything okay, Peach?"

The blue of his eyes looked more beautiful every time she looked at him, and she took in slow, deliberate breaths to try and calm herself. She was bracketed in his arms as he held one on the bike handle and one on the seat where he had propped the helmet. Gigi stepped closer into his space until she could smell the worn leather scent that felt more and more familiar, more like home to her with each passing day, her hands reaching out of their own accord and landing on his chest. She paused, enjoying the feel of the hard muscles there for a moment and closing her eyes, trying to let the feel of him being solid and strong beneath her give her the courage to make that last leap to lay it all out on the line right then and there.

Once she was staring into those beautiful blue eyes of his once more, Gigi took one last deep breath, finally feeling ready. "I love you, Cooper," she stated bravely.

Cooper's eyes widened for a moment and softened, his expression blissful as a wide smile came over his face. His hands moved to her waist and he lifted her up, pulling her body against his while leaning down for a deep kiss. Gigi wrapped her legs around his middle, the side of the bike hitting the back of her legs as he leaned her up against it, their tongues delving into each other's mouths as they explored one another hungrily.

Finally, Cooper pulled back and rested his forehead against hers, his smile one of gratitude and wonder. "I love you, too, Peach." He sounded so sure of himself then that Gigi's heart squeezed with happiness.

Gigi smiled and kissed him briefly. "I'm so glad you said that because the ride home would have been real awkward otherwise." He chuckled and held her tightly against his body. Gigi felt his hard length brush against her center and she moaned, grinding herself against him. Cooper pressed her body closer to his until they seemed to melt into one another, an occurrence she welcomed happily. Gigi moved her hips again to get a better angle, but noise from the other side of the parking lot froze her in place. She smiled at him, slightly embarrassed at just how singularly focused she seemed to be any time they got physical, and leaned up to his ear. "Take me back to your place?"

Cooper slammed his lips against hers one last time, placing her on the ground. "As if you even have to ask." He smirked, plopping her helmet on her head and helping her onto the bike. She giggled as he slammed on his own helmet, climbed on the bike, and kickstarted it, pulling out of the lot like it was on fire.

"In a hurry, are we?" Cooper peered over his shoulder at her, spearing her with a look so hungry she almost worried he would eat her alive. She gulped, suddenly feeling hot all over and grateful for the rush of air against her skin as he drove them through the streets. "Forget what I just said. You go as fast as you want," she called over the sound of the bike motor.

Cooper grabbed her hand and brought it up to his mouth to kiss it before moving it back down to his stomach. "Only while I'm driving. When we're back home, I plan on taking my time with you."

Gigi smiled, not at the promise of going slow, although that idea had her feeling all kinds of tingly, but at his use of the word home. Whether they went to his place, her place, were out at a bar, or even having lunch at the picnic tables outside the shop, as long as Cooper was there with her, home was exactly where she was.

Chapter Sixteen

Cooper

The ride back home from the bar couldn't go fast enough. Cooper needed this woman under him, on top of him, next to him, basically any way he could get her. Cooper needed Gigi like he needed air or water. She had become essential to his survival now, and he couldn't wait to express his love for her with more than words. It wasn't just the potential for sex that had him feeling like he was filled with warmth and light that could burst out of every pore, though he was absolutely looking forward to that and was currently breaking about three traffic laws to get home in record time for that purpose alone. The fact that she loved him was what was causing all the gooey feelings in his chest.

Gigi Davenport was the most phenomenal woman he had ever come across. She had it all—beauty, brains, humor, and a way about her that drew everyone into her orbit whether she realized it or not. The fact that she found him worthy of her love made him feel about ten feet tall. Cooper couldn't hold back from telling her how he felt after she had declared her feelings, it just wasn't possible because his love for her had been aching to get out of him for the last week at least, maybe longer.

The moment his carport came in sight, Cooper breathed a sigh of relief. *Finally,* he thought to himself. He parked the bike and propped up the kickstand, hopping off and tossing his helmet into the bed of his truck. It seemed like he wasn't the only one in a hurry because he hadn't even needed to help Gigi off the bike. She had already ditched her helmet and was walking up to his front door backwards, crooking her finger at him. "You coming, baby?"

"Not yet, but hopefully soon." His reply had her shaking her head, but she was smiling at his silly words.

Cooper hurried to unlock the door, and once it was open and the two of them were inside, they were on each other, mouths crashing, teeth gnashing together, and hands roaming all over each other's bodies like they would die if they weren't touching some part of the other person. Gigi slipped her hot hands under Cooper's blue t-shirt and he broke their kiss just long enough to whip it over his head and toss it to the side. A strange whimpering sound drew their attention away from themselves and over to where Shep was currently struggling to remove Cooper's shirt from over his head.

Gigi laughed at the poor animal, going over and helping his dog out of his predicament. "Sorry, boy," she cooed, tossing the shirt to the floor. "I think we forgot about you in our hurry to get to…" she peeked at Cooper over her shoulder, her hazel eyes sparking with fire. "Other things."

Cooper rubbed his hand over his beard. He really wanted to just pick up where they left off, but he needed to take care of his dog or they would most likely get interrupted, and he didn't want anything coming between the two of them for at least the next twelve hours. He patted his hand against the side of his leg to call the dog over to him. He would grab him by the collar, but he knew his hands would be busy soon enough and didn't want to have to make another stop in the bathroom to wash up before joining his woman.

Cooper nodded at Gigi. "Let me take him out real quick and then I'm coming back for you."

"I'll be waiting." Her voice was throaty and filled with need as she unzipped her dress, letting one shoulder strap slip down to give him a peek at her bare shoulder. With a sultry smirk, she disappeared into his bedroom.

"Don't be starting without me now." He took Shep out the front door, giving his best dog friend a pointed look. "This better be the fastest damn bathroom break of your life," he muttered, nudging the dog with his ankle so he would go do his business. Like the amazing doggo that he was, Shep took about two minutes before trotting back over to Cooper. He led his dog into the laundry room and made sure to set him up with water, his dog bed, and plenty of toys, But as he went to shut the door, he stopped at the look of betrayal on his dog's face. Cooper smiled at the dog sadly and shrugged. "Sorry, boy. I'd say you'd understand eventually, but seeing as how you're neutered … I guess you won't." He shut the door, kicked off his shoes and socks, and made his way over to his bedroom with a fierce determination, but the sight that greeted him when he got there had him suddenly feeling weak, so much so he had to grip his door frame for support.

There, lying casually on his bed and leaning up on her elbows, was Gigi in nothing but her lingerie, a coy smile playing across her face and her fingers dancing over the white sheets. "You okay, baby?" She knew full well what the sight of her was doing to him. The evidence was currently pressing up against his jeans, probably leaving a zipper indent on his dick at that very minute.

"I might take a minute here if it's all the same to you." His voice was low and thick with emotion, and he would use that minute to gather himself, but also to take a long look at the woman in front of him.

Gigi looked like everything he'd ever wanted but didn't have enough imagination to ever conjure accurately. Cooper's heart practically ached at her beauty. Gigi had pulled her hair down from her ponytail, the auburn waves spilling back over her shoulders and rested lightly on the sheets. Her peach strapless bra and matching panties were elegant and set off her ivory skin. She was peaches and cream, and his mouth flooded with moisture at the thought of taking a bite of her. Cooper wasn't sure if she already owned the set or if she had bought it specifically for him. Either way, he was pleased that she was embracing her nickname because she would always be Peach to him.

Gigi lifted a hand from the bed and ran over the slope of one breast down to her panty covered pussy, stopping there and turning to face him, her expression challenging. "When you're done with your minute, maybe you can lose the jeans and join me before I have to take care of things myself." She teased at the waist of her panties with one finger, licking her lips like a seasoned seductress.

A low growl escaped Cooper's throat at the image of her pleasuring herself. "That's not the threat you think it is, Peach." He popped the button of his jeans and pulled down the zipper. "In fact, you can go ahead and put me down as requesting that show for later on tonight."

Gigi's eyes lit up and followed the movement of his hands as he peeled the front panel of his pants back, revealing a peek at his black trunks. She bit her lip and leaned up higher on her elbows, her earlier threat to take things solo all but forgotten. Cooper could tell she wanted more, but she had teased him enough, so he thought he would give a little back in kind. He walked over slowly, his pants hanging low off his hips, and Gigi rolled over to him, eagerly kneeling up on the bed to meet him. "I think you forgot the most important part about getting naked." She tugged on the waistband of his jeans, an adorable pout he wanted to kiss right off her face. "You have to actually lose your clothes."

Cooper grabbed her wrists and pushed them

behind her back, holding onto them to keep her from moving. The movement had her pupils blowing wide, a whimper coming out of her mouth, and he made a note for them to try tying each other up sometime because clearly it had a positive effect on her. He didn't need to be in control that way, he simply wanted to do anything with her that would give her the kind of pleasure she deserved. There was another fun bonus of having Gigi's hands behind her back. The position had also caused her full breasts to push out toward Cooper and rub against his bare chest. The cool, silky material of her bra felt nice against his overheated skin. He'd had every intention of drawing things out, but he was barely holding on, so when Gigi started grinding her hips against his erection, he nearly lost it.

"I'm trying to take my time with you, Peach, but you're not making it easy," he ground out through his clenched jaw. Pleasure was shooting up and down his spine with each shift of her body, the motivation to go slow quickly dissipating as primal need took its place, and Cooper wasn't so sure he could push it back down or that he even wanted to.

Gigi moaned and kept rubbing up against him. "Not sorry in the least." Swirling her hips, she leaned up to nip at his jaw and bottom lip, the small stings making his blood hum happily. Damn, she didn't even have use of her hands and she was already getting him there. Granted, it had been a long time, but Cooper knew it was being with her that was causing his body to feel so much at the moment.

Cooper took a deep breath to try and shake off the need to claim her right then and there, but he couldn't manage it. "Fuck it," he muttered, crashing his lips against hers. He released her wrists and her hands immediately started to explore the planes of his chest, tracing the lines of his pecs and ridged abdomen with her fingers. While she explored, he kicked his pants off and reached behind her back to unhook her bra, doing it in one swift movement.

Gigi pulled back and studied him, her eyes still full of heat and want, but her brow slightly furrowed. "I don't think I want to know how you were able to do that so easily."

The tiny pout was back on her face, but when Cooper reached up and cupped one of her heavy breasts, flicking his thumb back and forth across the nipple, it disappeared instantly. Gigi's eyes rolled back and he brushed his lips lightly against hers, savoring the sweet taste. "I used to practice on a bra strapped to a throw pillow when I was a teenager."

A raspy chuckle left her mouth, but it turned into a groan when he teased her rosy peak once more. "I'd tease you about that," she breathed as he reached up to do to her left breast what he was doing to the right. "But at the moment, I can't think about anything but having you inside me."

Cooper leaned his forehead against hers. "Careful, Peach, or I might just come from your words alone."

"I don't want that. I want to feel you go off inside me." Reaching down, she cupped him through the thin material of his underwear, the pressure only amplifying his need. They had discussed tests and birth control after their little dalliance in her entryway and subsequent messing around, and because they were both clean and she was on the pill, they were free to get to it.

Gigi continued to stroke him through his trunks and he felt himself shifting his hips to give her better access. He needed to stop doing that or they wouldn't ever get to the main event. Cooper grabbed her hand and pulled it away, kissing her palm. "Lie back on the bed for me." Gigi smiled seductively and did as he told her, the trust she had in him making his heart squeeze. "Good girl."

As he spoke the words, he could swear he saw the damp spot on her undies grow, and he made a note to praise her in bed as often as possible if it increased her pleasure even the slightest bit. Cooper stood next to the bed and shucked his trunks, watching Gigi's eyes widen and her mouth form a little "o" at the sight of him. She'd seen him before, had his thick cock in her mouth, but only for a quick blowjob. There was no hiding how he felt about her now, and while he didn't need the ego boost, seeing her looking pleased was nice.

Gripping his dick, he gave it a good tug. "It's all for you, Peach."

Gigi licked her lips and smiled. "Then why don't you come give it to me," she begged, her husky voice shaking slightly.

"I plan on it." Crawling up the bed and between her legs, Cooper reached up and grabbed the top of her panties, slowly peeling them down to reveal her alluring center. She kept things nicely trimmed, and once he had removed her underwear entirely, he leaned in and kissed the area just above the small patch of auburn curls. "I'll be tasting you later."

The promise had Gigi chuckling, and he loved that they had as much fun in the bedroom as they did outside of it. "You planning on having a conversation with my lady bits, or can we get them more closely acquainted with that python you smuggle around in your jeans?"

Cooper shook his head, trying not to laugh as he continued to move up her body, stopping every now and then to kiss her hip bone, her breasts, her collarbone, and finally her neck as he settled himself between her legs.

He placed his hands on the sides of her head, running his dick through her folds while making sure to hit that little bundle of nerves with the tip. Gigi was wet and ready for him, but he drew it out a little anyway, wanting to memorize the way it felt to be with her for the first time. She moaned and moved her hips, trying to get him to slip inside, but he kept changing the angle every time she did.

Her hips stilled as she huffed at him. "Are you going to fuck me or what?"

Cooper smirked at her swearing, something she rarely did. Clearly she was more than ready to get started. "I'm going to fuck the sass right out of you is what I'm going to do." After tapping her clit one more time, he finally slid inside of her in one slick movement. Gigi cried out, but it turned into a moan as he started to move in and out of her, the slow drag of his dick against her walls giving them both immeasurable pleasure. God, she was tight. Luckily she was worked up enough to where it wouldn't be an issue for her, but Cooper felt like he was getting gripped in a vise and didn't want to disappoint either of them by having this be over too soon. "Damn, Peach. You feel like heaven."

Gigi nodded and babbled incoherently, sliding her hands down to his ass to grip him tight and pull him further into her. He thought he heard the words "you too," but he couldn't tell and he wasn't about to stop what they were doing and ask her to enunciate. They moved together, their hips colliding and sparks shooting all throughout his body. Gigi moaned each time he slammed back into her, grinding the base of his cock against her center. The sound was so alluring that Cooper started counting backwards from one hundred to try and stave off his orgasm, but it was coming on like a freight train. He needed her to get there first, so he leaned down and teased her nipples with his tongue, licking and sucking on the rosy buds as he thrust into her over and over until he felt her pussy fluttering around him. Cooper leaned back up and looked at his woman, knowing she was close as her eyes drifted shut, looking like an absolute goddess as she chased her release.

He kissed her lips briefly and sped up his movements, close to tipping over the edge but still wanting her to come first, so he lifted her hips higher, hitting a spot that had her crying out. "Oh, my god," she breathed out quickly, her chest heaving up to meet his. "So close."

Cooper pounded into her, not able to hold back his grunts of pleasure. "Open your eyes, Peach," he commanded. "I want your eyes on me as I make you mine."

Cooper's words seemed to be enough to tip her over the edge and she came hard, her eyes flew open as her legs shook, her breath seeming to stop altogether, and her insides gripping him so tightly he swore he would need the Jaws of Life to pry them apart, not that he was complaining. The only thing his body felt was bliss, and when the tingling in his spine intensified, he joined Gigi in their shared gratification, spilling into her with each thrust of his hips. When the pleasure started to fade, he slowed his movements and slipped out of her, rolling to the side and lying on his back, trying to catch his breath. That was the best sex he had ever had in his life, and as soon as he got his energy back, they were going to do it all over again.

Cooper reached over and tugged Gigi to him until she was resting her head on his chest, her own breath coming rather quickly. "That," she said as she took a deep breath, "was amazing."

"You're amazing." Cooper rubbed his hand up and down her back, her skin warm and damp from the exertion of what they had just done. He tipped his head down and kissed her forehead brushing a few damps strands of hair from her eyes.

Gigi leaned up and rested her chin on his chest, her hazel eyes searching his. "I already was, you know. Before the sex."

Cooper tried to blink away the spots that were floating in front of his eyes. "You were already what?" His orgasm addled brain was having a hard time putting two and two together because he couldn't make sense of what she was saying.

"Yours," she explained, smiling and scooting up to kiss his lips. "You said you were going to make me yours, but I have been for a long while."

Cooper smiled back, her words solidifying what he also felt. "And I'm yours." Hugging her closer to him, he enjoyed the feel of her in his arms as much as he did the sex they'd just had. The pleasure they had shared had felt larger than life, but the love he felt flowing through him at that moment was indescribably larger.

"Good," she replied, resting her head on his chest. "Because I love you a lot, Cooper Ellis."

Cooper smiled and tightened his arms around her, hoping he would hear those words from her every day for the rest of his life. "I love you a lot, too, Gigi Davenport."

Cooper felt her hum of contentment against his chest and they laid together peacefully for a few moments. Cooper had almost drifted off to sleep when he felt Gigi stirring. "Um, Cooper?"

"Yeah?" He was tired and wanted nothing more than to drift into a deep slumber knowing that Gigi was there with him, but she always came first.

Gigi's body left his and he felt her pulling a sheet up. "I think your dog got out." Cooper's eyes shot open and he looked to the side to see Shep staring at the two of them, his head tilted to the side and his tongue lolling out of his mouth. "Do you think he saw anything?"

Cooper sat up and looked over at Gigi with a smile. "Well, the nice thing is that if he did, he won't be telling anyone." Gigi slapped his arm and he chuckled. "I'll get a lock for the laundry room door for next time," he promised, pulling her back down into his arms and shifting their bodies so that she was the little spoon. "Let's get some rest. I have plans for a repeat performance, but I need a few minutes."

"That's good with me." Gigi brought his hand closer to her chest while holding it there tightly. It was as though he was cradling her heart, a privilege he wanted to work hard at making sure he didn't squander. "As long as the next performance doesn't have an audience."

Cooper laughed and kissed her shoulder. "No audience, but I can't promise you won't want to give me a standing ovation at the end."

Gigi snorted and they dissolved into laughter before settling back down into one another. As they both drifted off to sleep, Cooper realized he couldn't remember a time when he had ever felt this happy, and he wanted the feeling to last as long as possible. An image of Gigi in a white gown and holding a flower bouquet sprang into his mind and caused a smile to pull across his face. Soon, he told himself. Soon.

Chapter Seventeen

Gigi

Gigi bounced on her heels with excitement at the thought of her impending date with the man she loved as she finished packing a cooler with the fried chicken, coleslaw, and sliced peaches that Millie had helped her make. She had been wanting to go out on a picnic with Cooper for a while now, but the weather just hadn't cooperated on the days they had available. That all ended today as Gigi peeked out the window and smiled. The sun was shining, the skies were clear and as blue as Cooper's eyes, and the temperature was a beautiful seventy three degrees—perfect picnic weather. When Cooper mentioned bringing along some of his fishing equipment, Gigi knew the date would be an even bigger success. They were heading into the state parks area where the foot traffic wasn't nearly as bad and the fishing was better. All in all, the day looked to be filled with fun and time well spent with her man.

Gigi smiled at the thought of Cooper being her man. She had been thinking it for a while now, but ever since last week when they told each other how they felt and finally had sex, things between the two of them were starting to feel more and more permanent. Her parents still weren't talking to her much, only texting her now and then with formalities like reminders about upcoming weddings or other celebrations for relatives. It was still all a bit strange, but she was slowly getting used to it. Whether getting used to it was ultimately a good or bad thing, she hadn't decided.

Instead of having dinner with her whole family like she had in the past, she had lunch with Ford and he filled her in on any of the latest gossip from their mother and father. It was good to know she still had the support of her brother. He had asked to meet Cooper soon and she was planning on when that would be, but not sure of how soon was too soon. Gigi knew Ford would be great, but she was still a little wary of introducing new variables into their relationship. She liked the little bubble they found themselves in and worried that adding to that would increase the pressure on their relationship too quickly. Gigi loved Cooper deeply and saw a real future with him, and she didn't want to risk losing him because they rushed things.

"What do we think of this dress?" Millie asked, coming out of the walk-in closet where she had been trying on dress after dress of Gigi's in preparation for a date of her own. Millie had gotten a match on one of her dating apps, and she was meeting the man for drinks later that night.

Gigi sealed the cooler and placed it in her picnic basket, coming out from behind the counter. She and Millie were the same height, but Millie had an even more prominent hourglass figure, so a lot of Gigi's dresses ended up not leaving much to the imagination when draped over her friend. Case in point, Millie walked to the kitchen wearing a midnight blue wrap dress that, while looser on Gigi, hugged Millie's every curve and was cut low enough that there was definite potential for a nip slip.

Gigi frowned at Millie's awkward posture as she stood in front of her. "I think it all depends on how comfortable you are in it. I think you look really good, but I can also tell you'll need to wear a strapless bra and thong, and I know you hate both of those."

Millie sighed and slipped onto a stool next to the kitchen island. "Ugh, I do hate those, but every outfit I have at home doesn't feel right."

"And this one does?" Gigi gazed at her friend, knowing how she was feeling was less about the outfit and more about her nerves at going out on a date. Millie was putting so much pressure on herself with the dating thing that Gigi wondered if maybe her whole challenging themselves idea had been premature in her friend's case.

"I mean, not really, but it doesn't feel wrong exactly." Millie hung her head in her hands and huffed a breath. "Remind me again why I have to go out on dates. I need some motivation."

Gigi rubbed soothing circles on her friend's back. "You're going on dates because you love romance and you wanted to try and be a little more proactive in finding it for yourself." Gigi left out the part where she and Jo had maybe pressured her into it because deep down she really believed that Millie could do this.

"I guess." Millie blew a raspberry between her lips, her eyes looking around the room with no particular interest. "Why is this so hard?"

"Because anything in life worth doing isn't easy." Gigi used the words her Grandma Mae had told her plenty of times in her life, knowing it was true, too. Things with Cooper hadn't been all easy, certainly not where her parents were concerned, but the happiness she felt when she was with him was definitely worth any hardships.

Millie nodded and pushed her glasses up her face. "How are you doing on your challenges?" She scrunched up her face and waved her hands around. "I mean the professional one. Obviously the personal one is going well if your perma-smile is anything to go by." Gigi grinned and Millie pointed to it. "See? That's the one."

Gigi chuckled and poked her friend in the shoulder. "Things with Cooper are going really well. As far as the tearoom, well, things are great and I got into contact with Heidi Haux, you remember from our birthday outing? I invited her and some of her friends to come to the tearoom and do a short performance before dining with the customers." She ran over to her writing desk near the window and grabbed the flyer she printed out earlier. Marketing was always more Jo's thing, but Gigi did her best and was proud of the work she'd done. "We're still working out what the exact performances will be and the menu, but this is what I had made to hang in the windows at The Kettle, and maybe give it to some other businesses to advertise as well."

Millie's eyes ran over the flyer for a moment before meeting hers. "This is fantastic, Gi." Millie hopped up from her stool and gave Gigi a big bear hug, the press of her soft curves always feeling more maternal than any hug she'd ever gotten from her mother. "I'm so happy for you. It seems like everything is coming together nicely."

There was a knock on the door and Gigi's smile widened, knowing Cooper was there on the other side. "Thanks, Mills." She bounced over to the front door and opened it to find Cooper holding a bundle of daisies, looking like her every teenage and adult fantasy come to life. He wore his typical jeans and a t-shirt, but both hugged every muscle in his body in just the right way that had her blood flowing straight to her lady bits.

"Hey, Peach." Cooper grabbed her lower back, pulling her into him for a deep kiss, the paper from the flowers making a crinkling sound as it was pressed between the two of them. Their lips and tongues tangled for a while before she heard a throat clear behind her. Gigi broke the kiss, feeling slightly dazed, and stepped to the side. Cooper frowned and looked up, but after spotting Millie he straightened up and waved. "Nice to see you again, Millie."

"You, too" Millie stifled a giggle as she grabbed her purse and the outfit she arrived in, hurrying past the two and smiling on her way out the door. "You guys have fun," she called over her shoulder.

"Thanks." Gigi was still slightly dazed from her kiss with Cooper before she remembered what Millie was doing that night. "Text me to let me know how your date goes." Millie waved over her shoulder and kept walking down the long path to the front of the main house. Gigi really hoped the night went well for her friend. She looked up at Cooper who was staring at her with a smile. "Are those for me?" she asked, pointing to the flowers.

"Of course." Presenting her with the pretty bundle of happy flowers, he leaned down and brushed his lips against her cheek. "I'm not out here buying flowers for just anyone, Honey."

Gigi batted her lashes at him and walked into her house. "Let me just put these in some water and we can go."

Twenty five minutes later, the two of them arrived at Willow Creek Ponds. It was a state park that housed a series of ponds created from a small offshoot of the main river. They left Cooper's truck, gathering a blanket, the picnic basket, and a couple of fishing rods and made their way along the trail to a prime spot. Cooper leaned the rods against the trunk of a large hickory tree spreading a big flannel blanket out in the abundance of shade the tree provided. Eager for some fun and relaxation, Gigi kicked off her tennis shoes and planted herself on the middle of the blanket. She had dressed a little more casually today in some cut-off shorts and a yellow, peasant tank top, and her hair was in a high ponytail which was great for keeping cool in the warmer weather, the shade of the old hickory making her feel much nicer than the blazing sun had.

Cooper kicked off his boots and sat down next to her, watching her every movement as she opened the picnic basket and started pulling out food, rubbing his hands together. "That looks amazing. Thanks for doing all this, Peach."

Gigi smiled as she pulled out a Thermos filled with sun tea. "Don't give me too much credit for all this. Millie came over and helped me in the kitchen in exchange for borrowing a dress." Gigi wasn't completely hopeless in the kitchen, but she wasn't a whiz like Millie, and her friend always insisted on repaying help, even if it was something silly like borrowing clothes.

Cooper opened up the container filled with sliced, macerated peaches. He inhaled the smell and groaned. "Tell me you brought whipped cream."

"I brought whipped cream," she sang as she held up the container, displaying it like it was a prize on a game show.

"Good girl." Leaning over, Cooper kissed her as she reeled from the praise she loved to hear from him. He put the container of peaches to the side and grabbed the fried chicken. "I'm saving the best for last." He took a bite of the crispy, breaded poultry and Gigi watched him chew and swallow, the bob of his Adam's apple melting her insides. When he started licking his shiny lips, she grabbed a napkin and dabbed some sweat that had formed on the back of her neck. Cooper looked over at her and smirked. "You okay, Peach?"

"I'm great." Her voice cracked slightly, and when she caught him smirking at her, she balled up her napkin and tossed it at him. "Eat your food," she scolded, grabbing a fork and taking a bite of the coleslaw.

"Yes, ma'am." Cooper winked at her, making a big show of taking another slow bite and licking his lips. Gigi chuckled at his behavior and luckily he toned it down before she attacked him with her mouth.

As they ate, they talked about their weeks, exchanging stories that made them laugh or others about customers that tested their patience. Cooper asked Gigi about her drag show brunch and she filled him in on all the details, her excitement for the event growing with each bit of information she shared with him. He promised to stop by and be there if he could, a promise that had her chest feeling warm and slightly tingly. Gigi loved having someone that supported her so much. It was a nice change from how she had grown up. Her parents never seemed to think she was good enough, but she never felt even the slightest bit of that with Cooper.

After they finished most of the food, they relaxed on the blanket. Cooper was on his elbows, currently looking up to the sky, and Gigi was leaning above him, dipping peaches into the whipped cream and feeding him. She enjoyed providing for him as he did for her, and while every brush of his lips and tongue against the tips of her fingers had her wanting to ditch the picnic entirely, she also wanted to enjoy this beautiful day with him. The mid-day sun would have been brutal if not for the canopy of leaves that shielded them, but as it was, they had a view of blue sky and the occasional wisp of cloud as they lazed about together.

"Today has been pretty perfect," Gigi confessed to him as she took a break from feeding him the peaches and drank some sun tea, enjoying the sweet flavor.

"It has been." Cooper agreed readily with a smile, leaning over to kiss her shoulder. He looked up into the sky, his expression thoughtful. "I didn't think my life could ever be this happy."

"What do you mean?" Scooting closer to him, she stared into his eyes seeing the happiness he was talking about, but also a lingering pain.

Cooper's eyes flicked to her, then back at the sky. "I don't know. I guess I just always assumed my life would be one way. I would work in a garage or at a dealership, maybe eventually I'd settle down with someone, have some kids if I was lucky." He turned to her, his beautiful, baby blue eyes boring into her eyes. "But I always figured it would be, I don't know, unexceptional. Ordinary. Nothing particularly special." Cooper brushed her ponytail over her shoulder and smiled at her, the small amount of sadness that was in his eyes gone completely. "I guess what I'm trying to say is that I've been pleasantly surprised with just how much more than special my life has turned out to be recently."

Gigi melted a little at his honesty. Something about this muscular, handy man being vulnerable with her shot a joyful feeling straight to her heart. She loved that he trusted her with his thoughts and feelings, and Gigi wanted to be just as vulnerable with him in return. "I know what you mean." Running her hand over his beard, she cupped his cheek, wanting to always be touching him. "I thought my life only had one way to go. Married to a lawyer or doctor, going to social functions I had no interest in, and raising kids to continue the cycle of unhappiness." Gigi looked at him and felt her heart swelling as she thought about just how wonderful her life had been for the last two months. "I never expected to ever feel as happy as I do now. I never expected you."

Gigi brushed her lips against his lightly, but Cooper slipped his hand to the back of her neck and held her to him, demanding more. They opened up for one another and moaned into each other's mouths. He tasted like peaches and cream, and she wondered if it was the same flavor he enjoyed smelling on her all the time. If so, she could see why he seemed to be addicted to it. Cooper rolled their bodies so that she was laying on the blanket and he was bent over her, his forearms on either side of her head. They continued to kiss, reveling in their happiness.

Cooper leaned back and his blue eyes shined with adoration as he searched hers. "I love you," he said firmly. Gigi gasped lightly. She had already heard it a few times now, but every time he said it, her heart expanded more than she thought possible just to make room for all the love she was feeling.

With her heart full and a bright smile to showcase just how blessed she felt to be with him, Gigi said those three important words back to him. "I love you, too." She rubbed her hand against his chest, enjoying the solidness beneath it. "I don't think I'll ever get tired of saying it."

Cooper smiled and kissed her briefly. "I'll never get tired of hearing it."

He leaned down once more and they were back at it, exploring one another, their mutual declaration only heightening the pleasure she was feeling. Gigi's hand found its way between them and to the hem of his shirt. She slipped it underneath, enjoying the hard planes and light dusting of hair beneath her fingertips. Cooper slipped a leg between hers and she parted for him automatically. When his body was fully between her legs, he ground their fronts together and she moaned appreciatively.

The friction caused by the fabric of their jeans as they moved against one another had her getting all kinds of turned on. One of Cooper's hands moved up to her shirt and pulled it down, giving him access to the tops of her breasts. He kissed along the outline of her bra, pushing one cup down and pulling her nipple into his mouth. His mouth felt cool against her warm skin, and she shivered in response. Gigi arched into him, threading her fingers through his dark blond locks to encourage him to keep going. She wanted, no needed, to feel more of him. She started to pull up his shirt, but laughter in the distance caused both of them to stop.

Cooper pulled back to look at her, alarm and amusement in his eyes as he fixed her shirt and tugged down his own. "I forgot where we were for a minute," he huffed out, rolling off of her and onto his back.

Gigi looked over at the large tenting at the front of his jeans and whimpered. If only they'd been in a bedroom and not out at a public park. A few hikers passed by and they waved hello. Once their visitors had passed, the two of them dissolved into giggles, clutching each other as they laughed. "That could have been really bad," she said as she clung to him.

"Yeah, those hikers definitely would have gotten more than they expected when they set out on the trail." Cooper wiped a hand down his face and leaned over to kiss her briefly. "To be continued?"

"Absolutely." Glancing over at the two fishing rods, Gigi decided to use them as a distraction from her runaway libido. "Should we do some fishing?" Before Cooper could answer her, her phone pinged. Normally she would ignore it, but she wondered if it might be Millie needing some encouragement for her date tonight, and she didn't want to leave her friend hanging. "Let me just check to see who this is. I'm worried Millie's going to chicken out of her date."

"Sounds good." Leaning back on his elbows again, he basked in the warm April air.

Gigi grabbed her phone from near the picnic basket and looked at the notification, balking slightly when she saw that it was from her mother. Curiosity got the better of her and she swiped the phone open to read the message.

Mama: **Your father and I would like you and your**

new beau to join us for family dinner this evening.

Gigi's mouth fell open in shock as she stared dumbly at the message.

"What is it, Peach?" Cooper asked her, his voice threaded with concern.

Gigi glanced over at him, confused and a little suspicious of her mother's motives. "My mom is inviting us to their house for dinner tonight." She bit her lip as she turned over the new information. On the one hand, she didn't want to expose Cooper to possible vitriol from her family. On the other, she didn't want to turn up her nose at what could possibly be an olive branch. "Maybe they've come around."

"Maybe." Cooper's voice was low and filled with the disbelief she herself was just feeling. "What do you want to do?"

Her phone pinged again with another message from her mother.

Mama: **We'll be cordial.**

Gigi held up her phone to show Cooper the message. When he looked at her, Gigi could tell that he was still hesitant. "It's your call, Peach. I go where you go." Gigi knew he was telling the truth. He would leave things up to her, and as much as she was nervous that nothing good would come of introducing Cooper to her parents, the possibility of being able to have him and her family, not matter how problematic they could be, in her life was too good to pass up.

Gigi took a deep breath and grabbed Cooper's hand. "Let's go and see what happens. Who knows? Maybe my parents will surprise me and be totally okay with our relationship." Even as she said the words, Gigi knew that probably wouldn't be the case, but she smiled at Cooper anyway, trying to be brave for the both of them. "At the very least, Ford will be there as a bit of a buffer, and he's already told me he's happy for me and is excited to meet you."

Cooper nodded slowly, a small smile playing at his mouth. He looked down at his clothes and back to her. "I'm guessing I should change into something a little more Sunday dinner appropriate?"

"Only if you want to." Gigi leaned over to kiss his lips, just happy that he was coming. "You look good in whatever you're wearing and it doesn't matter anyway. I just want you to be comfortable."

Cooper blew a harsh breath through his lips. "I think I will. Better not to start off with more of a deficit than I already have," he mumbled and started to pack up their things.

Gigi helped him, feeling the need to give him another out if he wanted. "If it's going to be that rough for you, we can skip it. Or I can go alone," she offered.

When he looked at her, she could tell he was determined to see things through. "No way, Peach." He gripped her chin and planted a firm kiss on her lips. Every time he touched her, it was like a brand on her soul, one she would gratefully accept. "Like I said, I go where you go."

"Okay." They packed up their things quickly and walked back to his truck. Cooper dropped her off at her place so that he could go get ready at his house. Gigi was still so happy after having spent another afternoon with the man she loved, but the whole time he was gone, she couldn't help but wonder if that feeling would disappear the moment they stepped foot in her parents' house. All she could do was get ready and hope for the best, but the sinking feeling in her stomach was telling her that she should probably also prepare for the worst.

Chapter Eighteen

Cooper

The drive to the Davenports' house wasn't long, a fact he lamented the closer they got to it. Cooper wished they had lived further away because it would have given him time to gather his thoughts, form a more solid game plan, or do something to ease this feeling that joining her family for dinner was a colossal mistake. He didn't know her parents, but he knew their type. He'd spent his whole life being judged by people who saw themselves as better than him, and he had a hard time believing that Gigi's upper class parents were suddenly okay with their only daughter dating a lowly mechanic.

Cooper pulled at the collar of his shirt, feeling like the damn thing was choking him. He glanced at himself in the mirror and frowned at the light blue button down shirt and pair of brown slacks. He even wore a tie, an item of clothing that had been buried in his closet for years, not having seen the light of day since his interview with Bob at the shop, but he wasn't the least bit comfortable. He felt distinctly unlike himself, like he was wearing a second skin that had little to do with the real him, and he hated the feeling.

Cooper glanced sideways to look at Gigi who looked more herself than ever dressed in a light pink, filly dress, her hair down in curls and a pearl necklace around her neck. She looked great, as though she absolutely belonged in a house like the ones in the ritzy neighborhood they were driving through. The truth was, she could have been wearing a drop cloth covered in grease and she still would have belonged there because that was the world she came from, the world she still lived in despite her involvement with him.

Cooper looked the part this evening, but he didn't belong. Not really. He didn't have a fancy college degree or a lot of social connections outside his gran and coworkers at the garage. All Cooper had were his own two hands and the skills his grandad taught him. It was enough for him, more than enough, but it wouldn't be enough for Gigi's parents. Was it really enough for her? She's always said so, but the further into the neighborhood they got, the more he started to doubt that she could live her life in his world and the one she'd known her whole life. Eventually she would have to choose, and who wouldn't stay in a world this beautiful where everything came easily?

Cooper shook his head to try and dispel the thought of him not being good enough, but it kept nagging at him. Gigi told him she loved him, and he believed her, he just didn't know if that was enough to sustain a relationship in the long term, and that's what he wanted with her. When it was just the two of them and a few select others, he didn't feel so insecure about their relationship. Now that their little love bubble seemed to have burst, exposing the two of them to scrutiny from the outside world, he was starting to feel differently. Cooper squeezed the hand he had been holding the entire drive, and when Gigi squeezed back, he felt a little bit better about the whole thing.

She shifted in her seat and he peeked over at her, seeing the trepidation he was feeling advertised in her expression. "We can still cancel if you want," she told him, her tone completely serious. "I can practically see the anxiety rolling off of you in waves, baby."

Cooper chuckled humorlessly at her astuteness, but he wasn't turning back now. If it was a trial by fire he needed to face, at least he had her by his side to help weaken the flames. Tugging her hand up to his chest, he held onto her a little tighter to shore up his courage. "Nah, Peach. We're going. It's important to you, so it's important to me."

He saw her smile sadly, wondering just how happy she was to be going herself. "I appreciate that, but it's not more important than you being comfortable with what we're doing." Her declaration gave him that little extra boost he needed to get through the evening. Gigi was making him a priority, and the least he could do was return the favor.

"I'll be totally at ease the entire night," he promised as they pulled up to the address that was in his phone's GPS.

Cooper flipped the truck into PARK and looked out his windshield at the opulent home. Gigi had described it as "cabin-like," but it looked more like a small lodge you would see in an expensive mountain town. Cooper knew his way around a building supply store, so as he took in the home's masonry, wood paneling, and custom lighting, all he could see were dollar signs flashing through his mind. This home probably cost more money than he had made in all the years he'd been working. He'd spoken too soon. There was no way he was going to feel at ease in a house like this. Hell, he didn't even feel comfortable looking at it for too long.

Gigi cupped his cheek and pulled his head to look at her, studying him with a concerned expression. "Are you sure you're going to be okay? You look a little sick to your stomach."

In all honesty, Cooper felt a little sick to his stomach, but she didn't need to worry about that. She had her own worries about the evening and he didn't want to pile onto them. "I think I'm just a little hungry," he told her. "That fried chicken was hours ago."

Gigi's eye's narrowed and he could tell she wasn't buying his load of bull, but she didn't press him on it. "Okay, but if you change your mind at any time, just tap your nose so I know you want to leave."

"Will do." Cooper hopped out of the truck, trying desperately not to start tapping his nose already. He rounded the hood of his truck and went to hold out his hand for her, but she was already reaching for him. He linked their fingers together and smiled at how naturally they fit together. Maybe things wouldn't be so bad after all.

They walked up the steps of the porch, and Cooper tried his best not to keep a mental list of all the expensive materials he had eyed on the home as they did. Gigi knocked on the large, wooden door and when it swung open a moment later, Cooper sighed in relief at the sight of a man around his age, a man he assumed was Gigi's brother, Ford. "Ginny," the man said, leaning down and pulling her into a hug. "Good to see you."

"Good to see you, too, big brother." Gigi leaned back and smiled up at the other man. No matter the state of affairs between her and her parents, it seemed like she and her brother were close at least. Gigi stepped back next to Cooper and made introductions. "Cooper, this is Ford. Ford, this is my boyfriend, Cooper."

Ford extended a hand to him and Cooper shook it heartily. The light bounced off the expensive wristwatch he wore and his suit was clearly bespoke, but the smile on his face was genuine enough that Cooper was reserving judgement. "It's nice to meet you, Ford. Gigi has nothing but nice things to say about you." He spoke the truth. Any time Gigi spoke of her brother, she was always talking about how he was always there for her growing up and was an all-around standup guy.

Ford's wide smile reminded Cooper of Gigi's. "I

highly doubt that, but I'm happy that she's saving most of the trash talk for after the two of us have gotten to know one another a little better." Ford stepped to the side and ushered them in. "Gigi tells me you work down at Bob's. Is that right?"

"It is," Cooper admitted, preparing to hear a snide or sarcastic comment about his job. It had happened often enough in the past. "I've been there for about five years now."

"Nice." Ford sounded sincere as they walked deeper into the house. "Maybe you can convince Bob to get you guys up to speed on electric cars. I hate taking my Audi to the dealership in Atlanta. It's quite a drive and I gotta say, I don't know shit about cars, but I don't think the guys there know what they're doing."

Cooper tilted his head, considering what Ford had just told him. "That's a really good idea, actually." He loved his job, but it wouldn't hurt for the shop to update a thing or two. Cooper made a mental note to discuss it with Bob at their next shop meeting.

Ford smiled. "I am known to have a few on occasion." Gigi's brother led them into a dining room that looked like it was designed to impress and intimidate, or maybe that was just the effect it had on him. The walls were lined with ornate crown molding and wainscoting, and the furniture seemed to be highly maintained antiques. A sideboard sat on one side of the room and a drinks cart on the other. If he wasn't positive he was going to need all his wits about him, Cooper would have snagged a shot or two of bourbon to calm his nerves. "Mom and Dad will be down in a second. I figured I'd come greet you guys instead of having you wait on the porch," Ford said, distracting Cooper from his idea of taking a little liquid courage.

"Thanks," Gigi sighed. "I can't believe they're

pulling their power moves out already."

"Power moves?" Cooper inquired, not quite grasping the concept and not liking the sound of it either.

Ford winced. "Yeah. Sorry. It's something my dad does in meetings at work. The longer you have to wait for him, the more you overthink your strategy and are more likely to make a mistake." He shrugged and smiled apologetically. "I wouldn't take it too personally. They do it with everyone."

Gigi hugged his arm. "That's true. I was late for prom because they made my date wait around for fifteen minutes before letting him get past the entryway."

Cooper chuckled. If Gigi and Ford were able to joke about it, maybe things weren't all that bad. "Well, I guess that's something to hold on to while I'm getting grilled."

Gigi leaned against him, tilting her head up to look into his eyes. "My mom said they'd be cordial." Cooper just stared at her blankly and she winced. "Just remember our signal and we can go, okay?"

"You guys have a signal? Can I have one, too?" Ford asked and the three of them chuckled together, but their laughter quickly died at the sound of a throat clearing behind them.

Cooper turned to face the new arrivals, Gigi squeezing his arm just a little tighter than she had been before her parents had descended into the living room. Whether she was trying to give a boost of confidence to him or herself, he wasn't sure, but he appreciated the gesture either way. "Hi Mama. Daddy." Gigi stepped forward to give each of her parents a kiss on the cheek.

"Virginia." Her father spoke in a smooth, cultured voice, one Cooper had heard his entire life in their small town, but it had only ever been directed at him with contempt. "Aren't you going to introduce us to your friend?" Clearly Cooper hadn't remained on the man's radar for longer than the brief interaction they'd had months ago at the shop, but Cooper remembered her father and the way he liked to look down his nose at him. There seemed to be a slight curl to the man's lip as he spoke as well, but he schooled his features too quickly for Cooper to be sure what he saw. Still, if he hadn't already been a little on edge, he certainly was now.

"Of course." Gigi's voice wavered slightly, and as much as Cooper wanted to bolster her confidence he was having enough of a hard time with his own. "Cooper Ellis, these are my parents Clifford and Theodora Davenport. Mama. Daddy. This is Cooper Ellis, my *boyfriend.*"

Cooper didn't miss her emphasis on the word boyfriend, and he appreciated it. Gigi's willingness to clarify their relationship status, even though her parents knew perfectly well they were dating, had the pressure he felt in his chest letting up a bit. Clifford extended his hand and Cooper shook it, noticing that the older gentleman seemed to be trying to grip his hand harder than necessary and was angry he was losing the battle. "It's a pleasure to meet you, sir." He turned to Gigi's mom and offered her his hand. "Ma'am."

Theodora placed her limp wristed hand in his and he didn't know what to do with it besides bob it up and down a couple of times. She withdrew her hand with a slight eye roll and moved to the table. "Shall we sit? I believe dinner is ready."

Cooper watched the parents take their seats at the head of the long table and Ford moved to the other side. Cooper carefully pulled a chair out for Gigi, pushing it in for her when she was ready. He caught her dad seem to nod his head in approval at the gesture, so at least he was doing something right. No sooner had he sat down in his own chair than a short woman with black hair came out pushing a cart covered in food platters.

Large plates filled with what looked to be salmon, beet salad, asparagus, and some kind of grain Cooper had never seen in his life made their way to the table. He watched as the woman placed the various platters atop the pristine white tablecloth and disappeared back into the kitchen not having spoken a single word. He glanced over at Gigi and she looked completely nonplussed. Were all of their family dinners like this? While Cooper was cooking hot dogs on the engine of a car, she was getting hand delivered fine dining like a member of some royal family.

"You must try the bourbon glazed salmon. It's simply divine," Theodora said while passing the platter filled with the bright, pinkish-orange fish to Cooper.

He nodded his gratitude to her and served himself a piece, passing the plate on. "Thank you, ma'am. Everything looks delicious and I truly appreciate the invite." Cooper could appreciate them trying to mend fences, but he still had the sinking feeling in his stomach telling him that he wasn't going to be a part of that.

Gigi's mother smiled coolly, her graying brown hair not moving an inch out of place as she shook her head. "It was no trouble. We figured that if Gigi insisted on dating you, we should probably get to know you better."

Cooper nodded slowly and filled his plate with the rest of the foods being passed around, using it as a distraction from the fact that he was pretty sure he had just gotten insulted, but he couldn't be totally sure. He didn't want to start trouble when he was sure it was going to be coming along on its own soon enough. Gigi grabbed his hand and laced their fingers together. "It's a good thing, too, because I plan on dating Cooper for a long time." Cooper peeked over at her and saw a shy smile on her face. "If he'll have me."

Gigi's father snorted derisively. "If he'll have you. As if you aren't a catch with your family history." Clifford cut into his salmon a little more forcefully than the tender meat required, but Cooper ignored him as best he could in favor of looking at the woman next to him. Cooper smiled at Gigi and mouthed *I love you.* She mouthed it back and the conversation moved on to other topics. Ford tried to focus the conversation with her parents onto himself, a move Cooper could have kissed the man for, but neither Gigi's mother nor her father could be deterred from asking Cooper all sorts of questions. They grilled him about his upbringing, his schooling, how he came to work at the auto shop, and how far back his family history went in its ties to Willow Creek. It was a good thing Cooper was dressed for a job interview because he sure as hell felt like he was in one. By the time dessert was over, Cooper felt like he had been put through the ringer, and then some. Every muscle in his body ached from being tensed up all night and his brain felt like it was about to start melting and leak from his ears. He couldn't wait to get out of this place and back to his own home where he could feel more like himself.

"So, Mr. Ellis," Gigi's father went on, blatantly refusing to call Cooper by his first name. "What are your plans for the future? Surely you can't be a mechanic forever."

"Daddy," Gigi scolded her father, but Cooper squeezed her hand to let her know it was okay. It was just like dealing with a difficult customer at the shop. Patience and an even tone could help diffuse any situation, even though Cooper's patience was currently running thinner than a low viscosity motor oil.

"It's a fair question." Cooper smiled at his woman, trying to let her know he could handle himself before he turned his attention to her dad. "I don't have any immediate plans for the future beyond spending as much time as I can with your daughter. Gigi is an amazing woman, and I feel lucky to have her." Cooper was pretty sure it wasn't the answer her father wanted to hear, but it wasn't one he could argue with unless he wanted to disparage his own daughter to her face, something he wasn't sure was entirely out of the realm of possibility.

"Hmm. Isn't that sweet." Gigi's mother smiled thinly, turning to Gigi where her smiled looked slightly more genuine, but only just. "Virginia. I have a charity event coming up and I was wondering if I could get your opinion on my dress."

Gigi's eyes shot to his. Cooper could tell she was reluctant to leave him and while he always wanted her around, her parents needed to see he wouldn't back down from their intimidation either. "I'm not so sure…"

"It will only be a few moments, dear." Her mother sounded slightly exasperated and Cooper wondered how such cold and unfeeling people could produce two warm and inviting children.

Cooper looked at Gigi and winked, hoping to convey that everything was okay even though he had been itching to tap his nose the moment her parents walked into the dining room. She smiled at him and stood hesitantly, her hand touching his shoulder one last time before she left, trailing after her mother as she walked out of the dining room, dragging her feet. It looked like she was headed to the guillotine, but Cooper knew it was really his neck on the line.

No sooner were the two women gone than Gigi's father leaned closer to Cooper, inspecting him with narrowed eyes, a somewhat hostile expression on his face. He knew the man practiced corporate law, but he really missed his calling because Cooper could only imagine how it would feel to be a criminal on the other end of the look he was getting now. "Mr. Ellis."

"You can call me Cooper, sir." It was the third or fourth time that night he'd offered it up to the man, but from the stern look on his face, he wasn't going to take him up on it this time either.

"I'm not going to bother to learn your first name because the truth is that you won't be around long enough for it to be necessary." He spoke harshly, looking Cooper dead in the eye with nothing but disapproval.

"Dad," Ford started to argue, but his father held up a hand and the younger man shut up, giving Cooper a resigned look. Boy, their parents really had the kids under tight control, afraid to speak out about even blatant rudeness on their part. It looked like Cooper was on his own for this one.

"With all due respect, sir, your daughter thinks otherwise," Cooper countered. Gigi's parents might not care for him, but Gigi loved him and it was what he had to cling to in order to get through this whole debacle.

Clifford snorted. "She may think that now, but she'll come around. She always does," he said confidently. The slight confusion Cooper felt at that statement must have shown on his face because her father smiled knowingly and continued. "Oh, you didn't know this was a pattern for her? Like in grade school when she wanted to quit dance lessons. That lasted, how long was it Ford? Two, three days?"

Cooper looked across the table to her brother and the slight wince on Ford's face was all the confirmation he needed to know that the story was true. "That was a long time ago," Ford rebuffed, but the father went on undeterred.

"There was also the time in junior high when she dyed her hair purple right before school picture day because she knew it would anger her mother. Or the time in high school when she refused to try out for cheer unless we let her spend the night at her friend Mildred's house."

"Jesus, dad. Her name is Millie." Ford sounded as exasperated with his dad as Cooper was, but even knowing he wasn't totally alone didn't prevent the pressure in his chest from coming back tenfold. If Gigi's best friend of over twenty years didn't rate with her father, what chance did Cooper really have?

Gigi's dad waved off his son's admonishment. "It doesn't matter what her name is because their friendship was not appropriate, and do you know what happened with Virginia's cheer career?"

"No." Cooper grit his teeth, trying his best to remain calm despite constantly feeling like someone was pressing their boots down on his chest, pushing him further and further into the ground as if trying to bury him. "But I'm sure you're going to tell me." The man really needed to just get to his ultimate point because Cooper was sick of all this chatter. The walls seemed to be closing in on him and he needed to leave, pronto.

Gigi's father smiled. "Virginia continued on the cheer squad all through high school, even making it to the state competition her senior year." Clifford leaned back in his chair and steepled his fingers in a perfect depiction of a comic book villain. "Then there was the time when she wanted to skip college and just start working for my mother."

Cooper's head was pounding with all this new information and from an evening spent in poor company. "Your point, sir?"

The man chuckled cruelly. "My point is that I have survived my daughter's little rebellions before and I will survive this one." Clifford stood and buttoned his suit jacket, picking off a piece of lint he would probably attribute to Cooper. "I wouldn't get too comfortable in this relationship if I were you, Mr. Ellis. I don't see it lasting all that long." With that, the man left the dining room like he hadn't a care in the world, like he hadn't just confirmed one of Cooper's worst fears about his and Gigi's relationship.

Cooper looked across the table to Ford, who looked just as tired as he did. "I'm sorry about that, man," Ford said, slamming back a glass of some amber colored liquid. "I would say they're not always like that, but..." he shrugged.

Cooper just nodded, trying to absorb all the information he'd just been told. "Is all that true? The stuff your dad said about her rebelling?" Cooper loved Gigi and wanted to be with her more than anything. She said she loved him, too, and he believed her, but how long would it really last? They'd talked many times about how important family was to the two of them. Could he really expect her to blow up what she had with hers just for him? That was a big ask.

Ford shifted his head from side to side. "Yes and no. I mean, all those things happened, but I think of it less as a rebellion and more like times where the real Gigi was trying to break loose. Eventually, the Gigi my parents pressure her to be shoves the other one down far enough that she doesn't get out again for a while."

He hummed as he processed her brother's assessment. It was the only reply Cooper could articulate after such a long, horrendous evening. Was the real Gigi the one he was with, or the one her parents wanted her to be? Everything felt like it had gotten spun sideways, and he wasn't sure how to make it right. Past insecurities that had been simmering underneath his skin boiled to the surface, clouding out all other rational thoughts until every judgmental comment ever thrown his way blended into a chorus that sang about his low worth.

Moments later, Gigi walked back into the room and looked around, seeming to know that something bad had happened during her brief absence. "What's wrong? What did Daddy do?"

Cooper shot her brother a look, letting him know not to say a word. He didn't want her to worry about what her dad had said, not until he had time to process it all anyway. If he could just push those feelings of inadequacy, the voices from the past down again, everything would be fine. "Nothing," Cooper told Gigi as he rose up and walked over to her, pulling her into a hug, her peaches and cream scent comforting him like it always did. Still, even that wasn't enough to squash the tightness in his chest. "Ready to go?"

Gigi looked up, scrutinizing him with her gaze. "Are you sure you're okay?"

Cooper nodded. "Just a bit of a headache. It's been a long night and I'll be fine soon enough." It wasn't a total lie, and he didn't like that he was still holding back some of the truth, but his head was still on a swivel and he needed to get it straight before he potentially ruined her relationships with her parents. She'd been so happy at the prospect of them coming around that he didn't have the heart to dash her hopes, not yet. He steered them to the door, hoping that the hit of fresh air would help clarify what it was he was supposed to do about all this.

"That's fair," Gigi said with a slight laugh. They said their goodbyes to her brother and left the house. After Cooper let her into her side of the car, he walked around to his, everything her dad told him repeating in his head until Cooper literally felt sick to his stomach.

Cooper started the truck and pointed it back in the direction of Gigi's house. "I hope it wasn't too horrible for you." She kissed his cheek and leaned against his shoulder as he drove, her body warming him after such a cold reception from her folks. "I'm sorry they asked so many questions, but they're always like that. I'm really glad you came." He grunted a reply. "I think they'll come around eventually," she said quietly.

Gigi might think they would come around, but after the little chat he had with her dad, Cooper knew that wasn't the case. As he drove, the ache in his chest became more pronounced as he wondered why it suddenly felt like their relationship had a ticking clock on it.

Chapter Nineteen

Gigi

The day had finally come for her drag queen brunch, and Gigi should have been excited beyond words as she finished setting up the tables and chairs in an arrangement that would allow for eating, socializing, and watching some amazing singing and dancing performances. She was really looking forward to the special event, even wearing one of her favorite dresses, a vintage floral swing dress with a red bust and white bodice to make herself feel a little more glamourous for her first foray into themed events. She also did her hair in 50s waves and wore thicker heeled shoes to complete the look. Gigi looked like a million bucks, but emotionally, she felt more like a handful of pocket change.

The last two weeks had been busy, with Gigi's days filled with preparation for the brunch and Cooper's with working at the shop more than usual. Bob's had been swamped as people took their cars in for a tune up in anticipation of the summer months, and while Gigi would like to blame packed schedules for the change in her relationship, she knew it as probably something else. Cooper had seemed different lately, not totally distant, but not completely present either. Sometimes his eyes would take a far off look, as though he was trying to see into a crystal ball but couldn't make out the images. Any time she brought it up, he told her he was just caught up in his head and needed to process a few things, but she knew it was more than that. Even their lovemaking had changed.

It was still hot as hell, both of them experiencing the same amounts of physical pleasure as they always had, but something in Cooper's demeanor was off. He held her differently, still as though she were something precious, but with a firmer grip, like he was afraid she was going to slip away from him. Cooper would also still gaze at her as they moved against one another, but it was like he was trying to memorize every line or freckle on her face, every aspect of her being. Gigi wanted to believe that it was because he was so in love with her that he couldn't help himself from soaking her all in, but it felt more like he was cataloging features to recall at a later time, like they wouldn't always be together.

The thought of no longer being with Cooper caused a sharp pain to slash through her chest and she gripped the edge of a nearby table to steady herself. Gigi wanted forever with him, and she had been certain he had felt the same way, but that certainty was wavering slightly and had been ever since their dinner with her family. Had Ford said something to spook him? Cooper had been very complimentary of her brother, so she doubted it for that reason and because despite being a lawyer and driving an unnecessarily flashy car, Ford wasn't a snob and didn't look down on people. That left her parents as the true culprit. The idea that they might have said something to make Cooper doubt her feelings for him wouldn't surprise her, but what would be surprising was if he listened.

Gigi thought she had made her feelings clear with every tender word spoken, every touch of her lips and hands, every time she looked at him like he was everything she'd ever wanted but never dared to hope for because that's what he was to her. Everything. Gigi had asked him how his talk with her dad went, and he said it was fine, that there was nothing unusual about it. Surely, Cooper would tell her if something had gone amiss, but maybe he hadn't dealt with his insecurities in their class differences as much as he led on.

Gigi had been raised in privilege, but had also spent most of her life around Millie and knew how money struggles could affect a person's outlook on life. Maybe in the whirlwind of their romance, she and Cooper hadn't talked about it enough. Gigi decided that today was as good a day as any to do it and would seek him out after work. Her nerves about how the community would react to her brunch event had only added to her paranoia, but luckily, the community seemed to be as supportive of her endeavors as she knew they would be.

Gigi sold tickets to the event to keep the numbers manageable and prevent any walk-ins from causing a ruckus should they be upset with the dazzling performances and more progressive topics of conversation, but other than that, no other measures had really been necessary to keep things calm. The tickets sold out rather quickly, and other than a few looks she got from some of the more outspoken and staunchly conservative members of Willow Creek as she walked down the aisles of the grocery store, she hadn't dealt with much blow back, a fact she was grateful for. Gigi wasn't sure she could handle the stress of putting on a special event, the weirdness from her boyfriend, and people outside with picket signs and bullhorns all at the same time.

Gigi glanced at her watch. It was approximately half an hour until her brunch was scheduled to start, so she unlocked her doors, smiling when she saw the first two customers waiting outside. "You guys could have texted me. I would have let you in." Her friends filed past her looking absolutely stunning.

Jo smiled and looked at her from beneath the wisps of blonde curls that had fallen into her eyes. She too had gone all out today, wearing a strapless, mint green cocktail dress and pink cloche hat. "We could have, but we wanted to wait until you were ready to let us in so we could get the full effect." Jo spun around and looked at the tables that were set up with tea service trays, folded cloth napkins, and were arranged in a manner to allow for easy movement between rooms. It didn't look much different from a normal service at The Happy Kettle, but Gigi had also placed flyers advertising upcoming shows for each of her special guests along with newly printed menus that advertised the day's special treats. "This looks amazing, Gi," Jo gushed, picking up a menu and snorting at it. "Bye, Felicia finger sandwiches? That's awesome."

"Isn't it great?" Millie read the menu over Jo's shoulder looking just as beautiful as she always did, wearing a light gray dress that was covered in large blue flowers, the vee neckline cutting lower than Millie would normally be comfortable with. Her shoes were tall heels with ribbons that wound around her ankle and ended tied in a bow, making her feet look cute and her legs look fierce.

"Speaking of great." Gigi gestured to her two friends, fanning herself. "You both look smoking hot. Did you dress up to impress the queens?"

Millie blushed and Jo answered the sly question for the two of them. "We may have video called each other a few times to approve outfits." She shrugged a shoulder nonchalantly. "When you dine with a queen, you must look like royalty after all."

Gigi chuckled. "Okay, your grace. Why don't you two find a seat? I need to be up here to greet my customers."

"Will do." Millie and Jo wandered off to find a seat near where the performances would mainly take place, their eyes still roaming the room as if it were the first and not hundredth time they'd been there.

Gigi turned to greet more customers as they filed

in, saying hello and thanking them for coming as she took their tickets and pointed out the various seating areas. When Mags came in, Gigi gave the older woman a hug, careful not to knock off the large brimmed hat she wore. She had been tempted to ask Cooper's grandma if she had noticed anything off about him, but she hadn't gotten a chance because the drag queens had arrived and needed to know where to hook up their phones to the music system.

Two hours and four amazing drag performances later, including an incredible duet from Heidi Haux and Miz Cheeky where they sang Cher's "Believe," Gigi was making her rounds, weaving through the room and checking in to make sure her customers had everything they needed from food, to drinks, to more time gossiping with the drag queens. That last part had by far been the biggest request with people not being able to get enough of hearing the performers chat with them and call other people out as they gossiped.

Gigi grabbed some empty teacups and walked them over to the busing station, smiling as she overheard Jo speaking with Sasha Royale about the coworker she couldn't seem to stop talking about. "Girl, I think you know what you need to do," Sasha told Jo, one perfectly penciled brow raised.

"Let all the air out of his tires? Move everything on his desk one inch to the left over the course of a week so he thinks he's losing his mind?" The more pranks Jo came up with, the more crazed she started to look.

Sasha scoffed. "No, girl. You need to bang the shit out of him. That will get rid of all the anger you seem to have toward the man. I think what you are experiencing is a supreme buildup of sexual tension between the two of you."

"Ew, no way." Jo's protest sounded flat, and Gigi

walked away with a smile, letting the conversation fade into the background and leaving Jo in the capable hands of the amazing Sasha.

The event was starting to wind down, but Gigi wasn't about to kick anyone out. Instead, she walked up to the front counter to check her phone, hoping to see a message from her man. Cooper had mentioned that he would try to show up to support her, but she knew that Saturdays at the garage were insane, so she hadn't counted on it. She pulled her phone out of her purse and saw a text from Cooper.

Cooper: **Shop is slammed. Working through lunch. Sorry I won't make it today, Peach, but I am so proud of you.**

Gigi smiled at the message and replied with two kisses. If he was slammed, she didn't want to bother him. She would pack up some leftovers from the brunch and take them over to his place for after his shift. If he had to skip lunch, he would probably be starving by the time the end of the day rolled around. Maybe when she saw him she could get a better read on his previous weirdness.

Gigi stowed her phone and started to head back into the event, but the warm breeze of outside air caused her to pause. She looked over and was shocked to see her mother walking in with Tanner Lawson of all people. Gigi smiled nervously at the pair and walked over to greet them. "Mama. Tanner. What are you two doing here?"

"Is that any way to greet your mother and an old friend?" her mother asked, leaning down to kiss her cheek.

"I'm sorry." Gigi wasn't exactly sure why she was apologizing, but it was a kneejerk reaction to either of her parents scolding her, not to mention she was totally thrown off by the appearance of these two people. "It's just that we're closed for a private event and I wasn't expecting anyone to come in."

Theodora flicked her eyes around the room briefly. "Oh, yes, your little show." Her mother had a tight smile and look in her eye that threatened to wilt the flowers on the counter she was glancing at disapprovingly, the very same flowers Cooper had brought her that morning when he came to wish her luck. "You decided to go through with that?"

Gigi swept her hand out to indicate the rooms filled with customers. "Obviously." She tilted her chin up, feeling proud and protective of all the hard work she'd put in. There was no way she was letting her mother ruin what had been a fun and fantastic event for her business. "And it's been a big success."

"Well, that's neither here nor there at the moment," her mother said dismissively, grabbing Tanner's arm and practically shoving him into Gigi. "I thought I would bring Tanner by so that the two of you could get reacquainted. You have so much in common and would make the loveliest couple."

Gigi pinched the bridge of her nose to stave off the headache that always accompanied a talk with her mother. "Mama, I'm with Cooper." She was growing increasingly frustrated with her mother's ridiculous behavior. Now that she'd seen how wonderful and easy life with Cooper could be, she couldn't remember why she ever put up with the demands of her parents in the first place. "No offense, Tanner. Feel free to grab some food or tea if you like. I need to speak with my mother."

"No worries." He spoke affably, walking over to Jo and Millie's table. Gigi watched as he sat next to Millie, knowing that she would make sure he had anything he needed, but she didn't have time to worry about Tanner at the moment. Right now, she needed to set a few things straight with her mother.

Gigi turned to face the woman, noticing but not caring about the displeased look on her face. "What are you doing bringing guys around here, trying to set me up on dates when you know that I'm seriously dating someone else?"

Her mother had the gall to roll her eyes. "Virginia, please. You've had your little moment of defiance. You've invited drag queens into your business and dated a carpenter. We're all very impressed with your ability to draw attention to yourself, but it's time to get back to normal."

Gigi fumed at her mother's words, feeling equal parts insulted and enraged. "Firstly, Cooper is a mechanic, and secondly, this is my normal. This is probably the most normal I have felt in my entire life." Gigi had spurts of feeling like herself, only to have to shove it back down to play the part of the perfect daughter of a lawyer and socialite, but she was done hiding behind who she was supposed to be, who other people demanded she be, and wanted to start living her life as the person she actually was. It was long overdue.

A disgusted noise burbled up in the back of her mother's throat, making her sound like a frog. Gigi would laugh if she wasn't so busy being pissed off. "This is not normal." She waved her hand around the room, gesturing to the very event that planning and hosting had brought Gigi a great deal of joy. "Dating beneath you is not normal."

Gigi felt her hands ball into fists as anger coursed through her body, setting her blood to boil. "I am not dating beneath me. If anything, I'm beneath him. Cooper's family has welcomed me with open arms and been nothing but polite. Can you say the same? He deserves to be treated with far more respect than what you or Daddy have shown him."

"Virginia." Her mom pinched the bridge of her nose, clearly as out of patience as her daughter was. "You need to end this now. It's gone on long enough."

Gigi could feel a heaviness settle in her chest as the knowledge that this moment was going to be a turning point in her life sunk in. Would she stand up for who and what she wanted, or would she cower back down and let herself settle for a life half-lived? A life she never ever wanted. Cooper's smiling face and loving words came into her mind, and she knew what she was going to do. In truth, she'd probably known this moment was coming from the moment she laid eyes on him.

"No, Mama. I'm not giving him up." Her mother opened her mouth to speak, but Gigi held up her hand. "You've said your piece, now I'm going to say mine." She took a deep breath and looked her mother straight in the eyes. "Cooper is a smart, caring, accomplished, amazing man. I'm not leaving him, and he's not leaving me. I love him. We love each other. We're going to get married and have half a dozen babies and everything. You can either get right with it, or you can get out."

Her mother narrowed her gaze at Gigi for a moment, turning on her heel and walking out the door. Gigi exhaled harshly, and held a hand over her rapidly beating heart. With any luck, her mom would eventually come to her senses, but she wasn't counting on it happening anytime soon. Either way, she would be okay. She had Cooper, her brother, her friends, and most of all she had herself, and right then she was feeling pretty damn proud of how she had finally been able to shuck off the cloak of pressure to be someone she never would be and stand up for what she wanted. Gigi looked to the side and saw Mags. The older woman winked at her, and Gigi wondered how much of the conversation with her mother she had overheard. It didn't matter because she would tell Cooper how much he meant to her later that night, and if she had her way, every night after that.

****

The door to Cooper's house was unlocked, so she pushed her way in, idly patting Shep after he had trotted over to greet her. "Hiya, boy. Where's your daddy?"

Cooper appeared from around the corner, freshly showered and wearing nothing but a pair of gray sweats that hung low on his hips. "Did someone call for daddy?" Cooper smirked, walking up to her and giving her a brief kiss on the lips, his damp hair dripping onto her and the drops of water rolling down her now heated skin.

Instead of dropping it to maul her man, Gigi held up the bag she carried that was filled with leftover sandwiches, raw veggies, and cakes from the brunch. "I brought you some food." She tried not to get distracted by all the muscles on display, but it was a trial.

"Thank you, Peach." His eyes shined with gratitude as he took the bag from her. "I'm starving." He turned and walked into the kitchen, his firm ass shifting back and forth under the cotton fabric of his sweats.

"You're not the only one," she muttered, trying to get her libido under control.

Cooper looked over his shoulder and grinned at her quip. "Calm down, Honey. Let me get some fuel and then we'll satisfy that hunger of yours," he promised.

Gigi sighed, but she was pretty hungry herself and she was happy to wait for the physical stuff since the promise was already out there, a promise she was definitely holding him to. "Fine by me, but can you at least put on a shirt?" She grabbed two plates and a couple of forks, having to peel her eyes away from his exposed torso. "A girl can't concentrate on food if she's having to stare at all that."

Cooper just chuckled and walked over to his dresser, grabbing a t-shirt and pulling it over his head. It hugged his muscles nicely, and she wondered if he was bulking up or purposefully shrinking his shirts in the wash. It was probably neither, the more likely explanation that she was just super horny for her man. "This better?" he asked, walking over to her and tucking a finger under her chin to pull her gaze to his. "My eyes are up here, Honey."

Gigi rolled her eyes at his teasing and the permanent smirk on his face. "Don't even try to tell me you're not happy that I find you incredibly attractive."

His smirk faltered a little as he reached into the bag and started to distribute food among their two plates. "As long as that's not the only reason you like me."

Gigi slapped his arm. "You know it's not." She thought he was joking, but his face looked a lot less amused than it should have been.

"Sorry, I guess I'm just tired," he breathed out. He did look rather weary, and suddenly she felt incredibly selfish for coming over and bugging him when he probably just wanted food and sleep.

"I can go if you want. I know it's been a long week and I don't want to keep you up if you're exhausted." Gigi made to stand, but he hooked his foot under her chair and scooted her closer.

Cooper looked at her, his blue eyes serious. "I want every minute with you that I can get while I can get it," he said, taking a bite of a sandwich. That seemed like a weird way to phrase things, but he said he was tired and she had a long day, too. She really needed to stop overanalyzing everything.

"Other than being crazy busy, how was your day?" She bit into a celery stick, trying to keep conversation light to try and stave off her worrying about everything.

Cooper ran a hand down his face. "It would have been a lot smoother if Bob would update some of the computer systems," he admitted with a weary shake of his head. "I swear sometimes it takes twice as long to get things done because those systems are so slow."

"Have you talked to him about it?" she asked as she continued to munch on the crunchy vegetable. It tasted bland already, but the expression on Cooper's face turned it to ash on her tongue

Cooper glanced at her like she'd just said the sky was neon pink. "It's not really my place. I'm not the boss."

She brushed off his look and shrugged a shoulder. "No, but you've been there for five years..." she started, but Cooper interrupted her.

"And so what? I should be higher up on the food chain so I can make more decisions?" His voice was a little harsh and she felt herself draw back at his tone, feeling like she was a scolded child. It reminded her a little too much of how she felt around her parents, her stomach lurching at the thought.

"No. What I was going to say is that you've been there a long time and I know Bob values your input, so he would listen if you wanted to talk to him about it." Jo's dad was the best and there was no way he would discount the opinion of any employee, let alone one that had been there as long as Cooper.

Cooper grunted in reply and bit into his sandwich again. Gigi ignored the knot forming in her stomach and kept talking. "You could be higher up if you wanted," she said, remembering a conversation she had with Jo earlier at the brunch. Jo had mentioned wanting her father to relax more and had hoped he would pass more responsibility onto Cooper. Gigi thought it was a good idea since she knew how much Jo worried about her dad's health.

"What?" His voice and eyes were filled with intensity, but not the kind that made her knees weak.

Gigi looked at his puzzled expression and felt the need to clarify. "Oh, I was just talking with Jo earlier, and she was saying how she was hoping her dad would retire soon and let you take over the shop if you wanted." She took a drink of water to quench her suddenly dry throat and set her glass down. "She's worried that her dad is working too hard and thought it would be better if he retired or had someone take over the big stuff so that he could go back to just working on cars."

"Just working on cars? Like it's that easy." Cooper huffed, shaking his head and snapping a carrot with his teeth.

"That's not what I'm saying and you know it," she protested, wondering where all this attitude she was getting from him was coming from. Gigi knew he was tired, but this seemed like a lot more than that. "Is something wrong?"

Cooper sighed and wiped his hand down his face. "Ignore me, Peach. I must have woke up on the wrong side of the bed this morning." He reached over and grabbed her hand to give it a squeeze, the touch making her feel slightly less off-kilter. "Tell me about your brunch. I'm sorry I didn't get to stop by, but from what I glimpsed from over at the shop, it looked like it was busy and people were leaving with smiles on their faces. I'm so proud of you."

The words of praise were nice, but there was still something about his tone that niggled at her brain. Gigi swallowed thickly, a feeling of dread starting to creep into her body. "It was great." Her voice lacked the enthusiasm she'd felt earlier that day, but she was happy to change the subject away from one that was obviously causing him distress. Gigi pushed her plate out of the way for a moment and rested her arms on the table. "The performances were amazing and everyone had such a great time. I'm pretty sure Mags has a friend for life in Heidi Haux—she was the main performer we hired for the day. I overheard the two of them talking about giving your gran a makeover."

Cooper chuckled, his eyes losing some of the exhaustion he clearly felt. "That sounds like something Mags would want to do. I can't wait to go over to the senior living community and see her blue hair and false eyelashes."

Gigi joined in his laughter. "I don't think she'd do the eyelashes because they're too fiddly, but I can totally imagine Mags with blue hair. Or maybe purple."

"I'm sure she'll try both before the end of the year" Cooper munched on a carrot, his mood seeming much lighter, and Gigi was glad of it. It wasn't that he couldn't ever be in a less than stellar mood, it had just seemed like he was taking offense to everything she said, and Gigi didn't love that. "Anything else crazy happen besides my grandma updating her beauty regimen?"

Gigi bit her lip, wondering if she should tell Cooper about what happened with her mom. She might as well. Gigi didn't want to keep things from him and there was the chance Mags would tell him anyway since she had overheard at least part of the conversation. "My mom stopped by when it was almost over."

Cooper stopped munching and leaned back in his chair, suddenly looking very apprehensive as his good mood vanished into thin air. "How did that go?"

Gigi picked at the bread on her sandwich, rolling it between her fingers and watching the crumbs fall to the plate. "I think it went well considering. She complained that I was going through another phase, but I set her straight." She hadn't gone into specifics, but she didn't want to be unnecessarily cruel and repeat what her mother had said word for word.

"She called us a phase?" he asked, studying her fiercely.

Gigi rolled her eyes, trying to play it off and get the smile she loved so much back. "Yes. She always calls the times when I'm not doing exactly what my parents want me to be doing phases or little rebellions."

Cooper twisted his mouth up. "Like when you almost skipped out on going to college?"

Gigi looked over at him, the blank expression on his face making her nervous. "Yeah. I told you about that?"

"It came up." Cooper's eyes darted away. His not directly answering the question, made her suspicious, so Gigi looked at him and raised her brow. She told him about her time at the university, but never that she almost didn't go. It wasn't something she was hiding, just not something they had gotten around to talking about yet. "Your dad might have said something."

Gigi sighed at the confession. "Of course he did." She was furious at her dad for airing her business behind her back. What Gigi chose to share and with whom was her business, not her parents'. "What else did he tell you?"

Cooper shrugged a shoulder like this was just a normal conversation and not one that seemed to be filled with potential landmines. "Just some other things that kind of spoke to a pattern."

"A pattern of what?" The slightly scornful tone in his voice wasn't something she welcomed or enjoyed. Gigi felt like she was walking a tightrope and any moment, she was going to make a wrong move and fall right off the side. She often felt that way with her parents and had come to think of Cooper as her safety net. Now, not so much.

"A pattern of doing things to piss off your parents. Wanting to quit dance lessons, not being a cheerleader, skipping out on going to college." He looked up at her, his face void of emotion. "Dating a mechanic."

"And is that what you think our relationship is? A phase, some rebellion to get under my parents' skin?" When he did nothing more than shrug a shoulder, Gigi fell back in her chair as if he'd slapped her across the face. He couldn't possibly be insulting her like this. "You can't be serious."

Cooper sat there another moment in silence before sighing. "Look, Gigi. I don't know if this is some rebellion or phase, but what I do know is that I don't want to wait around anymore for you to change your mind when you realize who you really are and that I'm not who you want me to be."

Gigi's lower lip trembled, tears welling up in her eyes. She blinked them back, refusing to let them fall in front of him when he was acting like such an ass. "What are you saying?" If he was going to be a coward and let her parents poking at his own insecurities drive them apart, he damn well better be clear about it.

"I'm saying that you'll have your fun and get your kicks with me, but then you'll realize that I'm just a mechanic with no ambitions beyond what I currently have." His tone was resigned, like he'd already decided their future for them without consulting her about it at all.

"Is this about what I said a few minutes ago? I was just relaying something Jo told me. I don't care what you do because I know you'll work hard and take pride in whatever it is and that's all that matters." Cooper could quit his job to paint crappy pictures of circus animals for all she cared, as long as he was happy and they loved and supported one another, what did it matter?

Cooper shook his head with finality. "You say that, but I think you'll figure out that I'm not worthy of you and you don't really love me."

As sad as she felt, Gigi was starting to get plenty pissed off, too. "I do love you," she told him passionately, wiping away a tear that fell down her cheek. "I know how I feel about you. You don't get to tell me what I feel, Coop.

"Maybe not, but I can tell you how I feel," he said ominously. "And I feel like this, whatever this is, has run its course."

Gigi felt all the breath leave her lungs in one go, like someone had pressed a fifty pound sack of flour on her chest. "So you want to throw away a loving, wonderful relationship because of a few ideas from me and some things my father said to you?" When he didn't respond, she barreled onward, determined to show him just how in the wrong he was. "Did my father also tell you that I stuck with dance because the teacher talked to me about not giving up on something because it was hard to do, and she inspired me to keep going? Did you hear about how I didn't want to try out for cheer because Millie was having a tough time at home and I wanted to spend more time with her? No? Well, maybe he told you that I ended up going to college because my gran said that I should take advantage of the opportunity because a lot of people didn't get one. You know how much she meant to me and you know I wouldn't want to let her down." Gigi slid closer to him and grabbed his hand, squeezing it but finding he was giving nothing back. "Did you hear anything I just said?"

"I heard it, but it doesn't change things. We're too different, and you belong with someone more like you."

Cooper's voice was low and it cracked slightly, but it was also resigned, as though he had no fight left.

Gigi nodded and stood, gathering her things and patting Shep as she walked away from the table. She was angry, but she wasn't getting through to him and wasn't sure she ever would, not as long as he thought so little of himself and of her. "You know what sucks the most about all this?" she asked, and he turned his head slightly but didn't look at her. "There are so many people out there, your gran, your boss, your coworkers, your friends, me. We all believe in you and think you are this amazing, wonderful person. The only one here who doesn't believe in you is you. We may come from different places, but we aren't all that different. The only real difference between us is that I think you're worthy of love, and you don't." She leaned down and kissed the top of his head, the tears flowing freely now. She walked to the door and turned around to look at him one last time. Gigi wasn't immune to feeling less than, but she'd grown to see those feelings for the remnants of past trauma that they were. If Cooper needed to the time to figure that out for himself, she would give it to him. "Call me when you finally realize that you are."

Gigi opened the door and walked out on shaky legs, not knowing how she made it across the street to her little blue Beetle, but she had. Now that she was alone, she let her restraint go and sobbed, folding in half as the pain of their break-up ripped through her body. She really hoped he came to his senses soon because she wasn't sure she could handle another minute of the sorrow.

Chapter Twenty

Cooper

Ice cold liquid splashing onto his face had Cooper jackknifing out of bed and sputtering as he tried to dispel some of the liquid from his nose. He groaned and clutched the side of his head. It was pounding from both the swift movement and from the fact that he had consumed a metric fuck-ton of alcohol the evening before. He'd been drinking himself to sleep every night for the past week, trying to ease the ache in his chest and forget the look on Gigi's face as he broke her heart. Cooper had acted like such a jackass, throwing her words back in her face like she was the enemy when all she was doing was making conversation.

He had used what her father had told him as a way to push her away, and while he didn't want to hurt her, he had been so sure that she would eventually hurt him that he turned the tables before that could happen. *Like a coward,* a voice whispered in his head. Cooper was a coward and a fool, letting the horrible words her father had said to him creep into his brain and take root, feeding into his insecurities and causing him to doubt their relationship. Her father wasn't the one who messed things up, though. Cooper was, and he had no idea how to fix it. The whole time they were together, Gigi had been rising above the judgement of others while he'd been wallowing in it, and it could cost him dearly. He'd wanted to protect her from everything, but it turned out the one thing she needed protecting from was his own misjudgment of her.

Cooper wiped a hand down his wet face and blinked against the bright light that streamed in through his bedroom window. When his eyes finally came into focus, he saw his grandma standing at the foot of his bed, an empty water pitcher dangling from one hand. "Mags?" he asked bewildered at the sight of his grandmother. "What are you doing?"

Mags raised an angry gray eyebrow at him. "What am I doing? I'm trying to knock some sense into you. What have you been doing?" Her voice was a little loud for how awful his head felt, but Cooper wasn't about to tell her that lest he get another ice bucket to the face.

"Nothing." Cooper had been doing a whole lot of nothing but stewing in the misery of his own making, his mind spinning in circles as he tried to figure out a way to fix the damage he'd done but not sure how to make it up to Gigi. There wasn't an apology adequate enough for what he'd done. Right now, though, he was trying to figure out why his grandmother was in his house. "How did you even get here and get inside?"

Mags scoffed. "I ordered a car, like I told you I knew how to do." She swept her hair back behind her ear, looking far more put together than anyone had a right to be at this early hour. "As for how I got into your house, well, let's just say you're not the only one who knows their way around a toolbox."

"You know how to pick locks?" Cooper shook his head at this new and slightly alarming development. Maybe it was time he got a keypad system instead, then no one would be able to interrupt him while he continued his downward spiral.

Mags pointed one bony finger at him. "Don't change the subject." She had barked the words and he straightened in his bed, not wanting to upset her further. It was amazing how she still had the ability to make him feel like a young boy when he was a grown man, not that he'd acted like it with his woman. "What did you do to that sweet girl across the way?" she asked, tipping her head in the direction of Gigi's tearoom.

Cooper looked down at his rumpled bedsheets to avoid her gaze, not wanting her to see the shame he'd been wearing as a mask all week long. "I don't know what you're talking about," he lied. He didn't like lying to his grandma, but he wasn't up for rehashing every moment of his stupidity with her either. He was doing that enough on his own and it had not been a pleasant experience.

"Bullshit." Mags called him out like he knew she would. "You can't lie to me." He huffed a breath and crossed his arms, frowning when he looked down and realized he had come to bed in his work coveralls. Cooper sighed. His gran was right, of course. He couldn't and had never been able to lie to her very convincingly. When he was twelve, he had been tossing a baseball around inside the house and when it broke a lamp, he tried to blame it on the dog. Not a bad plan except for the fact that they had never owned a dog. "Now, what did you do to Gigi?"

Cooper clucked his tongue, wanting to deflect from himself. "How do you know whatever's going on wasn't her fault?" It was a weak move, but that seemed to be all he knew how to do lately. Be weak.

Mags looked at him deadpan, her gray eyes not wavering one bit as she stared at him. "I know it was you because I've been over to her tearoom twice this week. The first day she wasn't there, having called in sick for the first time ever since I've known her, and the second day she walked around the place looking like a shell of a person, like her whole world had been ripped away from her and she wanted nothing more than to disappear into thin air. The girl might as well have been a ghost for as much presence as she had."

Cooper rubbed his chest right over his heart. It

ached at the thought of her acting like that and hurt even more knowing that he was the reason why. He'd let his insecurities sit for too long, let them mingle with his own ideas about the upper class until they became a potent mixture of doubt and mistrust that he turned against the woman he loved. Cooper's lack of self-awareness in that moment had been his downfall, and he had no idea how to make up for such a colossal blunder. He tried to swallow the thick lump of sorrow that seemed to be permanently lodged in his throat. "I messed up, Gran," he choked out.

"Well, no shit, Sherlock. The question is what are you going to do about it?" Mags tapped her foot impatiently as he sat there and stared off into space. Cooper had no idea how to fix it. Gigi had told him to call her when he could stop being an idiot, and while he realized his mistake as soon as the door shut after she left a week ago, he couldn't be sure it wouldn't happen again. The way people had treated him in the past, still treated him at times was something he thought he'd dealt with, but clearly he'd done a piss poor job. Mags sighed heavily and her gaze softened a bit. "Here's what's going to happen. I'm going to sit my brittle ass down in one of these plush chairs and then we're going to figure out what to do. Okay?"

He nodded, touched by how willing she was to help him after he'd so clearly screwed up, but that's what you did for the people you loved. Cooper got off his bed and sat in the chair across from his grandma. After taking a deep breath, he proceeded to tell her exactly what had gone down, not bothering to try and paint himself in a better light because she would see past that in a second anyway. Besides, he deserved every ounce of derision she could send his way. He told her about the way Gigi's parents had acted and what her dad had said, about how he felt inadequate in comparison to her and the type of guy she could get, and how he had treated her so poorly when all she had wanted was to spend time with him and share the details of her successful day. When he was finished, he looked over to his grandma, expecting to see her looking angry and disappointed, but instead she just looked sad.

"I think maybe your grandfather and I didn't do quite right by you," she said shakily, peering out the window for a moment before meeting his eyes again. "Gilbert and I wanted to teach you how to take care of yourself and give you the skills to get a good job. I thought we had also shown you that you were worthy of everything you wanted in this life, but now I'm not so sure we did."

Cooper sniffed, trying to stifle the tears that threatened to fall. He hadn't meant to make his gran feel bad. It wasn't her fault he felt the way he did sometimes. "It's not your doing. Most times I feel pretty solid. I'm a good person, I try to do right by others, and I work hard." He swallowed thickly as memories of being looked at like he was no better than a piece of chewed gum on the sidewalk still lingered in his mind, memories he'd buried instead of dealt with like he should have. "Everything Gigi's dad said just played into all my fears and I let them eat away at me. I didn't give her enough credit, wondering when she would leave me when she's shown me nothing but the truest affection. She never cared about my job or how much money I make, and now I've lost the only woman I've ever loved."

"Not the only woman, I hope," Mags sassed. Cooper chuckled lightly at the remark, the sound foreign to his ears. His voice had been left feeling a bit raw from the excessive drinking and lack of use, and he certainly hadn't laughed anytime in the last week.

Cooper smiled sadly at her. "You know what I mean." He looked down at his hands as he considered his horrible behavior. "And if I didn't feel worthy of her before, I sure as hell don't after the way I acted last week. I always knew she deserved better than me, I just thought it was about money or class, not about me being a total jackass."

His grandma leaned over at patted his hand. "While there is no arguing that you were a prime jackass, you're always worthy of love," she promised, looking knowingly at him. "And forgiveness." Cooper smiled and gave her hand a squeeze. "You'll get her back." She spoke with such confidence, and he wanted to badly to believe that was true, that Gigi would forgive him.

"Oh, yeah," he asked, not quite as certain of the outcome just yet. "What makes you say that?"

Mags's grin widened, showing off her straight but slightly yellowing teeth. "I say that because I was there when Gigi told her mama to get right with the two of you being together because she wasn't leaving you."

The corners of his mouth twitched, wanting to smile but not daring to allow himself to hope. "She said that?" He pictured his girl with her hands balled into fists and resting on her hips, righteous indignation fueling her as she gave her mother what for. Gigi had always been so confident in their relationship. He wished he had been the same when it really mattered.

"Among other things," his grandma said ambiguously. When Cooper looked up at her with curiosity, she smiled and waved her hand around like it was nothing. "She might have told her mom that she planned on getting married and having half a dozen babies with you."

Cooper couldn't hold back his smile at that bit of information. "Half a dozen, huh?" He could already picture the little rug rats, their auburn hair getting mussed as they horsed around with Shep. It was an image he wanted to be real so badly, and he kicked himself again for being such an idiot and putting that future in jeopardy.

"Uh-huh." His grandma stood and patted his shoulder as she walked by him. "You should probably get her back and get started on it then. I'm not getting any younger and I want to see at least three of those grandbabies."

Cooper nodded, standing and following her to his door. "Can I give you a ride home?" He didn't love the idea of driving his grandma across town with this hangover, but he would do it if she asked.

Mags snorted. "Absolutely not. Not only am I fairly certain you would fail a breathalyzer test, you have far more important things to do."

Cooper chuckled. "I can assure you I am no longer drunk, but you're right about that second part." He scratched at his beard, the hair having gotten much more straggly since he had stopped bothering to trim it a week ago. "I do have something important to do."

"Get to it," she commanded, leaning over to give him a hug. Cooper kissed the top of her gray head and smiled as she walked over the car that was waiting out near the side of his house.

"You kept the driver waiting the whole time?" Cooper would need to talk to her about that. If it was a regular occurrence, she could be throwing tons of money down the drain. Maybe he could sign her up for one of those senior technology classes so she could better protect herself.

Mags grimaced at him. "What do you take me for, a fool? This is a different driver."

Cooper blinked in disbelief. "When did you even have a chance to order another car?" He hadn't seen her pull out her phone once since the moment he glimpsed her at the foot of his bed.

"I did it from my pocket." Mags smiled proudly, sliding into the backseat of the small, black sedan. Cooper snorted to himself. His grandma was the one that would need to give him a tutorial on how to use technology better because she was already a pro.

Cooper walked back into his house and over to the corner where his dog had sequestered himself over the last week. It seemed that he wasn't the only one missing Gigi. He squatted down next to the animal and scratched his torso. His dog may not be happy with him for driving Gigi away, but he was putty in the hands of anyone who would give him belly rubs. Shep rolled over to give Cooper more access and he chuckled at his dog. "Does this mean you're not mad at me anymore?" Shep's long pink tongue lolled out and Cooper took that as a yes. "Tell you what, boy. How about you and me go out for a run and you can help me come up with ideas of how to best apologize. Does that sound good?" Shep barked and Cooper smiled at the animal. Definitely man's best friend.

Cooper stood up from his squat and his head spun. He gripped the wall and tried not to lose his dinner from last night. Come to think of it, he wasn't sure he had dinner, which explained how much the room was spinning. He walked into his kitchen and filled a large glass with water, drinking it down while he searched his cabinets for some ibuprofen. He finished his water and refilled it, slamming down some painkillers with the second glass. Cooper looked over at his dog who had already grabbed his leash and was wagging his tail excitedly. "First things first, Shep," he told the dog. "I need to eat something and then we'll go for a run," he stepped over to the fridge and winced as another dizzy spell overcame him. "Make that a walk."

As the morning went along, Cooper racked his brains trying to think of the perfect grand gesture to apologize to Gigi. She was used to the finer things in life and he wasn't sure anything he could do would live up to that. Of course, it was that kind of thinking that had gotten him in this position in the first place. Keeping that in mind, Cooper put together an apology that seemed a lot less impressive, but a lot more him. Knowing Gigi, as long as it was authentic, it would be enough.

Chapter Twenty-One

Gigi

A pile of used tissues was currently growing to unmanageable proportions on Gigi's coffee table, but she couldn't be bothered to care about it. It was Sunday, her day off, and she was going to spend most of it crying her eyes out if she wanted to. She had spent the work week holding back her tears as to not scare off her customers, but since there were none around today, she decided to feel her feelings and let the tears flow freely, and flow freely they did.

Gigi dabbed at her leaky eyes with another tissue, adding it to the ever-growing pile. She was watching *MasterChef Junior* because she didn't want to watch anything that would remind her of Cooper and start her crying again, but every now and then she would glance at the screen and her puffy, red eyes would see Gordon Ramsay and for a split second, he would look just enough like her boyfriend to get her going again. *Ex-boyfriend*, her inner voice corrected. Not wanting the reminder, Gigi told that voice to shut up and watch the show.

"Can we watch something else?" Jo complained from the other end of the couch. "I'm all for showing little kids how to cook, but seeing all that food is making me hungry and the only thing you have in your house at the moment is a half-empty box of bran flakes." Gigi turned to her friend and Jo held up her hands in surrender. "Hey, I'm all for bowel regularity, but a bowl of bran doesn't sound appetizing when you've been watching plates of roasted chicken and potatoes all day."

Gigi sniffled and looked over to the door. "Millie said she would be back in a minute." Millie had seen the state of Gigi's home and gone to the store to buy her food. Gigi had tried to refuse, but there was no deterring Millie once she got into mom mode.

As if she had been waiting outside for her cue, Millie walked into the door carrying an armful of groceries. She set the heavy looking bags down on the counter and sighed, wiping her brow with the back of her hand. "Phew. It's really warm out there."

Gigi paused the show and watched as Jo immediately hopped up from the couch and ran over to the kitchen, rummaging through bags like a starving raccoon, pulling out a box of brown sugar toaster pastries, and yelling triumphantly. Gigi stood up from the couch and trudged over to the kitchen, giving Jo a weary look when she got there. "How are toaster pastries any better than bran flakes?"

"The sugar, obviously," Jo mumbled around a bite of the hand pie that she had managed to rip from its wrapping with lightning speed and shove into her mouth.

Millie chuckled at Jo's antics as she unloaded the other groceries. "I also got a bunch of produce, some milk, and a few ready to eat meals so you won't need to cook anything." She put away the rest of the food and closed the refrigerator. "I'm also going to make you some casseroles that you can freeze, heat up, and eat whenever you like."

Gigi smiled sadly at her best friend. "Thanks, Millie, but you shouldn't have to do all that for me." It was nice to have someone taking care of her, but she hated the reason for it was that she no longer had Cooper.

Millie gave her a knowing look. "Just like you didn't have to give me half your lunch on the days when I didn't have any, but you always did." Millie walked over to Gigi and squeezed her side. "That's what friends are for." Gigi leaned into the hug, enjoying the familiar comfort of her friend. Millie leaned back, and spying the pile of tissues on the coffee table, grabbed one of the empty grocery bags and walked into the small living area to sweep all of the evidence of Gigi's heartbreak into the garbage. "I'll just walk these out to the trash."

Gigi smiled as Millie walked to the door, but when she pulled it open and Gigi saw who was on the other side, her smile faltered, her heart rejoicing and shuttering at the same time. Standing on her doorstep with a grocery bag of his own was Cooper. He looked good, but even from where she was standing Gigi could see the tired set of his eyes and his slumped posture. Maybe their break-up had been just as hard for him as it was for her. Well, good she said to herself. He broke her heart, so if he lost a little sleep because of it, she was all for that.

Millie peered over her shoulder and looked at Gigi. Whatever expression was currently on her face had a small smile coming across Millie's, and she backtracked into the kitchen to grab her purse and Jo's arm. "Hey," her other friend squeaked as Millie dragged her toward the door. "I kind of want to see how this plays out."

"We can find out later," Millie whispered loudly as she pushed Jo past Cooper before leaving herself. "Call us later, Gi"

After a nod to Cooper, she and Jo walked away, leaving Gigi all alone with the man who had taken a hammer to her heart. Despite the way they had left things a week before, hope for reconciliation bloomed in her chest like a flower in springtime. Could he have come to his senses? Gigi certainly wanted that to be the case because even after the other night when he had been so unreasonable, so stubborn, she missed him and wanted him more than she had wanted anything in her entire life. Relationships were never all rainbows and sunshine, and if Cooper was finally ready to weather the storms together instead of separately, she knew they could make things work.

Gigi walked toward the door, trying to smooth out what was probably a fairly bad case of bed head, and she winced slightly when she remembered what she was wearing. A pair of ratty pajama shorts and a threadbare t-shirt that read, "Namaste in bed." She probably looked as horrible as she felt, but she couldn't find it in herself to really care. Cooper was here, and that was all she could focus on at the moment. When she was just in front of him, she tilted her head up to look into his eyes. They were a duller blue than usual and were slightly bloodshot, but they beheld her with the same love and affection as they always had.

"Hello." Gigi wasn't sure what to say, only that she couldn't take the silence any longer or she would start crying again.

"Hey, Peach." His lips rolled inward and his face was full of remorse. "I brought you a few things."

God, it was good to hear his voice, the low timbre soothing her frayed nerves, but as much as her heart wanted her to just let him in and see what happened, it also remembered just how harshly he'd acted, how much the last week had sucked and wanted an apology before he stepped one foot inside her door. Gigi crossed her arms over her chest and jutted out her chin. "Unless you have a big, fat 'I'm sorry' in that bag, I'm not interested."

A small smile formed on Cooper's lips. "Well, it just so happens that a big, fat 'I'm sorry' is item number one on the list."

"Really?" The ache in her chest already felt lighter and less debilitating now that he was here with her and trying to fix things, but Gigi schooled her features, trying to look less pleased. "I guess you can come in, but no promises on whether or not you can stay."

Cooper nodded and walked into her kitchen. "Totally fair." Dropping his bag on the counter, he turned to face her, his eyes focused on hers. He reached out to grab her hand, and when he did it was almost like the last week hadn't happened. The touch of his rough hands grounded her, brought her back to herself from wherever she had disappeared to over the last seven days. When he laced their fingers together, she felt her eyes well up with tears again. Gigi had missed him so much, missed this, the two of them together, more than she could ever put into words. Cooper swept his finger under her eye to brush away the tears. "Don't cry, Peach. It breaks my heart seeing you like this."

Gigi sniffled and shook her head. "I'm not crying," she insisted, blinking away the moisture. "And you broke my heart first, so it's only right that you feel it a little bit, too."

Cooper pulled her closer to him and gathered her in his arms. She didn't resist him in the slightest and instead, she leaned her head down against his chest and tried to let the steady rhythm of his heart quell the sadness. "I did feel it, Honey. I felt it all week. Now, I know that saying that doesn't take away just how badly I hurt you, but I hope it helps to hear that you weren't alone in that."

Gigi nodded against his chest. "I know I shouldn't feel good about you feeling bad, but it does help a little bit." She wasn't happy that he had suffered or anything, just that he wasn't as cavalier in his feelings for her as he had acted.

Cooper chuckled slightly and she felt the vibration of it against her cheek. "I'm glad." He held her tighter and swayed her slightly. The motion was soothing and he did it for a couple of minutes before leaning back to look at her. "I'm sorry, Peach. So very, very sorry." He cupped her cheek, looking more remorseful than she had ever seen anyone look in their whole life. His lips turned downward and his eyes begged for forgiveness, something she'd been prepared to give to him since the moment she left his house. "I forgot that the thing about peaches is that if you treat them harshly, they bruise. I know you've been bruised enough by being held onto too tightly by your parents, and I'm sorry I forgot to treat you like you deserve to be treated. You're precious to me, Peach and I won't forget it again. I was an idiot, and while I am sure that I will be an idiot many, many more times over the course of our lives, I can assure you it won't be about me doubting myself or you when it comes to whether or not we belong together. The next time I feel even an inkling of that again, I'll talk to you."

Gigi searched his eyes and saw a confidence there that had been absent for those two weeks before their break-up. She also saw a good amount of love mixed in with all that certainty, something that had her smiling bigger than she had in the last seven days. "Thank you for saying all that, and for promising to talk to me first next time." Gazing up into his handsome face, she smirked at what she had to say next. "You were a pretty big idiot."

Cooper huffed a laugh. "That I was, and I'm going to make it up to you." He twisted to the side, pulling over the grocery bag he had brought with him. "Starting with this. Now, my gran told me how you stood up to your mom, I spent the better part of this morning trying to think of a grand gesture to show you not just how sorry I am and how much I love you, but how proud I am of you for being so brave.."

"Brave?" Gigi supposed someone could look at it that way, but what he saw as brave had just felt natural at the time.

Cooper smiled softly. "Yes, brave. You are the bravest person I have ever met, Gigi. And I am proud of you and proud to know you." His mouth ticked up in the corner. "Do you want to your grand gesture now?"

Gigi's chest warmed from his words and the loving way he was looking at her. "Absolutely. What did you come up with?" She was eager to see what was in the bag. Gigi didn't need a grand gesture, but she wasn't going to turn one down either.

"This." Cooper reached into the bag and revealed a pint of butter pecan ice cream with a flourish.

Gigi looked at it and smiled. "Butter pecan? That's your grand gesture?" In truth, the apology and a promise that he knew better was enough for her already, but the ice cream was a nice bonus.

"Well, yes." Cooper's smile wavered and he looked a little nervous, but he reached back into the bag and pulled out another pint, this one the same flavor but a different brand. "Not just one pint of butter pecan, or even two." He reached into the bag and pulled out at least a dozen pints of ice cream, all different brands and set them out on the counter for her inspection. "I know it's your favorite flavor, but you never mentioned which brand you liked best, so I went to the store and got every brand there is." Cooper gathered her back in his arms and stared into her eyes. "I'm sorry for how I acted, what I said, what I did. I can't promise I won't ever do something that requires another apology again, but I can promise that I will always deliver one and along with it, some ice cream."

Gigi smiled at him, feeling all the love she had for him solidifying in her heart once again. "So all this ice cream is so I can figure out my favorite?"

Cooper nodded and leaned down to kiss her forehead. "Yes, and then when I inevitably am in the wrong again, I will know exactly which one to buy you."

Gigi wrapped her arms around his neck and reached up to kiss his cheek. "Thank you. Thank you for saying you're sorry and for all the ice cream, but what I really want to thank you for is realizing that you're worthy of love because all I've ever wanted to do was love you."

Cooper's eyes glazed with moisture. "Thank you for loving me, Peach. I won't question it again."

Gigi smiled, but wanted to give him an apology of her own. "I want to say I'm sorry, too, for all the talk about the auto shop and stuff. I wasn't trying to pressure you, but I can see how it might have come off that way."

"While I appreciate the sentiment, your apology isn't necessary," Cooper sighed, shaking his head. "That was all me. I know you weren't pressuring me and I'm sorry I took it that way. Truth is I've been wondering why I haven't tried to move up a little myself, but that's something we can talk about later."

"What do you want to talk about now?" she asked slyly. If she was reading the look in his eyes correctly, he wasn't wanting to do much talking at all. Gigi had never had make up sex before because she had never seriously dated anyone long enough to experience it, but she was definitely looking forward to trying it out now. The apology had been necessary and wonderful, but Gigi wanted to feel his body against hers, experience the physical intimacy she'd been missing the last week.

Cooper's eyes shot to her chest and she remembered that she hadn't bothered to put on a bra. The blue in his eyes burned brightly as he looked at her, his tongue peeking out and running along his lower lip. "I want to talk about this t-shirt and shorts combo of yours and why I've never seen it before." He groaned and leaned down to run his nose against her neck, his fingers teasing the bottom hem of her shirt. "It's been driving me crazy since the moment the door opened and I saw you."

Gigi shivered against him, the ache no longer in her heart but settled between her thighs. "What do you think we should do about that?" she asked, shifting her hips and feeling his hard length up against her belly.

Cooper nipped at her ear with his teeth and ground into her a little, his arousal pressing against her belly. "I think you know what I want to do about it." He went to kiss her, but Gigi pulled back quickly once she had remembered that she spent the better part of the day crying and probably tasted like a weird mix of salt water, snot, and bran flakes. Cooper leaned back, a question in his eyes.

"I'm really gross today," Gigi explained, covering her mouth with one hand and shaking her head. "Can you give me like five minutes to brush my teeth and grab a quick shower?"

Cooper spun her and trapped her up against the kitchen counter with his arms on both sides. "You're always beautiful, Peach, but since you so generously forgave me, I can be generous as well." His eyes were alight with mischief as they stared into hers. "I'll give you exactly as much time as it takes me to put all this ice cream in your freezer to do whatever you need to, and then I'm coming after you."

"I need more time than that," Gigi protested, but Cooper just shook his head in reply, stepping over to the ice cream and grabbing onto a couple of pints. "Can I at least get like a thirty second head start?"

"Sorry, but the clock's already ticking, Honey." Cooper slowly backed away to the freezer, raking his eyes up and down her body the whole time.

Gigi squeaked and turned around, running to her bathroom, hearing Cooper's amused laughter as she did.

She nearly slammed into the door in her haste, but she was able to flip on the water for the shower, and grab her toothbrush at the same time. She would brush her teeth while the water heated up and then wash up as quickly as possible. There was a lot of ice cream out there, so she should have time. She spat and rinsed her mouth and was just peeling off her shirt when Cooper came into view, breathing quickly and staring at her like he was a predator and she was his prey.

The warmth turned to fire in her belly the longer she looked at him. "Did you run?"

Cooper smirked. "Hell, yes, I ran, and it's a good thing I did, too." He leaned against the door frame, his eyes roaming over her lazily. "I almost missed the show." Gigi lowered her shirt and he pouted at her, but when she leaned over to stop the water, he shook his head. "Leave it on." He stepped closer to her and lifted the hem of her shirt, his fingers trailing up her skin lightly as he slipped it over her head and tossed it behind him. "We're going to get real dirty and then we can get clean."

"O-okay," Gigi breathed out huskily, too turned on for more words than that. He peeled her pajama shorts down, smiling up at her when he saw that she wasn't wearing any panties. He leaned in and sniffed her center, a low growl coming from his throat.

He stood up and spun her around, smacking her lightly on the behind. "Get in the shower, Peach. I'll be right behind you."

Gigi stepped into the area that enclosed the shower. It was much more spacious than the average shower as it was custom built by her wealthy landlord, something she'd always enjoyed but was extra appreciative of today. She closed her eyes and leaned her head back into the spray, letting the warm water cascade over her hair and body. When she opened them again.

Cooper was standing in front of her, his body on display in all its naked glory. He cupped her wet face and tilted his head down, slanting their mouths together in a passionate kiss, her toes curling with the intensity of it. Gigi reached her hand up into his hair and held him to her. She had almost lost this man once, and she wasn't going to let it happen again. He would be an idiot sometimes, and so would she, but they would come back to each other because that's the way things were meant to be. The belonged together, and now that Cooper knew that in his head as well as his heart, nothing could separate them.

Gigi groaned into his mouth as their tongues danced against one another's. She slipped one of her hands between the two of them and gripped his slippery erection, pumping her fist up and down a few times. Cooper broke away and grabbed her hand, bringing it up to his mouth to kiss it. "Not yet. There's something else I want first." He kissed her lips briefly, trailing his own down her body, nipping at her breasts, her stomach, and her hips as he went. When he was kneeling on the tile in front of her, he grabbed one of her legs and lifted it over his shoulder. "Hang on to something, Honey," he commanded, and when she placed one hand on the wall and the other in his hair, he looked up at her with fire in his eyes. "Good girl."

Gigi's head raised to the ceiling, her pleasure ramping up about three notches at the phrase, not realizing just how much she had missed hearing it from him until he's said it. She like being good for him, but only him, and when she glanced down once again, she saw that he was about to be very good for her. Cooper parted her folds with this fingers, running the flat of his tongue from her center to the bundle of nerves at the top and repeating the action a few times until she was squirming, pushing his face into her.

Another minute went by and then he slipped one, then another finger inside her, pumping and curling the thick digits around until he found the hot button that had her moaning, the sound echoing off the tiles and sounding much louder than she had intended. Cooper pulled back, smiled, and winked at her, diving back in, attacking her with his fingers and tongue like he was trying to earn a gold medal in eating her out. If she was to be the judge, he would have already won because she felt better than she ever had, her whole body alight with hot, tingling pleasure.

Cooper's fingers gained speed and she gripped his hair harder, not wanting to lose one bit of the momentum that had started. She was close, oh, so close to hitting her high, and when he moved up to suck on her clit, she finally reached it. Gigi's eyes squeezed shut as the pleasure ripped through her body, her muscles tightening and releasing, fireworks bursting behind her eyelids until the bright colors had pushed out the darkness. She thought they were finished, but she should have known better. Cooper was not a selfish lover, always giving her what she needed first, and it seemed like this time he wanted to be more generous than usual. Instead of stopping or even letting up, he just kept going, gripping her ass and holding her to his face as he devoured her like a hungry lion. She came again and again, the third time having her wonder if she had slipped onto some other plane of existence with just how blissful she felt.

It was like she was floating, and when she couldn't take any more, she slapped at his shoulder and he leaned back to look at her, licking his lips and sporting a shit-eating grin. "Time to tap out," she said breathless, her legs shaky.

Cooper stood up and brushed a strand of wet air

out of her face. "You okay?" She nodded and held out a thumbs up, earning a chuckle from him. "You want to keep going?"

She reached up to grip the back of his neck and brought him down to kiss him, tasting the tangy flavor of herself on his lips and his tongue as she did. When she finally pulled back, she looked up at him, trying to express just how bad the need for him to be inside her was. "I want to keep going. I need you."

Cooper smirked and reached behind her, changing the angle of the showerhead so that it pointed against the wall. She wasn't directly in the stream anymore, but she wasn't cold either, far too worked up to feel anything other than heat all over her body. Cooper gently brushed his lips against hers, spinning her around. "Hands against the wall, Peach." She did exactly what he asked, and when he leaned over to her ear, she knew exactly what was coming and couldn't wait to hear it. "Good girl," he whispered as he seated himself inside her in one thrust.

Cooper pulled out slowly, slamming into her again and again, gripping her hips to a point where she was sure she'd have bruises tomorrow, but she didn't care. Gigi loved him and had missed him this last week, and she needed to be as close to him as humanly possible, needed to bear his marks that showed just how much he owned her. He reached his hands up and cupped her breasts as he continued to push into her over and over again, tweaking her nipples and causing sparks to shoot out all through her body. Gigi moved her hips back to meet him for every thrust, and every grunt he let out only fueled her desire more. He reached one of his hands down and started to thrum her clit, using his fingers to press that bundle of nerves like only he knew how that had the pressure building in her once again. His hand sped up as did his thrusts, and only after she cried out in ecstasy did he follow after, pumping into her and filling her with warmth until he finally softened and slipped free.

Gigi turned around to look at Cooper, his expression showing how very thoroughly pleased he was, and she was sure she had a matching look on her face. He reached over and pulled her into his arms for a hug, kissing the top of her head once she was there. "I love you, Peach. I plan on loving you for a very long time."

Gigi smiled against his skin. "I love you, too, Coop." They stayed in each other's arms for a moment, basking in the afterglow of their releases and their renewed declarations of love. Time seemed to slow as they stayed in the shower, Cooper washing her hair and every part of her body before she returned the favor, and when the water turned cold, they dried themselves off and went out to the bedroom where they clung to one another and warmed themselves up all over again.

Chapter Twenty-Two

Cooper

The Tap House Bar and Grille was fairly busy, but considering it was a Saturday night, that wasn't unusual. Cooper took a pull from his beer and swallowed the liquid down, enjoying the malty flavor as it slid over his tongue and down his throat. It was nice to be out and about with a friend after the last few weeks where most of his time had been spent either at work or with Gigi. The two of them had mostly been holing up in one another's houses, and while he loved spending all that quality time with her, when she had requested a night with the girls, he figured he would maybe go out and grab a beer with some of the guys from the shop. It had been far too long since he had hung out with any of them outside of work, and when it was Bob, his boss, who suggested they grab a pint, Cooper jumped at the chance. The man was as close to a mentor and father to him as he could get nowadays, so he figured, why not? Currently, the older man was nursing his beer, looking a little tired.

"You okay over there, Bob?" Cooper asked, hoping the tiredness had nothing to do with the man's health. Bob wasn't old, but he wasn't exactly young either.

Bob lifted his head from where it had been perched on his hand. "Yeah, I'm okay." Scrubbing a hand up and down his face, he raised his glass to his mouth again, but set it back down before taking a drink. "No, I'm not okay."

Cooper frowned, concern for the man building in his chest. "Is something going on with the shop?" If there was anything going on at the business, Cooper was more than happy to help figure things out. After his fight with

Gigi, Cooper seriously considered his options as far as his career went. What he found was that while he had been telling himself he liked where he was, he actually did want an opportunity to step up a bit and show himself what he was really made of. Gigi believed in him, and it was about time he did too.

"No. The shop is great." Bob shook his head, his graying hair falling into his eyes. Cooper took a closer look at the man and kicked himself for not asking the question sooner. Bob's hair was disheveled, like he had run his fingers through it one too many times and his usually clean cut face was covered in stubble. The man was a mechanic and never looked like a cover model or anything, but he usually looked a little more put together than his current state.

"Is it Jo?" He couldn't imagine it was Bob's daughter. Cooper had known the woman for a while and she was a force, so he knew she could more than handle herself.

Bob sighed heavily. "In a way." His eyes were looking a little glassy despite the fact that he had barely drank any of his beer. "She's headstrong, single-minded, stubborn, and impatient." He ran his hands through his already tussled hair. "She spends all her time worrying about me and my health when she needs to get out there and start living for herself."

Cooper shrugged a shoulder. "Have you talked to her about it?" If Cooper had just talked with Gigi more about his feelings in the first place, he could have avoided the whole temporary break-up mess he put them through. Maybe his advice could save Bob from causing himself similar grief with his daughter.

"I've tried, but I'm not sure what good it will do. Ever since her mama died she's felt the need to look after me. I'm not sure what would possibly change that." Bob grumbled, finally taking a pull from his beer. "She'll never listen to me."

"Maybe if you retire, she'll have less to worry about." Cooper wasn't angling for the man's job already, but he also didn't want to see Bob work himself into an early grave.

Bob scratched his jaw while he stared into his beer, his mind seeming to drift off. "Maybe."

Cooper didn't want to turn this into a conversation about himself, but as he had been thinking of asking Bob for more responsibility at the garage, this could be a way to broach that. He wasn't considering it because he thought he needed to in order to deserve his girl, but he had been thinking that it would be a great way to get a little more say in how things ran. He had a lot of ideas for the shop that could bring them up to date and draw in more customers, and he had another reason for wanting his job to be as successful and stable as possible.

Cooper patted the lump in his pocket that held the black velvet ring box. He had made the purchase the day after Gigi had taken him back and carried it around every day since, just waiting for the perfect opportunity to propose to her. He couldn't imagine a life for himself that didn't include her, and he wanted to make it official as soon as possible. He realized it seemed quick, and a lot of people would pass judgement, but he didn't care. All that mattered to him now was not letting what other people might think keep him from being happy, and being with Gigi made him the happiest he had ever been in his entire life.

Cooper's phone pinged and he pulled it out of his other pocket, smiling at the notification and sliding it open to check the message from his girl.

Gigi: **All done with girl's night and I'm at your place. You almost done?**

Cooper smiled and typed out a reply, eager to see her now that shew as available.

Cooper: **I'll wrap things up soon and be there in about forty minutes.**

He went to slide his phone back in his pocket, but another text came through, so he checked it out. Cooper's eyes widened at the picture Gigi had sent him and he clung his phone to his chest, looking over his shoulders to make sure no one else could see what he was seeing. When he was satisfied that no one was looking, he peeked back down at the message attachment, holding back a groan and trying to keep himself from sprouting an erection in public. The picture was Gigi propped up against a bunch of pillows piled at the base of his headboard, completely naked. Her red hair was spilling down her bare shoulders, just barely covering her dusky nipples and the bed sheet was pulled up just enough to cover her downstairs and one of her hands that was slipped underneath.

Gigi: **I might have to get started without you. ;)**

Cooper groaned and looked over to his boss who was looking better now that he'd had a full beer. "You okay if we call it a night?" He didn't want to ditch the man but was unable to quash the desire that was ramping up the more he thought about his woman, ready and waiting for him at home.

Bob looked at him with a sly smile. "I'm fine with that." He clasped his hand to Cooper's shoulder, giving it a squeeze. "Go enjoy a night with your girl."

"Thanks." Cooper slapped some cash on the bar, wanting to get his body across town to where his mind already was. "I plan on it. See you at work." Bob nodded and turned to signal the bartender for another drink.

Cooper's thumbs flew across the screen as he typed out a reply to Gigi.

Cooper: **Leaving now, Peach. Don't you dare get started without me.**
Gigi: **Too late. :)**

Cooper groaned and pocketed his phone, throwing his helmet on and hopping onto his motorcycle. Within minutes, he had kickstarted it and was flying down the streets of the city to get to Gigi as quickly as possible, a wide smile on his face the entire time.

****

The next morning as he was blinking his eyes open, Cooper smiled, flashes of the night before coming to his mind. He had caught Gigi in the act of pleasuring herself and he watched until he couldn't stand it anymore and had to join in. They spent the rest of the night alternating between making love and catching a few hours of sleep. He had to be at work in an hour, but as he peered down into the face of the woman he loved, a woman who was drooling on his chest at the moment, he couldn't muster up the energy to get out of bed and get ready for the day. Cooper smiled down at Gigi and lightly brushed his fingers through her hair until her eyes fluttered open. She looked up at him with a smile until she discovered the little pool on his chest, sitting up quickly and looking mortified while wiping at both him and her mouth.

"Oh, my god, I'm sorry." Gigi covered her face with her hands, mumbling through her fingers. "That's so embarrassing."

Cooper grabbed her hands and parted them so he could look into her eyes. They were bright and beautiful, even more so after a night of making love and sleeping in his arms. "A little drool never hurt anyone, Peach."

He smoothed over her embarrassment with a kiss to her lips, grinning when she looked much more content, if not a little turned on. As much as he would like to take advantage of that with the time they had left, he suddenly had the urge to do something else first. He whistled for his dog and Shep pranced into the room, his big tongue wagging around as he did. Cooper pointed to his jeans that were lying in a heap on the floor. He didn't exactly make it a priority to clean up last night when he had much more important matters to take care of.

"Bring me my pants, would you, boy?" Like the best damn wingman that ever existed, Shep grabbed the pants and brought them over to Cooper, dropping them in his hands before moving over to his bed in the corner and attacking a chew toy. Someone was getting cubed steak for dinner tonight.

Cooper dug around in his pocket while Gigi peered over at him with curiosity, her arm brushing against his. "What are you doing?"

Cooper's fingers closed around the smooth velvet of the box and he pulled it out, making sure it was completely hidden in his palm. "There's something I've been wanting to do for a while, and I've been waiting for the perfect moment to do it. I can't think of a more perfect moment than right now."

Cooper scooted over to her on the bed and used his free hand to grab hers, bringing it to his mouth and kissing it as he stared into her hazel eyes. "I love you, Peach. I want us to be together always, and I want always to start as soon as possible." He opened the ring box and presented the ring to her. It wasn't anything large or fancy, but he thought the simple design would suit her. Gigi didn't need something flashy to show off because she outshined everything anyway. Cooper took a deep breath and asked the question that had been on the tip of his tongue for a long time. "Will you marry me?"

Gigi looked up at him, her eyes welling with tears, but this time they were happy tears, at least he thought so because she was also smiling bigger than he had ever seen her smile. "I love you, too, Coop, and my answer is yes. I would be honored to be your wife."

Cooper's heart nearly exploded with joy and he pulled the ring from the box and slipped it on her finger with shaky hands. His whole body was filled with so much happiness and excitement he could barely sit still. "Perfect fit, just like Mags thought it would be."

Gigi admired the silver band with the aquamarine gem with a smile, looking up at him with bright eyes. "Mags helped you pick it out? That's sweet."

Cooper shook his head and pulled her close. "No, she didn't help me pick it out. It's hers." Gigi gasped and Cooper's smiled widened at her reaction. He knew she would be happy with whatever he got her, but knew that something coming from his family would be even more meaningful. "Rather, it *was* hers, but it's yours now."

Gigi was still smiling, but not quite as brightly. "Is she sure she wants to give it up? I mean, I love it, it's absolutely beautiful, but I don't want to take something from her."

Cooper kissed the top of her head. "That's sweet of you, Honey, but she was happy to give it to me. Mags said that was always the plan, I just needed to get my head out of my ass long enough to find the perfect girl.. And I did," he proclaimed, leaning down and kissing her soundly.

Gigi deepened the kiss and the bedsheet that was covering her body slipped away. They lost themselves in one another again, the feelings of love and elation coursing through them as they celebrated their engagement in one of the best ways possible. Neither of them ended up making it to work on time, but both had been too damn happy to care.

Epilogue

Gigi
Seven months later

The air inside the rock climbing gym was a bit too humid for Gigi's tastes, but as it was Jo's year to pick how they celebrated their birthdays, she did her best to suck it up and deal with it. It shouldn't have surprised Gigi that her sporty friend would choose a more active way to ring in their twenty-ninth year, nor did it surprise her that both Jo and her partner were already scaling toward the top of the hardest wall in the place like the showoffs they were. Gigi had a mind to drag Jo to a fashion show for a little payback, but she was too elated with the news she got earlier that day to really consider the matter seriously.

Gigi felt a presence behind her just before Cooper wrapped his arms around her and kissed the side of her neck. "You ready to try this thing, Peach?" He snuggled her back against his front and she sighed into the warm feel of him. Gigi would never get enough of her fiancé or the way he felt like home anytime he was near.

Gigi tipped her head up to look at him and smiled. "I think I could manage to give it a go." She slipped off her engagement ring, putting it on a chain around her neck. "I don't want anything to happen to this."

Cooper smirked. "Well, I should hope not." He lifted her now bare ring finger to his mouth and kissed it. "Though it won't matter much in a few months since you'll have a band here instead."

Gigi beamed at her future husband. He was right, of course. They were getting married at the end of May and she couldn't be happier about it. Her parents weren't exactly thrilled when she first reported her impending nuptials, acting about as well as could be expected for them. They still weren't the most open and judgement free individuals, but Gigi was hopeful that they could get there eventually. Her brother having made a few interesting decisions of his own would probably help speed that along as well, but change takes time and as it was, her parents weren't a big part of her life anymore. It was a relief in more ways than one, though Gigi would probably always grieve the relationship they could have had if things were different. Instead of dwelling on it, she chose to focus on the family she still had like her fiancé, brother, and friends.

"Ready, Peach?" Cooper asked, hooking her up to the safety line.

"I suppose so." Gigi glanced down at her recently manicured nails. "Well, ladies, it was fun while it lasted." Dusting her hands in powder, she reached for the first grip. She and Cooper continued to scale the wall, him helping her whenever she needed it. She appreciated his efforts, not only because she wasn't as athletic as she had previously thought, but because it was a great indication of how well he would probably take the news she had to share with him. After a little encouragement from Gigi and Mags, Cooper opened up more about how his past had affected his current feelings. Now he took everything in stride and had endless patience, so she wasn't worried about his reaction so much anymore.

Loud laughter pulled Gigi's attention away from what she was doing, and when she peered over her shoulder, she smiled as she watched Millie laugh from the seating area where her partner was tickling her mercilessly. The tickling stopped and her partner firmly planted a kiss on Millie's lips, resting both hands on her stomach. Gigi had never thought to see those two people together, but it was a pairing she probably should have seen coming a mile away. It didn't matter, though. All that mattered was that her friend was happy, that they were all happy.

Gigi tried to reach the next grip, but couldn't quite catch it and slipped. Luckily, the safety line tugged and she was able to reach the ground safely. Cooper hopped down immediately and rushed over to her. "You okay, Peach?"

"I'm fine, baby." Gigi caught her breath, reaching up to kiss his cheek. "Thanks for checking."

Cooper nodded. "You're welcome." He hitched his thumb over his shoulder, pointing to a small area with complimentary bottled water and granola bars. "Want to take a small break?"

"Yes, please." After washing their hands and grabbing a drink, the two of them stood, her back to his front once again as they watched their friends continue to climb.

Cooper nuzzled her neck and kissed the sensitive spot just below her ear. "So, Honey. You have any fun challenges for this year?" Once things between the two of them had settled, Gigi told Cooper all about how she, Jo, and Millie had set challenges for themselves. They laughed at how her going to a drag show had spurred her into finding the man she loved, the man that was currently staring at her with his eyes narrowed and a smirk on his face. "Obviously any dating ones are off the menu."

She chuckled. "Obviously." She thought for a moment and smirked as a new idea formed in her mind. "Oh. We could change it to sex challenges."

"I like that idea," he stated, his gaze turning heated. "I like that idea a whole helluva lot."

Gigi smiled at the man she loved more than anything, though he had a little more competition in that area now. She took a deep breath, hoping he would be just as excited as she was about the news she was about to share. "Besides, we should probably get in as much of that as possible, because in about eight months, we're going to be a little busy." Cooper's face scrunched with confusion, but understanding dawned in his ocean blue eyes when she slid his hands from her middle down to where their baby was growing.

A small smile played at his lips. "A baby?" he whispered to her, and when she nodded, his smile widened. "We're having a baby." He whooped happily, spinning her around in his arms and lifting her up in a hug, peppering her face and neck with kisses before putting her back down on the ground. "I can't believe we're having a baby. This is amazing!"

Gigi's cheeks hurt from how wide her smile had grown. They hadn't been trying for long, so it was a bit of a surprise. "I'm so happy you're happy," she gushed, reaching her arms up around his neck for a hug. "I can't wait to meet the little guy or girl."

Cooper pulled her close and swayed the two of them together. "Me neither. I'm going to teach them so many things."

"Like how to cook hot dogs on an engine?" Cooper had showed Gigi that trick on the Fourth of July, and while she had been skeptical at first, she had to admit they tasted pretty damn good.

"That and so much more," Cooper vowed, kissing her on the lips. His smile was bright and amusement played in his eyes. "I'm so glad my gran shoved that croissant in your tailpipe last year."

Gigi's mouth dropped open. "That was Mags?" It made sense that the sassy older woman would be capable of something like that, but Gigi was still shocked she would actually go through with the prank just to get the two of them together.

Cooper smiled, looking smug. "She did, and it's a good thing, too, or you wouldn't have come over to the garage and thrown yourself at me."

"I did no such thing," Gigi giggled, slapping his arm. "You were the one throwing yourself at me."

"I was." Cooper kissed her chastely, leaning their foreheads together. "And I would do it again in a heartbeat because it got the best thing to ever happen to me into my life." He reached down and brushed his hand over her still flat stomach. "Two best things."

Gigi smiled and covered his hand with her own. She and the baby might be the two best things to ever happen to him, but he was definitely the best thing to ever happen to her, and she was so glad she had the courage to fight for him and the happily ever after that was only just beginning.

The End

EVERNIGHT PUBLISHING ®

www.evernightpublishing.com